To my truest companion
Thank you for the auspices

MURDER AT A FLOWER SHOW

A 1920s Cozy Mystery

A Lady Felicity Quick Mystery
Book 7

ROSIE HUNT

ISBN: 978-90-834331-2-7

With thanks to early readers Michelle Clegg, Kelly Hodgkins, Jacqui, Deborah Jay, Lorraine Terrell, Nancy R Willis, and others

Cover art by DLR Cover Designs

A Note on Language

This book is written in British English. There are two reasons for this:

- the story is set in England, and
- I, the author, am British.

Part of my British writing style is the use of s where z is used in American English. For example: symbolise instead of symbolize, and terrorise instead of terrorize.

However, you may have noticed that in the blurbs and marketing for this book, it's called a cozy mystery and not a cosy mystery.

This is because the American spelling is standard for the genre. Spelling it this way helps people (and algorithms) recognise my book more easily.

But outside of book genres, it's cosy all the way.

Cast of Characters

Quick family

Lady Felicity Quick, journalist and occasional amateur detective

Lord Jasper Quick, Earl of Denbury, editor-in-chief of the Western Daily News and Felicity's brother

Lady Henrietta Quick, Dowager Countess of Denbury, grandmother to Felicity and Jasper

Pip, Felicity's Yorkshire Terrier

Rose breeders

Mr Clive Dingle, owner of Dingles Nursery

Mrs Edna Dingle, wife of Clive

Mr Tony Fox, owner of Champs Verts Nursery

Madame Blanche Ernault, assistant at Champs Verts Nursery

Monsieur Jacques Gobillot, assistant at Champs Verts Nursery

Mr Percival Colhayne, Lady Henrietta's protégé

Lady Leonora Templeton, heiress of the Templeton rose-breeding dynasty

Mr Michael Havelock, gardener at Templeton Manor

British Rose Association staff and volunteers

Colonel Simon Bolt, association president

Mr Ronald Merton, competition judge

Mr Elliot Etty, music-hall singer and competition judge

Mr Lucas Shakerley, rose expert

Mrs Gladys Broughton, volunteer

Mrs Enid Winterpole, volunteer

Others

Mr Alexander Cooper, reporter for the Western Daily News

Chief Inspector Luscombe, police detective

Mr Liam Finnegan, driver for the Quick family

Extract from the Western Daily News, 1922

Flower Breeders Compete For Top Award

New and established nurseries clash for the coveted Best in Show prize in Bickleford

EXETER, 13 June — Bickleford Rose Festival, Britain's most important floral contest, opens tomorrow in the West Devon village, and the competition is fierce.

Newcomers such as Champs Verts Nursery will compete with historic names like the Templeton family for Best in Show, an illustrious award that has launched several careers.

Celebrity judges, including Western Daily News journalist and renowned sleuth Lady Felicity Quick, will help the British Rose Association's experts allocate the prestigious prize.

Extract from the archives of the British Rose Association

Name of Rose: Rosa 'Gloire de Templeton'
Breeder: Lord Hector Templeton, Earl of Fernworthy
Year of Origin: 1874
Class: Hybrid Tea
Parentage: Rosa 'Souvenir de Reims' (Bourbon) and Rosa 'Royal Cobalt' (Portland)
Bloom Colour: Shell pink
Bloom Shape: High-centred, reflex petals, pointed bud
Bloom Size: 3 1/2 inches
Number of Petals: 16
Fragrance: Early morning rain, vanilla, jasmine
Foliage: Gentle gradient leaf colour from dark green to copper

Chapter One

BICKLEFORD VILLAGE, WEST DEVON, 14 JUNE 1922

Orange blossom. Sea spray. A hint of vanilla.

Lady Felicity Quick — journalist, amateur detective, and, for one day only, flower show judge — had put her nose to countless blooms that morning, but a rose's scent never lost its charm.

"Quite captivating, isn't it, dear?"

Lady Henrietta Quick, Dowager Countess of Denbury and Felicity's grandmother, wore a proud and knowing expression as Felicity straightened from the deep bow she'd taken to inhale the flower's perfume.

"We've more than a moderate chance for Best in Show, wouldn't you say?" continued the dowager.

Felicity touched a fingertip to the velvety petal of the sweetly scented cultivar. The pure white rose was one of dozens of flowers on the cloth-draped tiers of the exhibition stand and one of hundreds of plants in Bickleford Rose Festival's main marquee.

"I couldn't possibly comment, Grandmama," said Felicity as a light breeze flapped the white canvas walls of the tent and tugged at the embroidered hem of her cream-coloured silk dress.

Lady Henrietta drew her chin in sharply at the comment and reached under her arm. Tucked between her lace-trimmed sleeve and the fitted bodice of her Edwardian-style dress, Felicity's three-year-old Yorkshire Terrier, Pip, had almost fallen asleep. A burst of strenuous under-the-chin caresses from the dowager snapped the little dog's tufted ears to attention.

Felicity had recently left Pip in the care of her grandmother for a spell. The pair had developed a strong bond, and Pip had gained a second personality. With Felicity, the Yorkie was inquisitive, rambunctious, and often vocal. With Lady Henrietta, Pip was the perfect lap dog, quiet and interested only in treats.

"I must remain neutral," added Felicity as she observed her once boisterous canine companion lean into her grandmother's caresses, his eyelids drooping.

Lady Henrietta straightened, perhaps remembering the company she kept. "Of course, dear. In your current role, you simply have to be impartial." Continuing to stroke the Yorkie, the dowager glanced warily to her side.

Positioned beside Lady Henrietta, Mrs Enid Winterpole was a small-statured woman in her seventies, with puffy white hair and a penchant for pastel shades.

"Impartiality is crucial," Mrs Winterpole agreed, her blush-pink bicorn hat bobbing as she nodded sagely at Lady Henrietta's comment. She looked harmless enough, but Mrs Winterpole was a dedicated volunteer for the British Rose Association, which organised Bickleford Rose Festival each year. Leaving her with the impression Felicity was playing favourites would have been risky.

"You must have been so proud when the association selected your granddaughter as a judge for this year's festival, your ladyship," continued Mrs Winterpole, her clipped consonants rising above the gentle hubbub of the marquee's well-attired crowd.

Lady Henrietta nodded haughtily, her ease and self-assurance quickly regained. "Proud, but not surprised, Mrs Winterpole," said the dowager, laying a firm hand on Felicity's forearm. "Certainly not surprised."

Ordinarily, Felicity might have objected to being discussed as if she weren't present. Instead, she simply smiled. It was best not to meddle in the delicate balance of Lady Henrietta and Mrs Winterpole's relationship. Whenever their volunteering endeavours overlapped, both widows behaved politely and spoke as though they held one another in high regard. In reality, however, and in the most genteel way possible, their rivalry was savage.

"Felicity is a young woman of many talents," explained Lady Henrietta, who had come a long way since her initial scepticism at Felicity's career aspirations. "Having begun as a newspaper journalist, she now writes for the periodicals. She has an editor in London, you know."

Felicity continued to smile graciously, though the mention of her obligations to the fortnightly ladies' magazine made her stomach twist. With a subtle tilt of her wide-brimmed straw hat, Felicity scanned the tent's slow-moving crowds. She'd expected the signal by now. Had she somehow missed it?

"I am a subscriber to the Gentlewoman's Gazette," said Mrs Winterpole, "so I'm familiar with her ladyship's contribution to the periodical, which, I must say, is exemplary. But then Lady Felicity has always been a writer of outstanding quality." Mrs Winterpole's rivalry with her grandmother seemed not to affect her opinion of Felicity.

"Lady Felicity is most well-known as a solver of crimes these days, though. Isn't she?" The uncertain addition to the conversation came from Mrs Gladys Broughton.

Slightly younger than the dowager and Mrs Winterpole, Mrs Broughton had soft, round features and large eyes that made her look perpetually surprised. As usual, she hovered at Lady Henrietta's side.

"Isn't she?" repeated Mrs Broughton, the red and green feathers on her bucket hat quivering as her gaze shifted between Mrs Winterpole and Lady Henrietta.

Mrs Broughton supported the dowager on most matters, although they differed in their attitudes towards Mrs Winterpole. Even in private, Mrs Broughton insisted she wished to be friends with everybody, which made Lady Henrietta shake her head and Felicity sigh in despair. It was impossible to be universally liked.

"That's quite correct, Mrs Broughton," said Lady Henrietta.

"Felicity has a reputation both as a sleuth and as a journalist. For a woman to reach just one of those achievements by the tender age of two-and-twenty would be an incredible feat." The dowager patted Pip firmly on the head, as if to emphasise the point.

"I wholeheartedly agree." Mrs Winterpole turned admiringly towards Felicity. "Lady Felicity can certainly be proud of her accomplishments."

"That's kind of you to say, Mrs Winterpole." Felicity continued to smile. Reluctantly, she'd acknowledged the growth of her reputation. Her status as a 'celebrity' had triggered her selection as a judge for the show, but it was only with Lady Henrietta's encouragement that Felicity accepted the invitation, Felicity's knowledge of roses being practically null.

"My granddaughter is indeed to be congratulated," added Lady Henrietta, a little boastfully. "She is more than worthy of the attention and acclaim."

Felicity maintained a modest smile. Whether she deserved her fame was by the by, but keeping a low profile had become increasingly difficult since the Gentlewoman's Gazette had published a striking portrait of her. Felicity had never posed for the image. She wouldn't have agreed to the ladies' deerstalker and the ridiculously large magnifying glass with which she was pictured. Regardless, the number of people approaching her in the street grew exponentially.

Felicity had been ready to ask the magazine to remove the portrait from beside her articles when her brother, Lord Jasper Quick, Earl of Denbury and editor-in-chief of the Western Daily News, gently reminded Felicity of how her contributions to the Gazette had helped increase the readership of the Quick family newspaper.

After some careful deliberation, Felicity kept her opinions on the portrait to herself. Her obligations to the magazine wouldn't last forever.

"Oh, yes," agreed Mrs Broughton, clasping her hands together. "Lady Felicity is a marvel."

Felicity's smile wavered. "You're being too kind now," she said. "Really."

A jot of occasional praise was acceptable, but Felicity had her faults. Writing for the Gazette had proved rather different from reporting for the newspaper. Sitting alone at one's desk, remembering things, and writing them down had become an awful slog. Felicity had been granted a second deadline extension, yet here she was judging a flower show while her typewriter sat at home on her rosewood desk with its cover still on.

Felicity swallowed as she pushed a little onto her tiptoes and scanned the sea of hats that filled the marquee, the air warmed by the sun through the canvas and filled with bees, butterflies, and sweet, floral scents.

The signal. She can't have missed his signal.

"But Mrs Winterpole, have you had the chance to meet Mr Percival Colhayne?" Lady Henrietta's rather ungainly redirection of the conversation came as some relief to Felicity, as it was never her preference to be the centre of attention.

"Briefly, yes," confirmed Mrs Winterpole. "Ahead of the show's opening."

Those involved in the running of the rose festival — including Felicity and the other judges — had been given a quick tour of the many marquees and fleeting introductions with each of the exhibitors. Felicity and Mr Elliot Etty, a doe-eyed music-hall singer who'd been chosen as the other celebrity judge, had then each been sent off with a clipboard to provide their feedback on the exhibits ahead of the show's opening.

With only thirty minutes to make their rounds, the celebrity judging hadn't the air of a serious process. In Felicity's amateur opinion, all the roses she'd seen were of exquisite quality, so she'd given each of them full marks. If she'd only been engaged as a judge so her name could be added to promotional posters, it was for the best.

"Mr Colhayne is extremely talented," said Mrs Broughton, blinking nervously at Mrs Winterpole. Although not renowned for her distinctive viewpoints, Mrs Broughton was a loyal ally to Lady Henrietta. "He's a finalist for Best in Show."

The judging for the Best in Show prize was a different kettle of fish. Celebrities weren't actually involved. Entries were submitted to the British Rose Association months in advance, so that the plant's qualities could be observed over the growing season.

"That's rather impressive for a first-timer," said Mrs Winterpole, her eyes twinkling as she scanned the crowd for a sign of the newcomer. Best in Show from Bickleford Rose Festival was the most coveted award among breeders. Winning guaranteed an elevated profile, not to mention increased sales.

"Percy?" Lady Henrietta flailed as she struggled to locate the rose breeder in question. "Percy, dear?"

Pip's eyes were bright and his ears were pricked as the dowager swung from left to right. The little dog knew they were looking for something, but it was doubtful the Yorkie knew who 'Percy' was.

Thankfully, he wasn't far away and easy to spot among the crowds, with his reddish brown hair poking haphazardly from beneath his flat cap.

Felicity waved to attract Percy's attention, but he was deep in conversation with another cap-wearing fellow. It was Mr Clive Dingle, if Felicity's memory of the flying tour of the show's rose breeders served her correctly. Mr Dingle was one half of the ruddy-cheeked couple running the stand next door.

"Shall I fetch him?" offered Mrs Broughton, as Felicity at last caught Percy's eye.

Wearing a look of surprise and then of apology, the young man hurried through the crowd to arrive beside Lady Henrietta. "Awfully sorry," he said, although apologies weren't necessary.

Percy was the son of a cherished friend of Lady Henrietta's who was, sadly, no longer among the living. To honour her friend, the dowager was determined to help Percy in whatever way she could. Assisting him in his chosen career as a rose breeder had been the perfect opportunity.

"Percy Colhayne," he said, picking up the hints in Lady Henrietta's gaze and offering a hand to Mrs Winterpole. "How do you do?" he asked while tucking his cap under his arm, his copper-brown hair tumbling onto his forehead.

Mrs Broughton sighed somewhat dreamily at the sight of the young man.

Mrs Winterpole also seemed charmed. "Some rather impressive specimens you have here, Mr Colhayne."

"Oh." Percy glanced over his shoulder as though surprised by the roses on the display behind him, even though he'd bred the plants himself and the stand bore his name. "Thank you very much." He smiled warmly at Mrs Winterpole.

The dowager cleared her throat. "As Mrs Broughton mentioned, Percy is in the running for Best in Show. His white hybrid tea, 'Cloudless Dew', has a climbing habit."

Felicity had heard her grandmother's Percy-related patter countless times. Touching her hand to her hat, she again scanned the marquee. The show was too large and too busy to go looking for one another, and if there were two of them at the stand, it would be twice as difficult to get away. The agreement had therefore been for a signal from a distance.

In the far corner of the marquee, a slim, long-limbed woman of around forty with a dark brown chignon under a jade-green picture hat clutched herself protectively while being interviewed by a journalist.

Though the notebook and grey trilby had caught Felicity's attention, she didn't recognise the reporter. The elegantly dressed woman was, however, unmistakable.

Like Percy, Lady Leonora Templeton was a strong contender for Best in Show, but it was far from her first time at Bickleford Rose Festival. The Templeton family had a long and illustrious rose breeding legacy, and Leonora had several Best in Shows under her belt. While attitudes were changing, opportunities for women to establish careers remained uncommon. Regardless of one's interest in flowers, it was hard not to be intrigued by a woman who had propelled her family's business to new heights.

Yet Felicity had other priorities. She continued to scour the crowd.

The gathering of visitors on the other side of the marquee was dense. Another newcomer, Champs Verts Nursery, had also secured its place in the running for Best in Show and was doing brisk business at its stand, its flowers capturing the attention of the public as much as that of the show's expert judges. It wasn't possible to make out the nursery's representatives among the genteel throng, but it could be assumed they were taking numerous orders for the delivery of stock later in the year.

"Lady Henrietta, this is all very fascinating." Mrs Winterpole's reaction carried a distinct change in tone.

Felicity switched her attention back to the discussion at Percy's stand.

"I actually came to speak to you about something unrelated to today's event," continued Mrs Winterpole.

"Oh?" Lady Henrietta had been caught off guard. Pip received another round of energetic stroking. Mrs Broughton looked no more stunned than usual. Percy continued to smile somewhat absently, his hands in the pockets of his baggy checked trousers, his gaze drifting over the flowers on his stand.

Alerted by her grandmother's surprise, Felicity listened in. Lady Henrietta was already on tenterhooks about Percy's result in the show. If Mrs Winterpole had chosen this moment to discuss a controversial misalignment of opinion between the two women, then Felicity might have to step in.

"I hope you don't mind," said Mrs Winterpole, "but we should consider the preparations for the annual War Widows and Orphans Relief Society fundraiser. I was hoping you'd be available to attend a meeting in which we might discuss the division of responsibilities."

Felicity's shoulders relaxed with relief at the innocuousness of the topic. Sparks might fly at the upcoming meeting, but not at the flower show — and then there it was.

The signal. At long last.

Felicity needn't have worried. She could not possibly have missed it.

"Would you please excuse me for a moment, Grandmama?" said Felicity. "I shall return shortly."

Chapter Two

Felicity had recently completed an assignment as a teacher at an all-girls school. The experience had been memorable, but among the less life-altering outcomes was the widening of Felicity's vocabulary.

One term she'd grown accustomed to using was 'beau'.

It was the students' preferred term for a gentleman with whom a girl felt herself to be firmly associated but with whom she had no official connection other than sentiment. In most cases, a fairly powerful sentiment.

For Felicity, the term perfectly captured the new and exciting phase of her relationship with Mr Alex Cooper.

When they first met, Alex had been Felicity's professional rival. He'd developed into a reliable colleague and trusted acquaintance. Then a firm friend.

Now he was Felicity's beau.

Alex smiled at Felicity from the marquee's main entryway, flaps of white canvas drawn back like curtains to frame him against a cloudless cobalt sky. He looked typically dashing in a grey three-piece suit, his felt homburg tipped temporarily back to counter the heat of the June sunshine, the scar on his forehead and his slick dark blond hair revealed.

As Felicity eased towards Alex through the masses of flower show attendees, warmth spread in her stomach like butter melting on a hot crumpet, but Alex turned away. His attention was required by a man with a camera and a tripod over his shoulder.

Felicity halted her advance. Alex was working. The newspaper had deadlines, and what was a report on a flower show without photographs? Lady Henrietta would be happy to see Felicity back at Percy's stand, and Felicity would always respect Alex's commitment to his work, but might they not have even a little time together? The thought of it had kept Felicity going through the judging rounds and her grandmother's socialising.

Gesturing for the man with the camera to wait for a moment, Alex turned back towards Felicity. As the crowds continued to pass between them, Alex repeated the signal — the mime of a saucer and a cup being lifted to his lips — this time adding an extra action, pointing with his index finger.

Felicity gave a firm nod. She knew exactly what he meant.

As Alex hurried off with the photographer, Felicity started in the direction of the tea tent. They'd meet each other there.

"Lady Felicity?"

The interruption came from a pair of nervous young women with dark, curly hair and almost matching outfits. They'd recognised Felicity from the Gentlewoman's Gazette. It was a heartwarming exchange, the sisters impressed both by Felicity's endeavours and her writing. But just as Alex was rushing to squeeze a break with Felicity into his reporting schedule, so must Felicity be mindful of the time.

Having wished the sisters all the best with their respective endeavours — one planned to write a novel, the other hoped to work for the police — Felicity took the shortest route out of the main exhibition marquee. Deftly, she nipped around the side of the tent, away from the general flow of people and into the warren of passageways created by the many marquees erected to house the flower show. The white canvas walls gently undulated as the sun blazed overhead.

After pausing for a moment to gather her bearings, Felicity set off between the guiding ropes and tent pegs driven into the neatly shorn grass. Weaving between the marquees wasn't the most direct route, but by avoiding the slow-moving crowds and enthusiastic fans, it would surely be the quickest.

"You're only doing this to get at Leonora."

The words carried on the breeze. The voice was that of a man. He sounded rather angry.

Felicity stopped.

"You don't give a tinker's curse about roses."

Felicity couldn't see the speaker. It wasn't so much a voice as it was a growl.

"Otherwise you wouldn't have abandoned her."

It was beyond rude to eavesdrop, yet Felicity remained hidden beside the canvas wall of the nearest marquee. What should she do? If she continued her advance, she risked stumbling into a disagreement.

"Admit it. You're only here for Leonora."

Was the man talking about the rose breeder, Lady Leonora Templeton? To whom was he speaking? Felicity considered sneaking a look around the marquee's edge, but her priority was to reach Alex forthwith, and the man sounded angrier by the moment. Should she retrace her steps?

"What if it's true?" A second man spoke. A hint of wry amusement coloured his polished voice.

"What if I'm only here to cause a fuss?" continued the second man. "To embarrass your precious Leonora? I don't see what you can do about it."

A low growl rumbled. The noise was animal-like. It sounded dangerous.

Felicity gripped the skirt of her dress, ready to run and fetch help.

"Daisy!" shouted the first man.

The barking was ferocious but also immediately recognisable as belonging to a diminutive canine. It was therefore unsurprising yet still something of a shock when a short-legged white-and-tan Jack Russell Terrier came dashing around the tent's corner.

Woof! Woof! Woof!

The dog planted itself before Felicity and barked savagely. Attached to its sturdy collar was a braided leather lead, but there was no one holding onto the end.

"Good dog," said Felicity soothingly, but there was no quelling the Jack Russell's wrath. She tried edging away, but the dog followed Felicity's every move.

Woof! Woof! Woof!

What had set the creature off? Had it sniffed Felicity out and taken umbrage to her eavesdropping? Listening in was never polite, but how would a dog know that?

"Daisy!"

A stout man with hairy arms and a firm jaw appeared. He grabbed the still-barking Jack Russell and tucked her under his elbow. Another nearly identical dog struggled under his other arm, this one black where the other was tan. Both terriers barked furiously.

"Daisy! Flossie! Enough!" shouted the man. Shooting Felicity a fierce glare as he passed her, the stout man stalked away from the scene, his shoulders hulking under a checked shirt and braces, the end of Daisy's lead dragging across the grass, both dogs still barking.

Felicity let out a breath. Whoever the fellow was, she would be happy to never meet him or his dogs again.

Her relief, however, was short-lived.

A tall, slender man of around forty-five stepped out from behind the marquee. With dark hair tinged with grey and a scar on his cheek, he'd perhaps been handsome in his youth. A bright red rose was tucked into the lapel of his navy pinstripe suit.

"Lady Felicity Quick." The man's smile was oily. "How delightful to make your acquaintance."

Felicity's stomach squeezed with unease. She'd grown used to being recognised by strangers, but she couldn't forget what she'd just overheard. Was the man with the Jack Russells perhaps justified in his anger? Being caught eavesdropping added to the awkwardness of the situation.

"I was just—" began Felicity.

"You won't tell on us, will you?"

Felicity turned. Alex had appeared behind her, his hat in his hands, his dark blue gaze convincingly earnest.

How had he known where to find Felicity? When had he arrived? It didn't matter. Felicity was happy to allow Alex to rescue her. On this occasion, at least.

"We'd be awfully grateful if you were discreet," said Felicity, building on the ruse of being caught during a private rendezvous with a gentleman friend.

The dark-haired man narrowed his eyes at Alex. "Sly one, aren't you?"

Alex's jaw tightened. "I beg your pardon."

"Nabbing yourself the earl's daughter." The man's eyes twinkled mischievously. "Good luck to you, sir," he said as he strolled away, slapping Alex on the shoulder as he passed him.

Alex's nostrils flared, and his grip tightened on the brim of his hat. There wasn't much that irked Alex. He usually remained calm when others lost their heads. Yet this encounter riled him.

"What a deeply unpleasant character," said Felicity once the man was out of earshot. The accusation of Alex's social climbing was too ridiculous to be worthy of discussion.

"Rather," agreed Alex, his grip still tight on his hat.

Felicity slid her hand over Alex's, entwining her fingers with his. It was, by now, a familiar gesture between them but no less meaningful for it. "Thank you for saving me," she said.

Alex shook his head. "Poppycock." He squeezed Felicity's hand. "You hate being rescued." He beamed at her somewhat teasingly.

Felicity squeezed back. "Not today. Although you can't save me from everything."

"Regretting your decision to judge the flower show? Still thinking about that magazine article you aren't writing?" Alex quirked an eyebrow. "Maybe both?"

Felicity sighed deeply. He knew her far too well.

"I believe I've made my grandmother proud today. And I can't ask for another extension to the magazine's deadline, so I'll be up till rather late tonight. But at least I'm not suffering alone." Felicity cocked her head. "Unless reporting on roses beats reporting on crime?"

"If it means I get to see you, then it absolutely does."

Felicity's stomach fluttered with joy. The more time they spent together, the closer they became. And while her grandmother's meddling wasn't always welcome, Lady Henrietta had insisted Alex be assigned to the flower show, which boded well for them in case they decided to announce their relationship. But there was no rush for that.

Felicity tapped a fingertip on her chin. "Plants and crime aren't necessarily mutually exclusive, though, are they?"

"Here we go." Alex squeezed Felicity's hand and released it. "I knew I was right to come and find you." He replaced his hat on his head and reached into his jacket for his notebook. "What's the scoop?"

Felicity frowned. "What makes you think I've got a scoop?"

Alex paused and raised his eyebrows. "You've got that look in your eye."

"Are we going for that pot of tea or not?" said Felicity, mildly annoyed that there was hardly anything she could hide from Alex.

"Should still be able to squeeze it in." He held out an arm, which Felicity took, and they started towards the tea tent.

"Did you see the man with the two Jack Russells?" she asked.

Alex shook his head. The passageways behind the tents were a labyrinth. "I heard dogs barking. Then I found you."

"I came upon a confrontation between a man with two Jack Russells and the rather unpleasant fellow we just encountered. I overheard them talking about 'Leonora'. I presume they were referring to Lady Leonora Templeton. How many other Leonoras do you suppose are at the show?"

Alex turned to Felicity, his eyes widened slightly. "Do you know who that unpleasant fellow was?"

Felicity frowned. "Should I?"

"Champs Verts Nursery?"

"I was at their stand briefly this morning," said Felicity as she navigated a guide rope. "I shook hands with an older woman and a younger chap, both French, but I don't remember being introduced to Mr Unpleasant, and I somehow doubt I would forget."

"Mr Unpleasant is their boss."

"He is?" Felicity wrinkled her nose with distaste. "Goodness. I hope I didn't give any of his flowers full marks."

Alex flicked through his notebook. "Goes by the name of Fox. Wasn't there for the set up or the judging rounds. Only parachuting in for the prize ceremony. And—" Alex lowered his voice and leaned towards Felicity as they rejoined the flowing crowds of flower show visitors. "—there's a rumour." As a journalist, Alex was exceptional. You could drop him into any situation, and he'd dig up the most intriguing stories in no time.

"Do tell," said Felicity.

"That Champs Verts fellow and Lady Leonora—"

"Lady Felicity?"

Felicity let go of Alex's arm and turned towards the voice. Would they ever reach the tea tent?

"Apologies for the interruption," said a thin man with a pince-nez and a serious expression that conveyed an air of urgency. "Colonel Bolt requests your presence in the main exhibition tent."

Felicity cast a forlorn glance at Alex. He sighed.

"Now?" asked Felicity of the man in the pince-nez.

"Yes, your ladyship," he said. "Right away."

Chapter Three

"It pains me to say it, but year after year, we see the same old Templeton roses. No innovation."

Mr Ronald Merton was a portly man of about fifty-five, with a waxed moustache and a paisley cravat. One of the expert judges tasked with selecting the Best in Show, he paced the stage at the centre of Bickleford Rose Festival's main exhibition marquee.

"There's that couple who put in the hard work, bless them," continued Mr Merton, "but their quality this year is down." He stopped pacing, his gaze softening with fondness as he turned towards the judges' seating. "Then there's Champs Verts."

"Once again, Mr Merton, you've forgotten Mr Percival Colhayne."

Mr Lucas Shakerley, the second of Bickleford Rose Festival's expert judges, was of a similar age to Mr Merton, although much smaller in stature. Mr Shakerley had wispy pale-grey hair and a yellow bow tie that picked up the check running through his moss-green suit.

He adjusted his crooked spectacles and spoke without looking up from a battered leather notebook on his knee, its pages dense with spidery handwriting. "Colhayne may be young, but his talent shouldn't be ignored."

Seated beside Mr Shakerley, Felicity maintained a patient and impartial silence. There had been time for several cups of tea with Alex since she'd arrived for the prize-giving ceremony, but it was encouraging to hear the praise for Lady Henrietta's protégé. It was, however, perhaps for the best that there was hardly anyone within earshot of the judges' disagreement.

Porters in brown coats were still unfolding rows of chairs and repositioning the speakers of the public address system in an area around the stage that had been roped off from the crowds visiting the show. Beside the rope, Mr Elliot Etty, the other celebrity judge, was signing autographs for fans of the music hall, of which there were many from all walks of life.

On the stage, Mr Merton tweaked the tip of his waxed moustache as he stepped closer to where Mr Shakerley was seated. "Academically speaking, you outshine us all, Mr Shakerley. But this year is different. If the association is to stay relevant—"

Mr Shakerley raised his eyes from his notebook. "Appreciation based on animal instincts differs from engaging one's intellect, Mr Merton."

Mr Merton looked puzzled, then chuckled. "Colonel, are you hearing this?"

Colonel Simon Bolt, a retired army officer and president of the British Rose Association, paused his work directing two porters in finessing the position of an ornate silver plate on a slender stand. The plate was the prize for Best in Show. It sparkled brightly even in the soft light that filtered through the marquee's canvas.

"Are the envelopes all there, Mr Ince?" The colonel had a commanding voice and was rather tall, even when leaning on his cane. With a starched white collar, highly polished shoes, and a sharp centre parting, his presentation was meticulous. An enamel badge on his lapel carried the image of a rose and the words *British Rose Association*.

At the lectern towards the front of the stage, Colonel Bolt's secretary — who had interrupted Felicity and Alex's trip to the tea tent — responded to the enquiry with a rustle of paper and an adjustment to his pince-nez. “Yes, Colonel. All here.”

“Then there’s nothing further to discuss.” The colonel threw a steely glare towards the two professional judges. “Is there?”

Mr Merton sighed with defeat as he dropped into his seat next to Mr Shakerley.

“Five minutes, Colonel.” Mrs Winterpole was in the front row below the stage, among the seats reserved for prize entrants. In the lap of her floral tea dress in pastel shades she held a rather battered-looking pocket watch.

The colonel stiffened, a flush appearing in his cheeks. “Positions, everyone,” he bellowed. “Positions!”

As the porters took down the ropes, visitors surged forward, and the seats quickly filled, the air awash with the scent of the roses from the stands at the marquee’s edges.

Mr Etty sprang lithely onto the stage to take his seat next to Felicity.

“Not too late, am I?” he whispered.

“I’d be surprised if the colonel noticed,” Felicity replied, nodding towards the rose association president, who watched with a furrowed brow as the last adjustments were made to the microphone at the lectern.

Excited chatter filled the air, and the prize nominees took their seats in front of the stage. Lady Henrietta nodded in Felicity’s direction as she settled next to Percy, with Pip on her lap. Mrs Broughton gave Felicity a little wave, which Felicity acknowledged with a smile. Mrs Winterpole maintained her position in the front row with her pocket watch, her gaze fixed on Colonel Bolt.

There was a flurry of whispers and knowing nods from visitors and rose breeders alike as the Champs Verts team took their seats behind Lady Henrietta and Percy. The tall, slender man with the scarred cheek that Felicity and Alex had encountered behind the marquees was there. Seated beside him were the young man with straw-blond hair and a flat cap and the older woman with painted eyebrows and deep-set eyes whom Felicity had met briefly at the nursery's stand earlier that morning.

Had their roses truly charmed the public, or was the attention more connected to the rumour Alex had hinted at but not had time to elaborate upon?

On the other side of the seating, towards the press area, Lady Leonora Templeton was getting settled. She had two leather leads held taught in her hand, the dogs too small to be visible through the crowds, yet there was no doubting which creatures were attached to the leads.

Taking a seat next to Leonora was the hulking man Felicity had overheard behind the tents. The glare he gave Felicity sent a chill up her spine, and she averted her gaze.

What was it Alex had wanted to share? A rumour about Lady Leonora and the unpleasant fellow from Champs Verts, wasn't it? Alex had said the fellow's name was Fox. Mr Fox. They were sitting some distance apart and didn't appear to be aware of one another. Leonora's back was straight and her expression serene. The dark-haired man from Champs Verts reclined in his seat with his arms folded and a mildly amused look on his face.

Mrs Winterpole held her pocket watch aloft and gave the colonel a meaningful nod. The colonel's eyes grew wide, his secretary dashing off the stage to wait in the wings.

Approaching the lectern, Colonel Bolt tapped the microphone. The horn speakers at the sides of the stage crackled into life and the crowd quietened.

"Ladies and gentlemen," he began.

The press section at the edge of the stage was bulging. Alex's photographer was in the huddle, but where was Alex? Late-comers continued to stream into the marquee. Mr Clive Dingle, the flat-capped rose breeder from the stand next to Percy's, arrived with his wife, but the seats were already full, so they had to remain standing.

"On behalf of the British Rose Association," continued the colonel, his eyes switching between the pages of notes on the lectern and the crowd before him, "I'd like to thank you all for coming to Bickleford for our annual rose festival. As we all know, the rose is the queen of the garden, which surely makes our event the highlight of the floral year."

There was movement in the press area. Alex had arrived, his notebook at the ready. He gave Felicity a wink. Of course, he wouldn't miss the prize-giving.

The colonel's voice continued to hum through the speakers. "And now, for the climax of our show's programme. The awards."

Polite applause filled the marquee. Flash powder ignited in the press area. The first accolade to be presented was Best Shrub. Then came Best Climber. Best Fragrance. Best Colour.

Felicity had to stifle more than one yawn. The awards list was long, and there were amateur and professional categories for each, but the flow of announcements was smooth. Winners were processed efficiently, collecting ribbons and certificates from Colonel Bolt, Mr Merton, and Mr Shakerley, all ably assisted by the association's secretary and with the rhythm set by subtle nods from Mrs Winterpole and her old pocket watch.

The sun beating on the canvas steadily warmed the marquee. Polite applause rose and fell at regular intervals. An intoxicating floral scent danced perpetually on the breeze. With nothing to do but sit and bear witness to proceedings, Felicity fought hard to prevent her eyelids dipping. She cared little for the art of rose breeding and even less for her status as a celebrity, but falling asleep on stage would have been a step too far.

"Mr Etty, would you do us the honour of announcing this year's Best in Show? And Lady Felicity, would you kindly assist with the presentation of the prize?"

The colonel's words jolted Felicity alert. As she rose from her seat, a sense of sharpened attention rippled through the crowd. The journalists and photographers jostled with one another for an optimal view of the stage, but the focus wasn't on Felicity or even Mr Etty for their celebrity status. Best in Show at Bickleford was the most important accolade of the gardening year.

"Thank you, Colonel Bolt." Even over the crackling horn

speakers, the music-hall singer's voice was as smooth as honey. "It's a great honour and a distinct pleasure to announce the winner of this year's prize for Best in Show."

As Mr Etty untucked the envelope containing the winner's name, Felicity stood with Colonel Bolt beside the silver plate. Alex was poised, his attention on Mr Etty, the tip of his pencil on his notebook. From where Felicity was standing, it was hard not to envy the thrill of his role. As soon as Alex had the winner's name and a few comments from the acceptance speech, he would sprint to the only telephone box in the village to call in the news. Arriving late to the press area had certainly been deliberate. From the edge of the group, he would have a head start on the race to the telephone.

Lady Henrietta's attention was also fixed on Mr Etty, her hand pressing onto Pip's head with caresses that intensified in accordance with the dowager's nervousness. Even Percy's eyes shone with keen interest. To secure Best in Show could be life-changing for a rose breeder.

"And the winner is—" Mr Etty fished the paper out of the envelope. Reading it, his eyebrows lifted with delight.

Chapter Four

"It's Champs Verts Nursery with Rosa 'Red Vixen'!" announced Mr Etty.

The applause was intense. Flash powder exploded.

As she assisted Colonel Bolt in lifting the silver plate from its stand, Felicity wore a convincing yet unwilling smile. It brought her no joy to see Mr Fox, the unpleasant man in the pinstripe suit she and Alex had encountered behind the tents, firmly shaking the hands of his colleagues and navigating towards the stage with a self-satisfied smirk.

Lady Henrietta couldn't be happy either, but her expression was stoic, and she wasn't withholding her applause. Percy, too, was clapping, albeit slowly and with a somewhat glazed expression. Even Mr Shakerley had put aside his misgivings and got to his feet beside fellow professional judge Mr Merton to applaud.

The only audience member not clapping was the burly man seated next to Lady Leonora Templeton. His thick arms remain folded tightly over his broad chest. Frowning a little, Leonora's applause was cautious.

Felicity continued smiling as the smirking winner collected his silver plate. When he shook Felicity's hand, he raised his eyebrows in a manner she found overly familiar.

"Do you wish to address your public, Mr Fox?" enquired the music-hall singer, inviting the winner to approach the lectern.

Fox. It was a name well-suited to a man who was undoubtedly sly and perhaps even predatory.

Mr Fox waved a hand as though uninterested in giving a speech, but then he appeared to change his mind. Straightening his tie and with the silver plate tucked under his arm, Mr Fox approached the microphone.

A hush fell over the marquee.

The horn speakers crackled. "For many of you, this—" Mr Fox held up the plate, indicating his win. "—comes as a surprise."

It was the same polished voice with an undertone of amusement that Felicity had encountered behind the tents. She glanced at Alex. His expression was serious, his attention on noting every word of the winner's speech.

"For me, well..." Mr Fox shook his head and smiled. "None of you know what I've been through."

In the audience, the woman with the deep-set eyes from Champs Verts nodded earnestly. The younger man from the nursery with the straw-blond hair covered a yawn with the back of his hand.

"Well, I suppose there's one person who knows part of it," continued Mr Fox. "Where is she?"

As the winner of the Best in Show scanned the crowd, Colonel Bolt swallowed. A flush had risen in his cheeks. This clearly wasn't a typical winner's speech. Mr Shakerley looked grave, but Mr Merton was chuckling to himself, although Felicity couldn't fathom what about the situation was amusing.

"Aha." Mr Fox pointed into the crowd. "There she is. My dear Leonora. Although whether she recognises her own brother after all these years, I couldn't say."

Gasps went up around the tent. Excited murmurs swelled. More flashes went off.

Was this the rumour Alex had tried to tell Felicity about, that the unpleasant man in the pinstripe suit and Lady Leonora were siblings?

Is this why Mr Fox hadn't been at the show's set up or the introductions that morning — was the surprise part of his plan?

Felicity tried to catch Alex's eye, but his expression was concentrated, his pencil moving rapidly across his notebook. He had his scoop.

A few camera lenses shifted towards the crowd. Leonora's serene expression and stiff posture were fixed like stone, but her cheeks were drained of colour. The burly man next to her went to stand, but Leonora put a hand on his arm and he remained seated, fuming with anger, like a bull waiting to charge.

Mr Fox looked pleased as the whole tent buzzed with surprise and excitement. He wheeled around to face Colonel Bolt, Mr Shakerley, and Mr Merton. Wildness glinted in his eye. "Did any of you old sticks at the British Rose Association realise it was me?" In redirecting himself, Mr Fox's voice missed the microphone. Only those nearest the stage could continue to hear him. "Some of you must have recognised me, surely." He stroked his scarred cheek. "I've aged well, have I not? I don't suppose any of you expected to see me again. Did you imagine I'd forgotten you all? Forgotten everything my parents ever achieved?" Mr Fox put an uncomfortable emphasis on the final word. "Am I not owed something? Some part of this wondrous success you all bathe in year upon year like pigs in muck?"

The smile under Mr Merton's waxed moustache had disappeared. Mr Shakerley regarded the pinstriped prize-winner with a narrowed, analytical gaze. Colonel Bolt was becoming a worrying shade of puce.

Half-muttering an oath, the colonel marched off the stage, his cane tapping as he passed his secretary, who stood frozen with shock in the wings.

This was far from a normal prize winner's speech.

Out in the audience, Lady Henrietta trembled from distress or rage, Felicity couldn't tell. Pip's ears flicked about. He was alert to trouble but wasn't sure of the source.

Mrs Broughton's eyes were wide, her hand clasped over her mouth. Percy appeared intrigued, although he wore a faint frown.

Mrs Winterpole looked anxiously about, especially worried now that Colonel Bolt had disappeared from sight.

What could Felicity do to help? Mr Fox's speech should surely be cut short, but what on earth was it all about?

"Mr Fox," began Felicity, raising her palms placatingly, "perhaps we ought to—"

"Let's have another round of applause for Mr Fox of Champs Verts Nursery." Mr Etty's honeyed tones crackled over the speakers. The music-hall singer had circumnavigated Mr Fox without his noticing and was back in front of the microphone.

"Oh, no." Mr Fox span towards the lectern. "No, no. I'm not finished yet."

Mr Etty hopped nimbly aside as the Best in Show winner charged towards the microphone and swiped it off the lectern.

"You see, it's not just the association or my family." Mr Fox's voice boomed through the speakers. "It's all you breeders—" He pointed a finger into the crowd, jabbing at Percy and the Dingles, his sense of amusement gone, the wild glint in his eye now expanded into a savage glare. "—imagining this means something." He waved the silver plate. "Imagining this whole charade means something. Well, let me tell you. From now on, there's going to be a—"

Crack!

A noise like the snap of a whip came from the speakers of the public address system.

"—new way of doing things." Mr Fox's voice was no longer carrying across the audience. The microphone was dead. "What the deuce..." He shook the apparatus angrily.

Colonel Bolt straightened at the side of the stage, the disconnected cables of the public address system still in his hands, his cane abandoned on the ground beside him. His cheeks were still purple, but his shoulders were slumped with relief.

"Blast it!" Mr Fox threw the microphone to the floor and marched off the stage. Whispers of disbelief and nervous chatter swept through the packed marquee. What had just happened? Was the prize-giving ceremony over? What would happen next?

The woman from Champs Verts squeezed through the crowd to meet Mr Fox as he roughly shoved people aside in an effort to storm out of the tent. A gaggle of journalists left the press area to follow him. Alex was no longer to be seen, his long limbs no doubt carrying him swiftly to the telephone box. The journalists of the Western Daily News never celebrated the misfortune of others, but the public had a right to know, and Alex would surely make the front page with this story.

Felicity would catch up with him later. For now, she sought her grandmother among the throng.

Lady Henrietta was out of her seat, Pip tucked tightly under her arm. If she'd been upset, then she'd made a quick recovery. The dowager was decisively on the move, with Mrs Broughton trailing after her.

Mrs Winterpole had also swung into action. As Felicity descended into the crowd to follow her grandmother, Mrs Winterpole had made her way onto the stage, her hands raised aloft to attract the attention of the distracted and scattering crowd. "Mr Shakerley's presentation on his forthcoming book on the history of English rose breeding starts at two o'clock sharp," she announced, her voice barely carrying without the microphone. "That's in thirty minutes. Here in the presentation area. Do join us if you wish to—"

Mrs Winterpole's voice faded into the hubbub as Felicity left the marquee, squinting in the bright sunshine. She still didn't have a thorough grasp of exactly what she'd just witnessed, but she couldn't prioritise the unravelling of the situation for her own understanding. She had to follow her grandmother.

Lady Henrietta was hurrying through the crowds, and a little further ahead was Mr Fox.

Felicity's grandmother was in pursuit.

Chapter Five

Adjusting the brim of her hat against the bright sunshine, Felicity did her best to follow her grandmother and Mrs Broughton, but she quickly lost sight of them among the streams of flower show visitors exiting the main marquee. Beyond the still-excited buzz of the crowd, however, came a distinct sound that might have escaped the notice of the untrained ear.

It was faint, but Felicity could hear her grandmother's voice. And the dowager did not sound happy.

After some hasty false turns, the breeze knocking the sound about the various tents, Felicity came upon a scene that made her stomach plummet.

"We Quicks have donated to the British Rose Association for generations. Your own ancestors were the founders. The founders!"

Sandwiched between an educational display on rose cultivation and an unmanned information kiosk, Lady Henrietta had somehow cornered Mr Fox and was in the process of giving him a dressing down.

"You've abused the association for your own gain. You've brought rose breeding into disrepute. You should be ashamed of yourself, not smiling and pleased."

The dowager still clutched a confused-looking Pip under her arm.

At her side, Mrs Broughton appeared mildly panicked. The woman from Champs Verts Nursery stood between Lady Henrietta and Mr Fox, her arms outstretched, her deep-set eyes firing warning glances at the dowager, but Lady Henrietta showed no interest in stepping back.

In his pinstripe suit and with the Best in Show plate glinting under his arm, Mr Fox seemed thoroughly entertained by it all.

"You should be ashamed," continued the dowager. "Do you hear me?"

Pip cocked his head and gave Felicity a questioning look. In signing up to become a lap dog, the little Yorkie perhaps hadn't imagined such pulse-quickening encounters to be part of the job.

As much as the smirking rose breeder deserved his comeuppance, Felicity had to intervene. Emotion had got the better of Lady Henrietta. Even if it felt good in the moment, she might later regret the outburst.

"Come now, Grandmama." Felicity put a gentle hand on her grandmother's arm. "Let's leave matters to be solved by the association."

"Y-yes," echoed Mrs Broughton, her eyes wide and fearful, the feathers on her hat trembling. "Let's leave matters for the association."

Felicity's touch was met with a tug of resistance.

"You should give that back," continued Lady Henrietta, unperturbed, nodding towards the silver plate.

"You cannot speak to Monsieur Fox in this way," cautioned the woman standing between the dowager and the Best in Show winner. Her French accent was strong.

The advice went unheeded. "You don't deserve it," continued Lady Henrietta. "Your mother and father would be ashamed."

The amusement in Mr Fox's expression disappeared quite suddenly.

The woman from Champs Verts twisted towards him, her expression fearful.

"No one but me decides how to honour my parents," growled Mr

Fox. His face changed as he took a step forward, the scar on his cheek creasing more deeply. "Or whether to even honour them at all." He barged past Lady Henrietta and went striding off into the show grounds, the Frenchwoman scrambling after him.

The push Mr Fox gave Lady Henrietta wasn't violent, but it was enough to unsteady her.

"Goodness!" she exclaimed.

Pip whimpered with alarm.

"Oh, dear!" cried Mrs Broughton, her hand brought to her mouth.

The dowager was toppling.

"I'm so sorry."

The bells of Bickleford's church tower had not long rung the hour. Lady Henrietta leaned heavily on Felicity's arm as they walked slowly across the neatly cut grass, leaving the bustling marquees of the flower show behind. Pip trotted ahead, his nose dipping to the occasional daisy missed by the mower.

Lady Henrietta was unhurt but exhausted from her encounter with Mr Fox. As expected, regret at the indecorous confrontation was setting in.

"I'm so very sorry, my dear."

"Hush now," cooed Felicity, patting her grandmother's hand. "You've nothing to be sorry about."

The dowager sighed wearily. "Where would I be without you, my dear?"

Felicity's firm grip on her grandmother's elbow had prevented Lady Henrietta from tumbling to the ground after Mr Fox barged past her. Had the knock from him been deliberate? Felicity's chest tightened with anger at the thought. Giving such a man the benefit of the doubt was difficult.

"If you go home now," continued Felicity, doing her best to speak soothingly, "you'll perhaps feel recovered enough to return later in the afternoon."

Lady Henrietta shook her head ruefully. "That poor boy has been through so much. Losing his father in the South African War. Then his mother, while he himself was away fighting. And Pamela was such a treasure of a woman."

Percy seemed to be all Lady Henrietta could think about, which was understandable. The dowager had spent months preparing his bid to win Best in Show, and it had ended in a most inglorious manner.

"Mrs Broughton is giving him all the support he needs," reassured Felicity. Despite being quite shaken herself, Mrs Broughton had thankfully agreed to remain at Percy's stand and assist him. Lady Henrietta might not have left the show otherwise, even though she was in obvious need of rest.

"That wretched fellow. Winning the prize and addressing the crowd like that. I don't care if he says he's a Templeton. He can't just suddenly reappear and do whatever he wants."

Felicity was concerned about her grandmother becoming agitated all over again, but the situation was exceedingly curious. "Is he really Lady Leonora's brother?"

"There was a wayward son who left home early on, but that was decades ago." The dowager wrinkled her nose with disgust. "If he is who he says he is, then thank goodness Leonora's parents are no longer here to witness his behaviour. It's utterly unacceptable."

"Do you know why he left home?"

Lady Henrietta's grip tightened on Felicity's arm. "I'm going to have words with the association." The dowager was no longer listening. She was getting het up. "The prize should be rescinded."

It wasn't right to pressure her grandmother in her present state. Felicity would have to wait for answers.

The Quick family's dark blue Rolls-Royce had come into view, parked at the edge of the village, where the thatched roofs of Bickleford met the show ground. The driver, Finnegan, held the door open for Lady Henrietta as Felicity assisted her onto the back seat.

Woof! Woof! Woof!

Pip was about to join the dowager in the Rolls, but upon hearing the barking, he hesitated, a paw lifted.

The two Jack Russells Felicity had met earlier were straining at their leads, their barking directed at Pip. Lady Leonora Templeton held both leads in one hand, her other hand steadying her jade-green picture hat against the breeze. Beside her lumbered the thick set man with hairy arms who Felicity had encountered behind the marquees.

The man scowled at Felicity as he passed, but Leonora didn't look in her direction. Heading deeper into the village, they seemed in rather a hurry.

Had the Templeton stand been abandoned? It was one of the most popular exhibitions at the show. Had the speech from the man going by the name of Mr Fox been too much for Leonora? Were they really brother and sister? Regardless of the veracity of his claims, the Best in Show winner's controversial outburst had thrust her into an uncomfortable spotlight. Surely, every journalist at the show wanted a reaction from Leonora.

Grrr... Woof!

Pip returned fire at Flossie and Daisy, just a single cautioning bark. He wasn't a fighter, but he had his pride.

"Master Pip," said Lady Henrietta. "Are you accompanying me or not?"

With help from Felicity, the little Yorkie turned his back on his antagonists and hopped up into the Rolls, nestling into his basket beside Lady Henrietta.

"And you, dear," said the dowager. "Will you join me?"

Felicity shook her head. Returning to her typewriter and focusing on the deadline for the Gentlewoman's Gazette would have been the right thing to do.

But not yet.

"I shouldn't abandon my post as a judge. The prize giving may be over, but the show hasn't finished."

"Very good, dear." Lady Henrietta squeezed Felicity's hand. "You'll check on Mr Cooper, won't you?"

Felicity smiled. Her grandmother's concern for Alex was touching. The flower show wasn't his usual beat, and the dowager was somewhat responsible for his presence there.

"Of course." Felicity would make a point of seeing Alex, although she had priorities other than checking on his welfare.

Felicity wanted answers.

Chapter Six

"Lord Anthony Templeton."

Alex flicked through his notebook as he walked. His stride was brisk, but it was Felicity setting the pace, carving a purposeful path along the flower show's main avenue and towards the tea tent.

Felicity had already dodged several autograph hunters before locating Alex in the midst of wrapping up an interview with the rose association's secretary. By keeping the brim of her hat low and her gait deliberate, it limited the opportunity for interruptions.

"Go on," she urged, mindful that Alex couldn't take too long a break from his reporting.

"Disappeared some twenty years ago," continued Alex, reading from the pages. "Not heard from since. Not till now."

"So where does 'Fox' come into it?"

The strains of Mr Shakerley's voice carried on the breeze as they passed the main exhibition tent, the public address system having been reconnected in time for the talk about his forthcoming book.

"Unclear so far," said Alex. "Could just be a pseudonym he adopted to avoid being found."

Felicity huffed. It was information, but it wasn't the whole story. "Can we be certain he's the missing Lord Templeton?" She moderated her tone to not sound too impatient. Alex was surely doing his best to piece the tale together.

Their exchange paused as they circumnavigated an enthusiastic gathering that had formed around the music-hall singer, Mr Etty. Mr Etty appeared at ease and even enjoying the attention, smiling handsomely as he shook hands and signed autographs. A short man with a moustache accompanying the singer — perhaps his manager — looked less relaxed as he attempted to usher the star onwards.

"The fellow insists he's Leonora's long-lost brother," said Alex as they approached the tea tent. "When asked where he's been all these years, he's tight-lipped. Says he and his parents had a disagreement and won't say about what. He has a female assistant, a Frenchwoman, who won't allow anyone to speak to him for too long."

Felicity nodded. "I know exactly to whom you're referring."

"But there's not a reporter that's been able to get a word out of Leonora."

"She's left the show," said Felicity, craning her neck as they joined the back of a snaking queue. All of the tea tables were occupied, the waitresses in their black-and-white uniforms run off their feet. Would they ever have that pot of tea together?

Alex's eyebrows lifted. "She has?"

Felicity angled the wide brim of her straw hat to lower the risk of being recognised. "I saw her leaving the show myself. With her assistant or whatever he is."

"Michael Havelock."

"That's the fellow's name?"

Alex flicked through his notebook. "He's a gardener at Templeton Manor."

It was easy to imagine the burly Michael Havelock swinging a spade or a fork. It was less easy to imagine the brute handling delicate roses.

Felicity gave her head a little shake. She needn't nurture her dislike of the man. They'd likely never see one another again. "I saw them leaving the show grounds when I took my grandmother back to our motor."

Alex turned sharply to Felicity. "Is Lady Henrietta all right?"

"Just a little shaken." As the queue shuffled forwards, Felicity lowered her voice and leaned closer to Alex. "She accosted Mr Fox or Lord Anthony Templeton or whatever he's called. She confronted him about his behaviour."

Alex's eyes widened. "Your grandmother is a force of nature."

The bells of Bickleford's church tower could be heard faintly across the show grounds. It was now a quarter past the hour.

"What did she say to him?" asked Alex with a quirk of an eyebrow.

"That he should give the prize back." The queue shuffled forward a little more. "That his mother and father—"

A scream ripped through the show grounds.

Felicity froze. Alex stiffened with alarm. The staff of the tea tent stopped in their tracks. A deadly silence fell across the tables.

There came another scream, unnerving and shrill.

Felicity was the first to move towards the noise. Pushing through dumbstruck crowds and ducking behind a display of rose care equipment, Felicity found a waitress sobbing into the sleeve of her black-and-white uniform. Alex arrived right after Felicity.

Felicity put her arm around the girl's shoulders. "What's the matter? What happened?"

The waitress continued to sob, her eyes squeezed tightly shut.

"What's going on back here?" A pair of show porters in brown overcoats arrived on the scene.

Felicity gently squeezed the girl's shoulder. "Try to breathe. It'll be all right."

"Felicity," said Alex gravely.

She looked over to where Alex was crouched.

A crate of lemonade bottles, perhaps what the waitress had been aiming to collect, had toppled on its side, the bottles lying in the grass. The crate had been removed from a stack against which lay a tall pile of hessian sacks, the sort used for carrying soil and wrapping root balls.

Perhaps disturbed by the removal of the crate, the pile of sacks had collapsed like an avalanche. Revealed was a sight that whoever had arranged the situation wished for no one to see.

A man's body lay lifeless, still partially covered by hessian sacks. There was a scar on his cheek. In the lapel of his pinstripe suit was a crushed red rose.

It was Mr Fox. Lord Anthony Templeton. That year's winner of the prize for Best in Show.

He was dead.

Chapter Seven

THE NEXT DAY, BRADLEY COURT, NEAR LOWER DIDDLETON

"It wasn't such a queer suggestion, was it?"

Waving a folding mother-of-pearl fan slowly before her face, Lady Henrietta blinked questioningly at Felicity from the other side of the wrought-iron table. With a large tasselled parasol at the table's centre offering welcome protection from the sun, the gathering for afternoon tea on Bradley Court's terrace appeared quite normal.

Mrs Broughton had chosen a wide-brimmed hat decorated with wax berries for the occasion. Percy Colhayne wore a loose-fitting brown suit. Having made good progress on her magazine piece that morning, Felicity had joined the gathering in a pale blue chiffon tea dress. Pip's little nose occasionally lifted above the edge of the table, sniffing the cakes and sandwiches from his vantage point on the dowager's lap.

The atmosphere at the table was, however, decidedly and understandably odd.

"Mrs Broughton, perhaps you can decide the matter," urged Lady Henrietta, fanning herself slightly faster. "Was it such an unusual suggestion?"

Lady Henrietta would never be so coarse or unkind as to celebrate anyone's demise. Even that of her worst enemy. But the sudden passing of the winner of Best in Show at yesterday's Bickleford Rose Festival seemed to have erased the dowager's anger at the speech he'd given.

Any relief felt, however, was tense and uncertain.

Having interviewed Felicity directly after the body's discovery, the police had been at Bradley Court that morning to speak to Lady Henrietta. It was the police's intention to talk with everyone who had visited the show and might have seen something. They were doing an extremely thorough job. But they were also asking all potential witnesses to remain within the county until further notice.

Felicity shifted in her seat as Mrs Broughton looked with mild panic from the dowager to Felicity.

"Well. I don't see..." began Mrs Broughton, the wax berries jumping a little on her hat. "I can't imagine..."

"Is that your assessment, Mrs Broughton?" Lady Henrietta was unashamed of putting her friend on the spot. "That my granddaughter isn't up to the job?"

"Grandmama," sighed Felicity. "Please."

Following the grim discovery under the hessian sacks, the suggestion had been made by several bystanders that, given her profile as a solver of crimes, Felicity would involve herself in the investigation of the rose breeder's untimely passing. Thankfully, the police arrived quickly, and the idea was put to bed. Felicity had no desire to jump aboard cases willy-nilly, especially not when she had magazine articles to write, and the Devon County Constabulary were more than capable of seeing to matters.

"But I didn't say Lady Felicity isn't capable of handling the investigation." Mrs Broughton's protest was immediate and adamant. "I would never say that."

Lady Henrietta allowed a morsel of scone to drop onto her lap. Pip pounced upon it. So that was how Felicity had lost her pet's loyalty.

"Percy," pressed the dowager. "What do you think?"

The young rose breeder was gazing towards the clipped yews that framed a view of the rolling Devonian countryside.

"Percy, dear?"

Somewhat dreamily, he returned his attention to the table, his smile gentle, his green eyes blinking slowly. "Yes?" It was clear he hadn't heard a word of the discussion.

Lady Henrietta pursed her lips. The veneer of politeness covering her exasperation was wearing thin.

As touching as it was that Felicity's grandmother had faith in her sleuthing abilities, the dowager couldn't be given too much encouragement.

"If my assistance is required," said Felicity, "I shall, of course, do my bit. But the police have the matter firmly in hand."

Lady Henrietta squinted at Felicity, unsatisfied.

"I still have magazine pieces to write," continued Felicity. "I can't let the editor down. Or Jasper."

The dowager's demeanour changed. The mention of Felicity's brother seemed to do the trick. It was fortuitous that he was travelling on business and unable to speak for himself.

"Of course, dear. Of course." Lady Henrietta patted Felicity's hand. "You know best, dear. Percy." She wheeled towards the rose breeder. "Did you tot up the orders you received at the show?"

Percy scratched the back of his head. "Not yet, although I'd say there's rather a lot. Perhaps too many."

"Too many? If you need help, you need only say so, Percy dear. Mrs Broughton and I would be happy to assist. Wouldn't we, Mrs Broughton?"

"Yes, yes." Mrs Broughton shook her head as she spoke, the berries on her hat jiggling. "Of course. Yes."

Pip sat to attention on the dowager's lap, his tufted ears pricked.

"Aha." Following the little dog's gaze, Lady Henrietta leaned back in her chair and smiled. "We have company."

Alex was approaching the tea table, his hat in his hands, the sun glinting on his pomaded dark blond hair.

Felicity's heart soared.

He'd been so busy reporting on the dramatic reappearance and demise of Lord Anthony Templeton — the police having confirmed his identity — she hadn't expected to see Alex so soon.

"Do sit with us, Mr Cooper," said Lady Henrietta after a round of polite greetings.

"That's awfully kind, your ladyship, but I'm only here for a quick word with your granddaughter, if I may? I'm in urgent need of her advice on the reporting."

Felicity pulled a discreetly doubtful face at Alex as she rose from the table.

The dowager nodded proudly. "By all means," she said, clearly enjoying the idea of Felicity's expertise being put to good use.

"You, a highly experienced Fleet Street crime reporter, need advice from me, a local journalist who cut her teeth on the parish newsletter," said Felicity as she and Alex progressed along the yew-lined walkway, out of earshot of the tea table.

Alex grinned. "You write for a London publication yourself, now, remember?"

"Please." They settled on a bench near an ornamental pond, the trickle of a small fountain helping to blur their words should anyone be listening in. "Are you here to tell me the latest or not?"

Alex balanced his hat on his knee and reached for his notebook. "The police are still interviewing everyone they can. They've no firm leads, but the inquest should at least be straightforward. It's unlikely he hit himself in the head with his silver prize plate."

Felicity sat up straighter. "Murder, then?"

"Someone else was involved, but it's unclear whether it was premeditated or a scuffle gone wrong." Alex flicked through his notebook. "They've fixed the time of death to between two o'clock and a quarter past."

Felicity narrowed her eyes. "Can forensic medicine be that precise?"

"Sadly not. The porters brought the sacks to the storage area at two. The unfortunate waitress arrived for her lemonade at a quarter past."

Felicity lifted her eyebrows as she digested the information. Her assessment of the situation remained unaltered.

"I informed the police of the disagreement I overheard between Havelock and Anthony Templeton," she said. That had to be it.

Alex shook his head and smiled. "Guess again. Havelock has a firm alibi. He was with Leonora the entire time."

Felicity furrowed her brow. It was a disappointment that her evidence hadn't helped solve the case, but then it wasn't her case to solve. "I suppose that speech earned Anthony Templeton more than a few enemies."

Alex sighed. "There are indeed numerous possibilities for suspects. That's why the police are focussing on alibis, and I'm afraid Havelock's is as firm as they get. The word of a titled land owner is difficult to dispute."

Felicity thought for a moment. "Have you spoken to Leonora yet?"

Alex shook his head. "No one has." His dark blue eyes twinkled. "I say, why don't you report on the story with me? Like the good old days."

Felicity huffed out a laugh. "You make it sound like it's been years since we last worked on a story together." In reality, they'd met only a year ago, practically to the day. "And you know I can't, as much as I'd like to."

Alex offered a commiserating grimace. "Magazine deadlines?"

Felicity nodded sadly.

Alex put his hand on hers. "I have to get back, but I shall keep you informed."

She squeezed his palm. "Please do."

Pip met them as they approached the tea table. The Yorkie gave Alex's shoes a customary sniffing, then went belting off towards Bradley Court's walled garden. Indeed, the table was now empty, meaning that after another clasp of each other's hands, Alex could make a clean getaway.

Felicity ought to have gone back upstairs to her typewriter. Instead, following Pip's lead, she headed to the walled garden. After an entire morning spent at her desk, a few more moments in the sunshine would surely do her good.

Percy and Mrs Broughton were dead-heading salvias. Pip was chasing a Red Admiral with absolutely no hope of catching it. Lady Henrietta had her gardening gloves on, but she'd paused, her secateurs in one hand, a piece of paper in the other. Beside her stood a young footman holding a silver salver upon which an empty envelope lay.

In contrast to her exuberance over afternoon tea, Felicity's grandmother's expression was now distinctly sober.

"Grandmama, what is it?" asked Felicity after politely dismissing the footman.

The dowager continued to peer down at the paper. "I don't understand it."

"May I?" asked Felicity, coaxing the letter from her grandmother's hand.

In black copperplate, the letter was headed as coming from the Lower Diddleton Plant and Floral Society. It gave notice of the cancellation of an event on flower arranging.

"Oh, dear," said Felicity sympathetically. "What a pity."

Lady Henrietta was a very active member of the local village's plant and floral society, and the cancellation had clearly come as a blow. The dowager was perhaps still fragile from the events at the rose festival the day before.

"I'm sure they'll reschedule it," added Felicity.

Lady Henrietta continued to look serious. "Read it again, dear."

Felicity squinted at the text. What had she missed? She read the letter aloud. "'We regret to inform you that your participation in the session on floral arrangements has been cancelled.'"

Mrs Broughton was approaching, a bundle of spent flower stems in her hand, her decorated hat a little lopsided. "Is everything all right?"

Felicity blinked at the paper. "They're saying you're cut from the event, not that the event's cancelled?"

Mrs Broughton frowned. "Who's cut from what event?"

"And who signed it?" Lady Henrietta's tone was clipped.

Felicity traced down the page with her finger. "'Mrs Enid Winterpole. President.'"

Mrs Broughton's eyes widened with shock. "She... She hasn't removed you from the flower arranging event. Has she?"

Lady Henrietta nodded. "She has. Mrs Winterpole's gone and done it. I knew the day she was elected president that it would come to this." The dowager was becoming shrill. "After everything that happened yesterday, and now this. She's just jealous. Jealous that I'm making a real difference by supporting young talent. And all she does is—"

Percy straightened from where he'd been bent over a thicket of clary sage. "Is everything all right?" he asked, his eyebrows drawn together.

"Thank you, Percy," said Felicity. "Everything's under control," she assured, although she wasn't quite convinced herself.

"But I-I don't understand it," stammered Mrs Broughton. "You were to be an instructor."

"I can't accept it," fumed Lady Henrietta. "I won't accept it. A woman of my seniority shouldn't have to endure such things. And she was talking to me yesterday — just yesterday — about the fundraiser for the War Widows and Orphans Relief Fund. What if she cuts me from that? It's the pinnacle of the fundraising calendar."

"Can Mrs Winterpole cut you from that?" asked Mrs Broughton fearfully, the wax berries on her hat trembling.

"I'm going to go to Mrs Winterpole," said Lady Henrietta, waving her secateurs, "and I'm going to tell her—"

"Grandmama," said Felicity, her tone calm yet stern. She had a duty to step in. "It's best you remain here at Bradley Court. Ring for a camomile tea and put your feet up. The last thing we need is you exhausting yourself." And a repeat performance of the confrontation with Anthony Templeton, but this time with a fellow widow and on Lower Diddleton's village green. "I shall speak to Mrs Winterpole on your behalf."

"Oh, my dear girl," sighed Lady Henrietta, relieved. "Would you?"

Felicity nodded. She didn't have the time to spare for social calls, but Felicity detested seeing her grandmother upset, and despite the dowager suspecting a vendetta, an amicable resolution could likely be achieved through polite discussion.

"I shall pay Mrs Winterpole a visit right away."

Chapter Eight

Mrs Winterpole's cottage was a thatched dwelling on the edge of the village. With white cob walls and leaded windows in a criss-cross pattern, the cottage was surrounded by some of Lower Diddleton's prettiest flowerbeds, which was quite the achievement. Taking care of one's garden was the village obsession.

Perhaps needing to offset the titbits consumed at the tea table, Pip opted to join Felicity on the walk through Bradley Court's grounds and along the hedge-lined lane to the village. Felicity hadn't objected to the little dog's presence. Mrs Winterpole knew the Yorkie and was fond of animals. Indeed, she was typically friendly with everyone and had always been pleasant towards Felicity.

Yes, Mrs Winterpole could be a firebrand at meetings for the summer fete and on the many committees for which she volunteered, but so could Lady Henrietta. It was perhaps why the dowager felt such friction with Mrs Winterpole. The two widows resembled one another in temperament and dedication to the various causes for which they volunteered.

Felicity tucked Pip under her arm as she pushed open the blue-painted wooden gate and navigated the cobbled path onto which clouds of Lady's mantle spilled. The tiny yellow-green blooms were a wonderful foil for Mrs Winterpole's pink and white roses, about which Lady Henrietta was — in private — often scathing, but which were undeniably charming when combined with informal drifts of purple geraniums and the tall blue spikes of delphiniums.

A tug on the doorbell brought a small, nervous maid to the cottage's blue-painted front door.

"Mrs Winterpole is preparing to go out, your ladyship. She informed me to tell you to come back—"

"Wait, Doris." Mrs Winterpole's voice rang out from within the cottage. "Who is it?" 'Your ladyship' had perhaps been the trigger for Mrs Winterpole to rethink her instruction to her servant to ask whoever was calling to return later.

Mrs Winterpole appeared in the narrow hallway behind the maid. She had on a jacket and skirt in primrose yellow and had a toque in the same shade in her hands.

"Ah, Lady Felicity and Master Pip. What a pleasant surprise. Are you here for the paper? I do so love your articles, but I haven't seen many in the Western Daily News of late. Might you need my input for the Gentlewoman's Gazette?" Mrs Winterpole handed her hat to her maid. "Doris, a tray of tea and biscuits, as quickly as you can."

The maid bobbed a curtsey and dashed off.

"I'm due in Exeter for a meeting with the donors to the Polio Rehabilitation and Prevention Trust," continued Mrs Winterpole. "But if you should like to talk, your ladyship, I can, of course, spare the time. I'm sure the donors won't mind starting without me."

"It's not for the paper, Mrs Winterpole." Under other circumstances, Felicity would not have wished to make Mrs Winterpole late for her meeting. "But I should still very much like to speak to you, if you can indeed spare the time."

"Of course, your ladyship. Of course."

In a low-ceilinged sitting room with walls in duck egg blue, they seated themselves on cream-coloured chintz sofas, Pip settling peacefully on Felicity's lap. An open window allowed the scent of Mrs Winterpole's roses to drift indoors.

As Doris brought in the tea and biscuits, Felicity and Mrs

Winterpole discussed the unfortunate events in Bickleford the day before. They praised the police for the excellent job they were doing in following up with all potential witnesses, both of them expressing the hope that the wrong-doer would be promptly found.

It was all very polite and normal. If Mrs Winterpole harboured resentment towards Felicity's grandmother, she was either excellent at hiding it, or the grudge simply didn't extend to Felicity.

As Felicity helped herself to a macaroon, Pip stood to attention and whimpered on her lap. Lady Henrietta had thoroughly spoiled him, but the Yorkie had to learn. Felicity wouldn't coddle Pip in the same manner.

"There we go, little fellow," said Mrs Winterpole as she broke off a piece of her arrowroot biscuit and held it out to him. Pip licked it up with glee.

Felicity gritted her teeth and smiled. Now was not the moment to school Pip and Mrs Winterpole in proper canine etiquette. There was a more pressing matter at hand.

"I shouldn't like to take up too much of your time, Mrs Winterpole. I'm aware you were on your way out when I called."

"Please, my dear. Take all the time you need. What is it I can help you with?"

Felicity pressed her lips together for a moment. "It's about my grandmother."

Mrs Winterpole's features hardened. "Go on, dear."

"She received a letter just this afternoon about an event with the Lower Diddleton Plant and Floral Society."

"Yes, dear." Mrs Winterpole's expression was difficult to read.

"The letter was signed by you. As the president of the society."

"That's right."

The sun was still shining outside, yet the temperature in the little sitting room felt as though it had dropped. Was Lady Henrietta not imagining things after all?

"My grandmother has been asked not to attend a lecture on flower arranging," said Felicity, stroking Pip's back to settle him. "A lecture she herself was to give, if I understand correctly."

Mrs Winterpole said nothing for a moment. Her lips pursed, the lines around her mouth growing deeper. She sat very straight and still.

"As you can imagine," continued Felicity. "Lady Henrietta was terribly disappointed by the news."

"I can quite imagine, dear." Mrs Winterpole's tone lacked the sympathy her words seemed to convey.

"And there was no reason given in the letter for the change of heart."

Again, Mrs Winterpole said nothing.

"May I ask about the rationale behind the decision?" said Felicity carefully. "I can perhaps help my grandmother understand the situation better. Her nerves are quite rattled, what with everything that happened in Bickleford yesterday."

Mrs Winterpole sat as still as stone. Pip whimpered, but he was out of luck. The moment for sharing biscuits had passed.

"Lady Felicity," began Mrs Winterpole. "I hold the Quicks in extremely high regard. I've known your grandmother for decades. We've worked together across many societies, associations, and charities. She has my deepest respect. Yet I know that if she were in my position, she would surely do the same."

Felicity blinked. "And in what position do you find yourself, Mrs Winterpole?"

The widow's eyebrows drew together, as if perplexed that her vague explanation wasn't enough. "The position I find myself to be in is one of wanting to — nay, needing to — protect the society and its members."

"Protect them from what?" Felicity had double checked with Lady Henrietta that there was nothing she might have said or done to cause her to be excommunicated from the plant and floral society. Lady Henrietta swore there was nothing.

Mrs Winterpole sighed heavily. "From the shadow of violence, your ladyship."

Felicity drew in her chin. "Violence?" Barring Lady Henrietta's unforgiving attacks on any greenfly daring to land on her prized rose bushes, Felicity had never known her grandmother to be violent. "I'm not sure I understand."

Mrs Winterpole's brow wrinkled slightly. "As you are aware, the demise of Lord Anthony Templeton is being thoroughly investigated by the police. We were all utterly shocked by the crime. Despite what he said during the prize ceremony and his many years of absence, his roses really were unlike anything seen before." Mrs Winterpole cleared her throat a little. "But until the police reach their conclusions on the case, we cannot be too cautious."

Felicity nodded. "Of course. Safety must be paramount." As long as whoever swung the silver plate at the victim was at large, it was indeed possible further disorder might follow. "The flower arranging event has been cancelled, then?" Of course, it had been a case of misunderstanding. The letter had been poorly worded. That was all.

A hint of pity entered Mrs Winterpole's gaze. "As far as I'm aware, your grandmother cannot be accounted for during the crucial time period in which the police say the crime took place. I was the time keeper for Mr Shakerley's presentation, and I didn't see Lady Henrietta there."

Felicity's heart pounded. Was this an accusation?

"I take no pleasure in contradicting you, Mrs Winterpole, but my grandmother's movements can certainly be accounted for. Lady Henrietta was with our driver on her way back to Bradley Court. I put her in the motor myself." Felicity shook her head a little. The conversation was becoming ridiculous. "Even if my grandmother had no alibi for the time period in question, what difference would it make? She's not a murder suspect."

Mrs Winterpole swallowed. "It was reported that Lady Henrietta had a rather forceful disagreement with the deceased not long before his passing."

Felicity's stomach sank like a stone. How did Mrs Winterpole know about the incident? Felicity had encouraged her grandmother to be transparent with the police about her confrontation with Anthony Templeton. Other than that, they'd kept the matter to themselves.

"Are you saying you believe my grandmother to be responsible for Lord Anthony Templeton's death?"

Mrs Winterpole's eyes widened with alarm. "No, I'm not saying that." She didn't like the sound of it when it was spelled out, because it was ridiculous. Thoroughly ridiculous. "But it can't be ruled out. Not yet."

Felicity stroked Pip, who was now standing on her lap, craning his neck for more biscuits. "I very much appreciate the time you've given me and the candour with which you've spoken, Mrs Winterpole, but I'm finding the situation a little hard to digest. Has Lady Henrietta been banned from the Lower Diddleton Plant and Floral Society until either the police throw her into gaol or the real killer is found?"

"Lady Felicity, please understand. The circumstances are so unusual. Unheard of. I didn't take the decision in isolation. I consulted with the board, and we were all in agreement."

Felicity bit her tongue. She didn't want to fall out with Mrs Winterpole, but it was nonsensical. Lady Henrietta wasn't a murderer. Surely anyone in their right mind could see that.

Tucking Pip under her arm, Felicity stood up. "Thank you for your time, Mrs Winterpole." The conversation in the cottage sitting room was over, but Felicity couldn't return to her grandmother and tell her she was now a murder suspect. Further action had to be taken.

Chapter Nine

Felicity managed to return to Bradley Court without being seen. Upon entering the house's gardens via a lesser-used gate, she'd scooped Pip up to prevent him bounding off to Lady Henrietta in search of treats. The walk to and from the village seemed to have tired the Yorkie, however. After entering the house through a side door and navigating the quietest corridors to Jasper's office, Pip fell asleep on Felicity's lap before she picked up the receiver of the candlestick telephone on her brother's desk.

"Lady Felicity." Chief Inspector Luscombe's tone wasn't exactly disappointed, but he didn't sound thrilled about having Felicity on the line. "I understand you've information pertinent to our investigation." Felicity had stretched the truth a little in telling the young constable who had answered the telephone that she had something important to share for the flower show enquiry. "Does that mean you've been playing detective again?"

"I have full faith in your men to bring the case to a satisfying conclusion," said Felicity with sincerity. "And I don't believe simply being present at the scene of a crime gives one the right to become involved in the investigation. What happened at the flower show has nothing to do with the magazine articles I'm writing, and they're keeping me busy enough," added Felicity.

"Well." The chief inspector sounded surprised. "I'm relieved to hear it. It's a complex enough case without multiple cooks spoiling the broth, so to speak. Journalists like your friend Mr Cooper give us a hard enough time as it is."

Felicity smiled to herself. Alex was a first-class news hound.

"So, what is it you have to share, your ladyship? Has something come to mind since we collected your testimony in Bickleford?"

"In a sense," said Felicity vaguely. "Would you be able to tell me if you have a suspect already in mind?"

There was a pause. "Does that affect the information you wish to provide? Or are you perhaps still writing for your brother's newspaper and wish to barter for an exclusive?"

"I'm not speaking to you as a journalist, Chief Inspector. And I would never withhold information that could help with your enquiries."

There was an audible exhale down the line. Chief Inspector Luscombe's attitude towards Felicity teetered between grudging respect and outright dismissal. Recently, she'd felt it tipping more towards respect — they'd been through so much together, after all — but there was always the risk of being regarded as a troublemaker. Being a woman certainly didn't help in that department. Or any other department, really, when it came to the perceptions held by the opposite sex.

"As eager as we are to make an arrest," the chief inspector's tone was guarded, his words carefully chosen, "we have to take the time to do a thorough job."

"I quite understand," said Felicity, adjusting Pip on her lap to prevent him from snoring.

"After the speech he gave," continued the policeman, "there's hardly a person at the flower show who wouldn't have some reason to lose their temper and strike out at the man."

Alex had mentioned the possibility of the crime being of a passionate nature.

"People have alibis though, don't they?" pressed Felicity.

"Of course, and we're piecing those together. It's slow work, though. Do you know how many people were at the show?"

Felicity swallowed. She was pushing her luck, but she had to stick at it. "My grandmother has no reason to be considered a suspect, does she?"

There was silence. The line crackled. "Is this the reason for your telephone call, your ladyship?" Chief Inspector Luscombe could be annoyingly astute.

Felicity might as well come clean. "The reason for my telephone call, Chief Inspector, is my grandmother's wellbeing. She faces exclusion from certain social events based on the belief that she's considered a suspect in the case. As I told you, and I'm sure she also informed you, Lady Henrietta was either with me or with our driver on the way home to Bradley Court during the whole period in which the crime was believed to have occurred."

The policeman remained silent.

Pip let out a dragon-like snore and woke himself up. Felicity put a hand on the little dog's silky back to steady him.

"So it's possible to rule my grandmother out as a suspect, isn't it?" pressed Felicity.

"As I said, your ladyship. We're taking this case slowly. We don't want to miss anything."

Felicity frowned. "Do you seriously believe my grandmother to be capable of murder?"

"It wouldn't be right for me to comment on such matters at this stage in the investigation." Chief Inspector Luscombe was practised at giving noncommittal answers. He regularly dodged questions from far harsher interrogators than Felicity, such as Alex.

"But my grandmother has two solid alibis."

"I can't comment on the intricacies of our investigations at this stage."

"So even if Lady Henrietta argued with the fellow — and I know she made a point of being honest with you about that — she certainly didn't do away with him."

Silence.

"And she wasn't the only one to argue with him," continued Felicity. "Have you properly checked Mr Michael Havelock's alibi?" Felicity couldn't let on that she'd heard from Alex that Leonora's gardener had been dismissed as a suspect. More to the point, she couldn't quite accept it. In his speech, Anthony Templeton had targeted Leonora. Havelock was clearly protective of her. He was an obvious suspect for the crime.

"I'm sorry, but you know I can't comment on that at this stage, your ladyship. We'll make statements on our progress in due course."

Felicity breathed deeply. After Mrs Winterpole's ridiculous assertions, being stonewalled by Chief Inspector Luscombe was enough to push her over the edge, but Felicity had to remain composed. The senior policeman respected her enough to take her call and respond to her questions, even if he wasn't really giving answers.

"Thank you, Chief Inspector," she said, controlling the tremble of anger in her voice. It wasn't Felicity's investigation, and she couldn't tell Chief Inspector Luscombe how to do his job. She would rely on Alex to keep her up to date on where the police were with the case.

But what could Felicity tell Lady Henrietta?

Felicity followed Pip to find Lady Henrietta bathed in the late afternoon sunlight in Bradley Court's conservatory. She was rather aggressively removing ragged and yellowing leaves from rows of potted pelargoniums, Mrs Broughton and Percy Colhayne both having gone home. On the conservatory table lay an opened letter, the empty envelope discarded to one side.

Felicity couldn't see its contents, but the paper's heading appeared to be from the volunteers association at the Polio Rehabilitation and Prevention Trust.

Pip ran up to Lady Henrietta and pawed gently at the hem of the voluminous skirt of her Edwardian-style dress.

"There you are, Master Pip." The dowager sniffed as she bent over to pick the Yorkie up. Then she turned and saw Felicity. "Oh, my dear." She forced a smile, but from her red nose and watery eyes, it was clear she'd been crying. "Now. What did Mrs Winterpole have to say?"

"Have you had another letter, Grandmama?"

Lady Henrietta's eyes shot to the table upon which the paper and envelope lay. "Oh, it's nothing, dear. Was Mrs Winterpole there to speak to?" The dowager stroked Pip under the chin. "She granted you an audience, at least, I hope."

Felicity approached the table. "May I read it?"

Tears welled in Lady Henrietta's eyes. "I don't suppose I can stop you."

Felicity unfolded the paper. It was worded very much like the last one. *In light of recent events, your presence among the volunteers at the Polio Rehabilitation and Prevention Trust is not required for the foreseeable future.*

Felicity's grip on the paper tightened. "This isn't right."

The dowager dabbed at her eyes with a lace-trimmed handkerchief. "Mrs Winterpole has influence in so many places. I knew this day would come. Ever since I called her out in front of the plant and floral society for suggesting wood spurge could grow in dry shade when it can only grow in the damp. And now poor Percy's caught up in it all." She blew her nose on the handkerchief. "I promised to introduce him to the Historical Garden Appreciation Society. How am I going to do that now? She's turned me into a pariah. They won't even want to speak to me."

Felicity dropped the letter back onto the table and went to her grandmother. She did her best to maintain her composure, but she was seething. "You shouldn't hide in shame. The mere suggestion that you could have swung that plate at Anthony Templeton is completely ridiculous."

Lady Henrietta tucked her chin, suddenly offended. "You don't believe I have it in me to render a man senseless?"

Felicity shook her head. This wasn't helpful. "You have two solid alibis, don't you? For yesterday afternoon. Myself and Finnegan."

Lady Henrietta blinked. "W-what are you saying, dear?"

"The police have a narrow timing for when the victim met his end. Between two o'clock and a quarter past."

"If you say so, dear. But what has that got to do with me?"

Felicity couldn't quite bring herself to inform her grandmother that she was, in essence, a suspected murderer. "We just need to be very clear and certain of your movements yesterday during that crucial period. You were with me, and then you were in the Rolls with Finnegan. Remember?"

Lady Henrietta frowned, still confused. "I do, but I... Well..."

"You told the police of your whereabouts, didn't you?"

Lady Henrietta looked pained. "Of course."

"Then we must spread the news. When the facts are understood, you'll stop receiving these horrible letters."

The dowager sighed, her grip tightening on the Yorkie.

"What is it?" pressed Felicity.

Lady Henrietta sighed again. "I went for a little walk, dear. In the medieval rose garden, to clear my mind. I asked Finnegan to wait for me. I thought it would do me good." She sniffed. "Little did I know."

Felicity's chest tightened. "Was this during the crucial period? Between two and a quarter past?"

Lady Henrietta nodded. "But I can't be the only one without an alibi." She shook her handkerchief and blew her nose. "Can I?"

Felicity took in a steadying breath. "Of course not," she agreed soothingly.

While there were surely others without alibis, who among them had argued with the deceased shortly before his death? There was no point reminding Lady Henrietta of the now-regrettable incident. It would only encourage her despair.

But how had Mrs Winterpole learned of the confrontation between Lady Henrietta and Anthony Templeton? There was no stopping the information spreading now it was out of the bag, and who knew what damage it would wreak on the dowager's reputation?

"Oh, my dear, what should I do?" Lady Henrietta's voice trembled as she stroked Pip. "What if the letters keep coming? What if I'm excluded from the fundraiser for the war widows and orphans? It's only next month, and we Quicks have always played a leading role in raising money for the cause. To not take part would be to betray past and future generations of our family."

An outsider might have dismissed Lady Henrietta's fears as trifling. Yet the dowager's social and charitable engagements had kept her going through the loss of her husband, the passing of her son, and through the Great War, when her grandson was at the front.

The significance of Lady Henrietta's philanthropic activities couldn't be overlooked, and Felicity couldn't stand by and allow the crisis to deepen.

She straightened. "Do nothing, Grandmama. Speak to no one. And certainly do not announce that you consider yourself still capable of knocking a man out with a silver plate."

Lady Henrietta looked hopeful. "Will you take care of the rest?"

Felicity nodded. "I shall, but you must promise to tell no one I'm on the case."

Chapter Ten

THE NEXT DAY

Alex sounded pleased when Felicity telephoned to accept his offer to join him in his reporting on the Anthony Templeton case. He had a condition, however. They would make an early start in Felicity's nippy two-seater Alvis instead of Alex's reliable Model-T.

"Thought you might be hungry," said Alex as he joined Felicity in her white two-seater outside his digs in Exeter. "So I popped out to the bakery."

As he pulled the passenger door closed, the motor's interior filled with a sugary cinnamon scent. Felicity had eaten breakfast before leaving Bradley Court and hadn't been feeling hungry until the delicious smell of the baked goods tickled her nostrils.

She glanced over at Alex's lap as she guided the Alvis out of the city.

"Chelsea buns," he said, peering into the brown paper bag. "And a flask of hot tea. Mind if I start?"

"Thank you again for allowing us a little detour," said Felicity, keeping her eyes on the road and her mind off the cakes, which she couldn't eat while driving.

Alex's day had already been planned out, but by starting off earlier — wisps of mist still rising from the rolling green fields beside the road — they'd accommodated an extra stop.

"It's simply awful what's happening to your grandmother," said Alex, grimacing as he carefully collected the granulated sugar that had fallen onto his pale grey suit. "But I'm curious to know what we'll say to Chief Inspector Luscombe if we run into him."

Felicity glanced at Alex. He looked vaguely amused. He was partially teasing Felicity, but the question was sensible. It was good to be prepared.

"The truth," said Felicity, her eyes on the road. "That I'm assisting you with your reporting."

Alex finished another mouthful of bun. "That's only part of the truth." He never pulled punches when it came to interrogation. Not even with Felicity. "And you told him you weren't investigating."

"I wasn't." Felicity drove slowly, waiting to overtake a cart stacked high with hay bales. Fragments of the hay drifted towards the Alvis' bonnet in the early morning sunshine. "Not when I spoke to him on the telephone."

"But you're investigating now."

Felicity safely passed the horse and cart, and the hedgerows began whizzing by. "I can't allow things to continue as they are. I appreciate the police are doing a thorough job, but who knows when they'll be done with the case? My grandmother is already miserable, and her reputation could be destroyed beyond repair. If I can speed things along —"

Alex smiled. "If *we* can speed things along, you mean?"

Felicity almost laughed. "I'm not here to steal your byline. I just want to help my grandmother."

"Help her how?"

"I already told you. By finding out who really killed Anthony Templeton."

Alex folded away the paper bag. "So you're still open to detective work."

Felicity shot him a glare. "And what do you mean by that?"

Alex said nothing and shrugged. He looked a little too pleased with himself for Felicity's liking.

"I simply wish to help my grandmother," she said. "If I find anything that could speed up the investigation, I shall hand it over to the police. Is that detective work?"

"Speaking of bylines," said Alex, judiciously changing the subject. "I suppose this means you'll need another extension on your magazine deadline."

Felicity tightened her grip on the steering wheel. "Mm-hmm." Alex had an irritating talent for detail.

To make time to investigate, Felicity had shifted her writing to the evenings. The plan was easy to poke holes in, however. Even when she had all day, it was a struggle to stay chained to her typewriter long enough to hit her weekly writing targets.

Thankfully, there wasn't long to dwell on the issue. The sturdy iron gates and tall stone walls of Templeton Manor came into view.

Alex had explained to Felicity how, since the flower show's unexpected end, he'd already made multiple requests for an interview with or even just a comment from Lady Leonora Templeton. Journalists across the land were desperate to hear from the aristocratic rose breeder on her brother's demise.

Alex's requests had, however, so far gone unanswered.

It was also much the same story with the two assistants who'd been employed by Anthony Templeton and had accompanied him at the show. Alex had their names — both were French citizens — and a reliable report that they still lived at the nursery where Anthony had bred his Best in Show plant, but no one there was picking up the telephone.

A detour to Anthony Templeton's nursery had also been on Felicity's wish list, but it was rather a long drive and not a fit with what Alex had planned for the rest of the day.

Templeton Manor, on the other hand, was just a short run from Exeter. It was nestled in a series of interlocking valleys fed by babbling streams at the foot of the moors. The climate was both damp and sheltered, which resulted in jungle like tangles of hazel, ferns, and meadowsweet lining the roadside ditches.

Having drawn the Alvis to a standstill before the estate's imposing gates, Felicity tugged her lightweight cream-coloured cardigan closer to her body. She was thankful for the warmth of her olive-green pleated skirt and matching cloche, for it was still early enough for there to be a chill in the air.

Alex placed his homburg on his head as he looked up at the gates rather doubtfully. "Well. Here we are."

"Indeed." It wasn't that Felicity lacked confidence in Alex's ability to land an interview. Leonora's reticence was perfectly understandable, given her brother's sudden reappearance and passing. It wasn't unusual for someone in such a delicate position to need time before talking to the press.

But Felicity's goal was different. It wasn't about scooping an interview before any of the papers did. It was even more urgent than that.

Felicity approached the gates. The glossy black paint flaked in places and the gilded ornaments were dull. The keyhole in the mortise lock appeared well used. Curving away between steep banks under the milky sky, the driveway offered no view of the house or rose nursery.

"Can I help you, miss?" An elderly gentleman with a broad Westcountry accent and white moustache had emerged from a small lodge with steep gables just inside the gates.

Alex raised an eyebrow. It was perhaps closer than he'd come to an audience with Leonora.

Felicity put her hand on a bar in the gate. "Is her ladyship at home?" she enquired of the lodge keeper, hopefulness evident in her tone.

Even if they hadn't spoken for years prior to Anthony's untimely passing, talking to Leonora could be the key to understanding the motive of whoever had wished harm on her brother. In his speech, Anthony had said Leonora would be the only person who could understand what he'd been through.

Was there even the chance that the guilty party was to be found at Templeton Manor?

Not that Felicity was reckless enough to confront anyone directly. But despite Havelock's apparent alibi, Felicity couldn't simply forget the disagreement she'd overheard between Leonora's gardener and her now-deceased brother.

She also couldn't forget seeing her grandmother weeping in the conservatory.

"Who shall I say it is that wants to see her ladyship?"

"Please tell her that Lady Felicity Quick is waiting at the gate."

The mention of an aristocratic title had a noticeable impact on the white-haired man, prompting him to hurry back to his lodge house. The wrought-iron gates, meanwhile, remained firmly closed.

Felicity and Alex waited by the Alvis as the lodge keeper contacted the main house. Felicity finally got to sample the wickedly sweet bun Alex had bought for her, and they both enjoyed a few sips of tea from the flask.

"Here we go," said Alex, turning his attention back to the gates.

A small works van with a canvas canopy came tearing along the driveway. As the vehicle drew to a stop, Michael Havelock, Leonora's gardener, descended from the driver's seat, his shirt sleeves folded above his meaty forearms, a scowl already on his brow. The two Jack Russells came flying out of the back of the van and danced before the gate, barking at Felicity and Alex.

Felicity did her best to maintain a courteous smile, but she had to fight a deep sense of unease. She wasn't one for taking a dislike to people, but Havelock's presence sent a shudder up her spine.

With his fists on his hips, the burly man stared grimly at Felicity and Alex. Perhaps naively, Felicity hadn't thought through the scenario of being presented with Leonora's gardener, although he was perhaps something more than just an outdoor caretaker. Had Leonora sent him to the gate on her behalf? Or had the message of Felicity's arrival not even reached Leonora? From what Felicity had overheard and seen of Havelock at the flower show, he was immensely protective of the lady of Templeton Manor.

"You again," growled Havelock at Felicity as the dogs continued their barking unchecked.

Felicity raised her brow.

On the one hand, Felicity had done nothing to incur the man's animosity. On the other, it didn't take a genius to deduce that Felicity would have told the police about the disagreement she'd overheard between Havelock and Anthony Templeton.

But unlike Lady Henrietta, Havelock had an alibi, didn't he? So it didn't matter what Felicity said about him, and it didn't give him a licence to speak to her so rudely.

Alex had hung back, giving Felicity the space to do things her way. Perhaps unhappy with Havelock's tone, Alex now joined Felicity at the gate, his arms folded across his chest.

"Is Lady Leonora Templeton at home?" asked Felicity confidently. "I should very much like to speak with her."

It was as if Havelock was deaf to the barking dogs. Either that or he approved of their barking at Felicity. She was happy there was a gate separating her from them, both from the dogs and from Havelock.

"Her ladyship doesn't want visitors." Havelock fixed an angry glare on Felicity as he reached into his pocket.

Felicity flinched as he drew his hand out. It was an instinctive reaction that she immediately regretted. The item the gardener withdrew from his pocket was nothing but a small length of thickly braided rope. Twisting his broad torso, Havelock threw the rope a fair distance into the long grass beside the lodge.

The two Jack Russells stopped barking to watch the rope arcing through the air. They then set off after the rope, their barking restarting as they ran.

Alex glanced at Felicity. He appeared confused. So it wasn't just Felicity who found the gardener's behaviour odd.

"Well," she said, her composure regained. "Would you be kind enough to pass on my condolences to Lady Leonora?"

Havelock looked baffled for a moment. He grunted. Would he do as Felicity asked? His response to the request was thoroughly unclear.

The dogs were growling now, tussling over the rope, both hanging onto an end.

Perhaps sensing Felicity's reticence to engage with Havelock any more than strictly necessary, Alex stepped forward. "Might I ask you a few questions for the Western Daily News, Mr Havelock?"

"Absolutely not." The burly man turned his back on Alex and Felicity and started for his van. "Daisy! Flossie!" he bellowed.

The dogs paused their tug-o'-war in the long grass, their folded ears tilting forward with interest. With the rope still held in both sets of jaws, they dashed after the van, which was already pulling away, and leapt into the back of the vehicle. The van then sped up, hurtling back along the drive.

Felicity sighed. "I can only apologise," she said to Alex as they returned to the Alvis. "You did warn me that would be a waste of time."

"I didn't like the way he spoke to you."

"His dislike is somewhat understandable."

"His behaviour is not," said Alex tightly, doing his best to control his reaction. He took his hat off as he ducked into the motor's passenger seat. "I did a bit of digging into the fellow, you know. Wish I'd dug deeper. It's not logical, because we've no reason to doubt the reliability of Leonora's alibi for the man, but I now understand your reticence to accept it, at least."

Felicity climbed behind the steering wheel. "Was there anything of note in his background?" she asked hopefully.

Alex flicked through his notebook. "Record as clean as a whistle. Always been a gardener here at Templeton Manor, except for a stint on the Western Front." Alex tapped his pencil on his notepad. "Even picked up a few commendations. Two for bravery. Hardly a criminal profile."

Felicity swung the Alvis away from the manor gates and back onto the narrow country lane. "Yet you saw how he reacts to things."

Alex looked out the window for a moment. "Some chaps thrive in the chaos and violence of the battlefield. The same men can find the normal proceedings of civilian life rather a challenge."

Felicity said nothing. She slipped the Alvis into a lower gear and they began the climb up a steep hill. To have arrived at Templeton Manor and been invited in. To have convinced Leonora to admit that her alibi for her faithful yet ultimately flawed gardener was false. It all would have been far, far too easy.

Yet Felicity had in some mad way hoped for it, hadn't she?

With his rage at the victim, his passion for Leonora, and his threatening, untamed behaviour, Havelock felt like the obvious suspect. But what if he were merely a distraction?

"I should still like to speak to Leonora," proclaimed Felicity. Whether Havelock was involved in the crime or not, giving up on speaking to the victim's sister was out of the question.

Alex nodded. "You and me both."

Felicity slowed the Alvis as they took in the view from the hilltop. Lush, undulating meadows stretched towards the shimmering blue sea far in the distance.

"Let's hope our next stop is more fruitful," she said.

Chapter Eleven

The bells in Chagstock's church tower struck a quarter to the hour as Felicity brought the Alvis to a gentle stop on the stannary town's main thoroughfare. Alighting from the motor, she lifted her gaze towards a beautifully symmetrical Georgian building with a large front garden and manicured box hedging.

Alex tugged on the brim of his homburg, shielding his eyes from the morning sun. "Not exactly what I expected, considering it's run mostly by volunteers."

"My grandmother is always keen to point out that while the Templetons can take credit for the association's establishment," said Felicity, passing ornamental ponds and stone vases spilling with sweet-scented roses, "we Quicks have been faithful donors for generations." Her tone was exaggeratedly proud.

Alex squinted at the brass plaque beside the front door, which read, *The British Rose Association. Established 1765*. "This is indeed the place." He pulled the doorbell.

"Please don't emphasise the Quicks' fondness for the association in your reporting, though," added Felicity, smoothing the pleats of her skirt, a frown creasing her brow. "We don't need to encourage any further consideration of my grandmother's potential motives," she added quietly.

Alex met Felicity's gaze and gave a serious nod. "Understood."

The rose association's secretary answered the door, his pince-nez balanced on the end of his thin nose. Thick carpet absorbed their footfall as he led Felicity and Alex past a huge painting of a woman with an intricate arrangement of curls and a single long-stemmed rose in her hand. *Lady Philomena Templeton, Countess of Fernworthy, 1765*, were the words elegantly etched into a flat section of the bottom of the elaborate gilt frame.

"The founder, I suppose," said Alex, gazing up at the woman's serene expression.

"Indeed," said the secretary without looking back.

After following him up an elegant wooden staircase with a highly polished banister, the secretary knocked at a panelled door before gently pushing it open. "Colonel Bolt? The Western Daily News is here."

"Yes, yes. Come in, come in."

"Please," said the secretary, swinging the door fully open and gesturing for Felicity and Alex to enter the association president's office.

Pressing on his cane, the colonel rose from his chair. He'd been seated at a desk upon which an inkwell, desk blotter, and correspondence tray were all neatly aligned with the desk's edges. Framed botanical drawings of roses were positioned symmetrically and at regular intervals on the walls. A bookcase filled with specialist rose-breeding tomes had all its spines ordered by height and perfectly flush. A small window overlooked a sunny courtyard, which featured covered walkways and a neat parterre garden.

"Back to writing for your brother's paper, are you, your ladyship?" enquired the colonel once the handshakes and greetings were complete and everyone was seated.

"Oh no, not just yet. I'm simply..." Felicity glanced at Alex. "I'm assisting Mr Cooper with his reporting."

The smile Alex gave her was one of private amusement. In the past, Felicity had often allowed Alex to be understood as her assistant when investigating. He'd never complained, which meant Felicity had no right to do so either.

Alex opened his notebook. "Would you like to update me on what's happened since we last spoke?" It was a gentle opener, building on the fact Alex had already interviewed the rose association's president at the flower show, both before and after Anthony Templeton's passing.

The colonel drummed his fingers on the desk, his forehead wrinkling under his razor-sharp centre parting. "We've had a great number of our members and donors contact us with questions about what happened, not all of which we have been able to answer, for obvious reasons. Then yesterday we had a visit from the police. They asked our staff and volunteers for what they saw leading up to the awful occurrence."

Felicity would have loved to have sat in on those interviews. "Anything suspicious reported?"

Alex shot her a look. *Steady on*. He had to lead the questioning, even though Felicity's goal was urgent. They'd discussed the point and agreed as much, not only for the benefit of Alex's reporting but also for the ruse of her being his assistant to be believable.

Clearly, for Felicity, the reality of the situation had yet to sink in.

She answered Alex's look with an apologetic nod. She would endeavour to do better.

The colonel squinted thoughtfully. "Nothing of note reported, as far as I'm aware. But then the police are keeping their cards rather close to their chests."

And did you, Colonel, witness anything noteworthy between two o'clock and a quarter past the hour on the day of the flower show?

It was the natural follow-on question, but Felicity didn't ask it. Pressing her lips together, she tilted her head towards Alex and did her best to look encouraging. He was in the lead. Felicity was merely assisting.

Alex eyed the colonel carefully. "Has the association decided what to do about the prize for Best in Show?"

Felicity raised an eyebrow. Alex had hardly given the colonel a moment to warm up, and here he was, already turning the screws.

Other than the trophy's use as the murder weapon, the prize's influence on the crime had yet to be established, but the press was abuzz with the scandal. And there wasn't just the winner's sudden demise to consider.

Alex's eyes dipped to his notebook. "Looking back at what Lord Anthony Templeton — known to us as Mr Fox at the time — said during his acceptance speech, do you suppose by 'this whole charade' he was referring to the prize giving or to the British Rose Association's activities more generally?"

The colonel winced. "There have already been several discussions between the association's board members," he said. "As I'm sure you can appreciate, this situation is unprecedented."

Colonel Bolt's answer was unsatisfactory, but Felicity relaxed a little. Alex's line of enquiry was relevant to her investigation. If someone particularly attached to the rose association had felt wounded by Anthony Templeton's speech, might they have been angry enough to cause him physical harm?

"Two days have passed since the incident," Alex asked, his pencil poised, "and there's still no decision on what to do with the Best in Show prize?"

The president's cheeks flushed. Alex's question embarrassed him. "Indeed. You'll be among the first to know when that situation changes."

"Is this scandal — and we can call it a scandal, can't we?" said Alex.

Reluctantly, the colonel nodded.

"You said this scandal is 'unprecedented'," continued Alex. "So you've not known anything like it in your time as association president. How long is it you've been president here?"

The colonel drummed his fingers. "This is only my second year with the British Rose Association."

"Founded in 1765, wasn't it?"

"Correct."

"That's a rather long time. Has there ever been anything like this scandal in all that time?" Alex was like a dog with a bone. He wouldn't let the colonel go.

"You would have to check with Mr Shakerley. He's the expert on our history." The colonel's cheeks grew redder. "But I believe not, no."

If it were up to Felicity, she would go a little easier on Colonel Bolt. Alex was perhaps close to riling him, but it wasn't her interview.

"Had you met Lord Anthony Templeton before his reappearance at Bickleford Rose Festival?" asked Alex.

"No, I hadn't," replied the colonel.

"But you were aware of him?"

The colonel shook his head. "I'd heard mention of him, but he left decades ago. When he was rather young, if I understand correctly. It's not like the fellow had time to make an impact. Not like his sister."

"Might you know any reason Anthony Templeton chose this year's edition of the show to make his reappearance?"

"I certainly do not." Colonel Bolt's cheeks were nearing purple. "I told you, I never met the fellow till this week."

Alex paused his questioning and scribbled in his notebook. Felicity waited, but he didn't look up. It felt like an invitation.

"How did you come to the position of president here at the association, Colonel?" she enquired gently.

Alex glanced up from his notebook, his eyes sparkling with curiosity. Felicity's questioning had been approved.

"Well, I, uh..." Colonel Bolt seemed a bit flummoxed by the change in direction. "I've always had a keen interest in roses. Entered the amateur ranks at Bickleford occasionally. The outgoing president suggested I might be suited for the role. We were at Sandhurst together, you see. Built myself a reputation for organising social events and the like. That was a long time ago, of course. And running an association is awfully different, and well." He gave an awkward shake of his head. "That explains it."

The colonel was perhaps too rattled by Alex's interviewing style to give a proper account of himself. Considering the power of the association, including the high profile of its donors and the life-changing nature of its awards, Colonel Bolt's qualifications seemed a little mismatched for the role of president.

Alex picked up the baton. "A few of the old hands I spoke to at the flower show suggested that Champs Verts Nursery came from nowhere to win Best in Show. Would you agree with that assessment?"

The colonel puffed his cheeks. "Certainly not. It may have been the nursery's first time at the festival, but the roses the winner presented were of outstanding quality. He and his team could only have developed them through years of hard work. Whatever the man's faults, his plants were impeccable."

Felicity frowned. How could the rose association president still stand by Anthony Templeton's entry into the very competition the rose breeder had sought to undermine? The colonel had nearly spat out an oath in front of the entire flower show crowd before disconnecting the announcement system during Anthony Templeton's speech.

Had the Best in Show winner's untimely death caused the colonel to reassess the situation? Or was the rose association president simply doing his best to prevent anyone from suggesting he had a reason to wish harm on Anthony Templeton?

"So as long as the roses are of a high enough quality," said Felicity, "there is nothing a prize winner could do or say that would cause his award being rescinded?"

"If you don't believe me regarding the quality of Rosa 'Red Vixen', your ladyship," the colonel spluttered, "our expert judges are here today. You can find Mr Shakerley and Mr Merton in our repository and ask them yourselves."

"We've no reason to disbelieve anything you tell us, Colonel Bolt," said Felicity quickly. She had no wish to derail Alex's reporting by upsetting his interviewee. That was Alex's job.

"The police say they're building a detailed picture of witnesses and alibis," continued Alex. "They say that attendance at—" He flicked through his notebook. "—the presentation given by Mr Lucas Shakerley is a cornerstone of their investigation. Is information regarding this event something with which the association has assisted the police?"

The colonel continued to drum his fingers on the desk. "I wouldn't know. The police have certainly spoken to Mr Shakerley. His presentation was surprisingly well—" The colonel coughed. "—extremely well attended, but neither Mr Shakerley nor the police have reported the contents of their discussions to me. Nor would I expect them to. And before you ask, I wasn't at the presentation myself. I was with my secretary counting the takings from the entrance tickets. There's a lot more to running the association than meets the eye, I can tell you."

Felicity had been interested to hear if Colonel Bolt had an alibi for the time slot in which Anthony Templeton had met his end. That he'd offered it without prompting was testament to his keenness to promote his own innocence, but who wasn't eager to be above suspicion? Conjecture could be damaging. Lady Henrietta's predicament was proof of that.

Alex nodded and wrote in his notebook. Felicity took the pause as a signal.

"This might be an awful thing to think about," began Felicity, her tone gentle, "but might you be able to imagine any reason someone would want to hurt Lord Anthony Templeton? Much of his speech seemed to be said in anger, and I'm sure if he were given the opportunity, he would take the words back." Felicity was unconvinced by this. She wished only to create an atmosphere of safety in which the colonel might share his true opinions.

"But while what Anthony Templeton said may have caused offence," continued Felicity, "do you believe his speech was enough to prompt someone to violence?"

The colonel leaned forward, his hands clasped on the desk, the redness in his cheeks ceasing to increase. "Lord Anthony Templeton's story is a mystery to us all, your ladyship. What happened to him in the years after he left Templeton Manor is unclear, although I'm sure both the police and the press are doing their best to piece together this story."

Alex nodded without looking up from his notebook.

"But whether there were hard feelings beyond the regretful choice of words for his acceptance speech, I couldn't possibly say. We'll wait for the police's investigation. That's all we can do."

"It's indeed all we can do," said Felicity with an understanding tone and just a dash of dishonesty about which she had no qualms.

Alex gave Felicity a look of approval. The beginning of the interview had been a little rocky, but they had their rhythm now. Felicity was the gentle questioner, and Alex was the attack dog. It was a natural balance that they frequently struck. Felicity had to keep her impatience to help her grandmother in check, although the rose association president had just reconfirmed Anthony's background as a Templeton as one distinctly interesting avenue of investigation.

Would Felicity and Alex ever be welcomed through the gates of Templeton Manor?

"Might you be able to—" began Alex, but his question was cut off by a knock at the door.

The association's secretary appeared in the doorway. "Your next appointment has arrived, Colonel."

Colonel Bolt reached for his cane and sprang out of his seat. "My apologies," he said, addressing Felicity and Alex. "I'm afraid I can't leave my guest waiting." The interview was abruptly over.

Upon leaving the president's office, Felicity and Alex found the man who had arrived to speak with the colonel waiting in the corridor. Tall and thin, he carried a leather satchel bulging with papers. He was a little too dully dressed to be a solicitor. An accountant, perhaps.

The association's secretary accompanied the fellow into the colonel's office and remained there, leaving Felicity and Alex alone on the landing at the top of the big wooden staircase.

"The repository?" asked Alex, raising an eyebrow.

Felicity smiled. "Where else?"

Chapter Twelve

Felicity and Alex set about gently knocking at the doors of the first floor corridor, but the approach had to be cancelled. The doors were mainly locked, so when they unknowingly came upon one that wasn't, Alex knocked, then leaned a little too hard into it before realising. As the door flew open, he stumbled into a classroom in which young ladies were receiving instruction from a matronly woman about how to deal with greenfly.

Faced with gasps, expressions of shock, and the teacher's brewing anger, Alex withdrew from the room without asking about the repository's location. The search was looking rather hopeless until Felicity spotted something of interest through a window beside the staircase.

Returning to the ground floor, Felicity and Alex found the doors to the central courtyard open. The scent of roses wafted through the building on the warm breeze. The repository wouldn't be found outdoors, but Felicity advanced into the sunshine of the courtyard with Alex close behind her.

"Good morning, Mrs Broughton," said Felicity brightly.

The straw hat with a large purple bow tipped skywards as Mrs Broughton jerked upright, the sleeves of her voluminous floral cotton dress rolled above gardening gloves. Her mouth fell open as she gathered her senses. “Your ladyship. Good morning.” Clearly, she had not expected to see Felicity at the rose association headquarters.

Another straw hat tipped upwards, this one decorated with a single pearl-headed pin. “Lady Felicity. What a lovely surprise.” Mrs Winterpole was, like Mrs Broughton, involved in the process of dead-heading the many rosebushes in the neatly arranged garden of the building’s central courtyard. The spent blooms, with their withered petals, lay in wicker baskets on a stone table at the centre of the garden.

Mrs Broughton continued to look sheepish while Mrs Winterpole eyed Felicity a little icily. Their last conversation had been rather awkward.

Felicity smiled politely at the two women, but her heart hurt a little. “How pleasant to see you both.” Under normal circumstances, would Lady Henrietta have been there, too?

“Ladies,” said Alex with a lift of his hat. “I don’t suppose you know the way to the repository? We’re looking for Mr Shakerley and Mr Merton.”

Felicity couldn’t fault Alex for wanting to move along quickly. He had deadlines to hit, and Felicity had already changed his schedule once that day. While it wasn’t the moment to challenge Mrs Winterpole about the rumours concerning Lady Henrietta, Mrs Broughton’s nervous reaction implied that the dowager had been excluded from rose association activities as well.

Mrs Winterpole explained how the repository was upstairs, towards the back of the building, and how the two expert judges were always present at that time of the month for the reconciling of the rose registrations.

“Registrations?” asked Alex.

“Each new rose that a breeder develops and wishes to commercialise must be registered with the association,” explained Mrs Winterpole. “We monitor attributes such as heritage, appearance, scent, disease resistance, and so forth.”

"Thank you, Mrs Winterpole." Alex took his notepad out of his jacket. Time could be made to ask the volunteers a few questions. "An enquiry for the Western Daily News, if I may — what do you believe ought to be done with this year's Best in Show prize?" Alex had already collected the reactions to Anthony Templeton's untimely passing. The story had to evolve to keep the readers' attention.

Mrs Winterpole nodded gravely, her secateurs clasped before her. "It's for the British Rose Association to decide. Mrs Broughton and I both work with the association, of course, but we're only volunteers. We're not experts in the running of things. I realise that's rather vague and perhaps not what your readers would like to hear. But I do hope you understand that it's the only answer I can give under the circumstances."

Alex scribbled down Mrs Winterpole's words in swift shorthand. He had no follow-up question on the topic as there was no point pushing further. Mrs Winterpole was as sharp as a tack and extremely polite about it, which was the deadliest of combinations.

Mrs Broughton looked nervously from Mrs Winterpole to Alex, the large bow on her hat trembling. "I thoroughly agree with Mrs Winterpole," she blurted. Mrs Broughton's consorting with Mrs Winterpole was rather disappointing, but was it reasonable to expect Mrs Broughton to give up her own engagements simply because Lady Henrietta had been unrightfully excluded?

"I must say, I'm rather curious," began Felicity, returning her focus to her investigation. "Did either of you witness anything suspicious at the rose festival?" She did her best to keep her tone light and friendly. "I understand the police are very interested in everyone's alibis."

"I was looking after Percy's stand, your ladyship." Mrs Broughton blabbed this out rather hastily. "Don't you remember?"

Felicity smiled calmly. "Of course." The idea of Mrs Broughton bludgeoning someone to death was even more ridiculous than the idea of Lady Henrietta committing such a crime. It was understandable, however, that Mrs Broughton wished to avoid the fate faced by the dowager and her unfortunately timed walk around Bickleford's medieval rose garden.

"I was awfully busy speaking to customers," continued Mrs Broughton. "So I saw nothing of any importance." She glanced at Mrs Winterpole. "Nothing at all."

Mrs Winterpole's composure remained serene. "As you are aware, your ladyship, I was the time keeper for the prize-giving ceremony, and I was also given that responsibility for Mr Shakerley's presentation. My dear husband was in the navy, as you know, and he left behind a rather splendid watch they used for timing manoeuvres."

Felicity recalled the battered pocket watch she'd seen Mrs Winterpole with at the flower show. "I see."

"Its buttons can be a little stiff," continued Mrs Winterpole, "but it's still in excellent working condition and awfully useful. I'm, of course, happy to bring it out whenever it's needed. The colonel is most appreciative. He holds precision in high regard."

Mrs Broughton blinked admiringly at Mrs Winterpole.

Felicity was also intrigued. The first fifteen minutes of Mr Shakerley's presentation overlapped precisely with the window in which the police said Anthony Templeton had met his end.

Felicity glanced at Alex. He'd ceased writing in his notebook, but he lifted his brow encouragingly. Felicity could continue her questioning.

Keeping her tone casual, for her investigation must remain discreet, Felicity asked, "I imagine you gave a good account to the police of who was at the event, Mrs Winterpole."

The widow clutched her secateurs to her chest. "Well, I couldn't possibly know the names of every person there. The show was very busy and the marquee quite packed."

Before committing to investigating Anthony Templeton's unfortunate end, Felicity had considered the sheer number of visitors, volunteers, and staff at the flower show and the obstacle it might pose for such an investigation. The volume of witnesses and testimony was certainly slowing down the police.

Felicity, however, was undeterred. She would start with the connections she had and exhaust every trail until it went cold. And given the timing of the crime, Anthony's speech was surely at the heart of what had happened.

"You recognised quite a number of them, I'd wager," continued Felicity with an undertone of reverence. Flattery was an incredibly useful weapon to have in one's arsenal.

"I believe my recollections were of some use to the police." Mrs Winterpole's tone denoted a degree of pride.

Felicity nodded, but could she ask for a list of names? If even a hint got back to Chief Inspector Luscombe that she was sleuthing, it risked damaging the already tense relationship she had with the police.

"And who did you see there?" Alex had his notebook readied.

Felicity fought the urge to grab his hand and bring it to her lips, so thankful was she that he was the one to ask the question she was dying to pose.

"Well," began Mrs Winterpole, her eyes searching the heavens. "Of the faces I knew, I saw Mr Shakerley, of course, Mr Percival Colhayne, and Mrs Edna Dingle."

Alex wrote the names down as Felicity reflected with some frustration upon how Lady Henrietta had been so concerned about her protégé's success, yet Percy had abandoned his own stand to watch Mr Shakerley's presentation.

But Felicity had to let it go. There were more pressing matters upon which to focus.

Mrs Winterpole's expression became one of concern. "It's not like the News to speculate over the identity of offenders, Mr Cooper."

Alex nodded and offered a reassuring smile. "The Western Daily News is indeed not that sort of publication, but I'm interested in speaking to people who weren't at the talk about their impressions of the atmosphere and goings on leading up to the fateful incident. Your reliable account will save me some time in tracking down the right people to interview."

"Oh, how clever." Were Mrs Winterpole's cheeks glowing a little?

When not ruthlessly cross-examining his interviewees, Alex could certainly charm them.

"I do so enjoy reading the News for that very reason," continued Mrs Winterpole. "It's refreshing not to have all that supposition. Just the facts."

Mrs Broughton nodded along, pushing her hat up from where it had slumped onto her brow. "Yes, just the facts."

With time pressing, Alex chose the praise for Felicity's family's newspaper as the optimal moment upon which to end the conversation. After a round of polite farewells, Felicity and Alex retreated from the sunny courtyard into the shade of the main corridor, under the tranquil yet watchful gaze of the painting of the association's founder.

"I wrote the names down, of course," said Alex, keeping his voice low, "but who's to say how many people were at Shakerley's talk? Fifty? A hundred?"

Felicity refused to become despondent. "Let's start with what we know," she said, her voice barely above a whisper. "The speech. The prize. Who had the most immediate reason to be triggered into action? You said the police hadn't ruled out a crime without premeditation."

Alex nodded. "All right. Quite some glaring omissions on the attendance list, then." Though he continued to speak quietly, excitement was evident in his tone.

Felicity smiled. "You're starting to understand." Alex enjoyed unravelling a mystery just as much as Felicity did. Or rather, he enjoyed seeing his scoop on the front page whenever Felicity was first to solve a crime.

Alex flicked back through his notebook. "The rose breeder Clive Dingle wasn't at the talk. The Dingles were up for the Best in Show prize, weren't they?"

Felicity nodded. "Mrs Winterpole didn't mention the other show judge, either. Mr Merton."

Alex stroked his jaw. "Merton didn't seem that affected by

Anthony Templeton's speech. He was laughing at the beginning, wasn't he?"

"He wasn't by the end." Felicity's eyes twinkled at Alex. "And if we find him in the repository, we can ask him about it."

"Ask who about what?"

The voice that echoed along the corridor turned Felicity's insides to ice.

Chapter Thirteen

Felicity wore her most charming smile as she turned to face Chief Inspector Luscombe. The chief inspector's expression was one of disappointment and barely hidden frustration. The younger detective beside him looked mildly amused. Alex also wore the hint of a smile.

There was, however, nothing droll about the senior policeman's sudden appearance. In terms of investigating, Felicity had been caught practically red-handed. Was there any wriggling out of this?

"Chief Inspector Luscombe," Felicity said cheerily. "Good day to you. And to your colleague. What brings you to the headquarters of the British Rose Association?"

"Perhaps I misheard you when we spoke on the phone, your ladyship." The chief inspector removed his trilby. "I thought you said you were busy writing articles for a London magazine."

"Oh, but that's quite correct. I've a deadline this week." Felicity continued to smile gaily. She was perhaps overdoing it.

Chief Inspector Luscombe frowned. "Did you not tell me the flower show had nothing to do with your magazine writing?"

Felicity adjusted her expression to look more serious. "That's quite right."

Alex watched from the sidelines like a spectator at a tennis match. Did he enjoy seeing her squirm?

The chief inspector narrowed his eyes. "Then the question should be, what brings *you* to the British Rose Association headquarters today, your ladyship?"

The younger detective folded his arms and lifted an eyebrow at Felicity.

To those with less experience of law enforcement, the two policemen were perhaps an intimidating pair. Felicity wouldn't crack, though. She couldn't.

"I'm assisting Mr Cooper," she said brightly.

At the mention of his name, Alex looked suddenly far less amused. What had he expected? They were in this together.

"Assisting Mr Cooper, indeed." Chief Inspector Luscombe sounded like he was enjoying himself. "Mr Cooper doesn't normally require your help, does he? He's usually on his own when approaching my men to dig up information for his articles."

Alex cleared his throat. "I sometimes require assistance when conversing with high-ranking individuals or moving in exclusive social circles."

At last, Alex spoke up in Felicity's defence. She hadn't doubted he'd support her, but he'd waited longer than was comfortable to step in.

He smiled at the detectives. "It's only speaking to the lower echelons that I can get away without her ladyship's assistance."

The younger detective laughed. "Touché."

Chief Inspector Luscombe eyed Alex coolly.

"Who are you here to see, Chief Inspector?" Alex flicked to an empty page in his notebook. "Any breakthroughs in the case?"

It was Felicity's turn to fold her arms over her cream-coloured cardigan and raise an eyebrow at the policemen. She might have reminded them of her grandmother's suffering and the importance of a swift resolution for the case, but any suspicion around Felicity's real reason for being in Chagstock mustn't be encouraged.

Luscombe took in a breath. "Not yet, Mr Cooper. But you will, of course, be the first to know when we have anything to report."

"Chief Inspector?"

Colonel Bolt's secretary had arrived at the bottom of the staircase. Behind him, the accountant-looking fellow was hastening to the front door, his satchel bulging with even more papers than when he had arrived.

"The association president will see you now," continued the secretary.

The detectives exchanged polite yet stiff farewells with Felicity and Alex and followed the secretary upstairs.

Upon hearing the door to the colonel's office firmly close, Felicity let out a slow exhale.

"That was close," she said in a voice not much more than a whisper.

"You know just how to handle him," said Alex, his smile reappearing. "It's wonderful to watch."

"You might have stepped in sooner," hissed Felicity.

"Sorry," said Alex, no longer sounding amused. "I shall do better next time."

"I am grateful to you, though," added Felicity, not wanting to become overly snippy. "I couldn't do this by myself."

Alex's gaze took on a dreamy air. "If the News were another type of paper altogether, it could be a story in its own right. *Amateur Sleuth Takes On The Professionals*. Or *Female Detective Outwits Boys In Blue*. With a picture of you going toe-to-toe with Luscombe."

"Alex, please." Felicity had worked well with the Devon County Constabulary in the past and may need them again in the future. She didn't want to get in the police's bad books for any reason. At least not too seriously.

"I won't," affirmed Alex, although he sounded deflated. They were indeed attention-grabbing headlines. "What do you suppose they're here to discuss?"

Felicity tapped a fingertip on her chin. "The colonel said the police already spoke to everyone at the association. Perhaps they've uncovered a contradiction they need to check. Or something directly related to the colonel." Had the rose association president been hiding something? He'd certainly been nervous during their interview. Was the accountant bundling incriminating documents out just in time before the police arrived?

"Whatever it is," said Alex, "if we want to talk to those judges, we better get to the repository."

Felicity nodded. "Before our dear friend the Chief Inspector interrupts us again."

Chapter Fourteen

The voices were hushed, but they carried through the wooden panelled door of the British Rose Association's repository. Felicity couldn't make out what was being said, but the discussion sounded heated. The voices stopped abruptly when Alex knocked on the door.

A throat was cleared. "Come in."

Sturdy shelves filled with thick books lined the walls. Tall filing cabinets with labelled drawers stood like guardsmen beside the bookcases. At the room's centre, pages lay open on the glossy surface of a broad mahogany table. Voile curtains gently filtered the light from slender windows looking onto the street below. The air carried notes of worn leather, old paper, and beeswax polish.

As Colonel Bolt and Mrs Winterpole had both indicated, the professional judges from the flower show, Mr Ronald Merton and Mr Lucas Shakerley, were present in the repository. Adjusting his cravat, Mr Merton smiled at Felicity and Alex as they entered the room. Straightening his spectacles, Mr Shakerley regarded them with suspicion, a manila file squeezed to his chest.

"I hope we're not disturbing," said Alex.

"Not at all, not at all," said Mr Merton warmly, prompting a round of handshaking and polite greetings. They'd all met before, although Mr Shakerley seemed less pleased than Mr Merton to see Felicity and Alex again.

"Mr Shakerley and I were almost finished with our monthly review," said Mr Merton. "Weren't we, Mr Shakerley?"

Mr Shakerley mumbled something half unintelligible — "...too stupid to listen..." was all Felicity could catch — as he set about returning the books and files on the table to the shelves and cabinets. Mr Shakerley was slight of build, but he slammed the drawers of the filing cabinets with particular force.

Mr Merton's eye twitched as he watched his colleague. "Every month, we gather to assess the new entries into our catalogue. Not a selling catalogue, you understand." He winced as Mr Shakerley nearly yanked a drawer clean out of its cabinet. "It's simply a register so we can keep track of all the varieties, old and new."

Alex nodded. "The president of the association already explained it to us."

"Ah," said Mr Merton nodding, "very good. Very good. Please." He gestured towards the chairs pulled up at the table. "Take a seat. I suppose you're looking for comment for the Western Daily News. I'm sure Mr Shakerley and I can—"

Bang!

The door to the repository had slammed shut behind Mr Shakerley. He was gone.

Felicity glanced at Alex. It was one thing to not want to speak to the press. It was another to storm away without a farewell. But given the tense discussion overheard through the door, Felicity and Alex's arrival was perhaps not the reason for Mr Shakerley's behaviour.

Mr Merton blinked at the repository door, his waxed moustache quivering. "Please excuse my colleague," he said as he took a seat at the table. "Mr Shakerley can be a little... Eccentric, shall we say? And since that awful business with... You know." He smiled apologetically at Felicity and Alex as they seated themselves on the opposite side of the table. "I believe we're all a bit on edge."

"Quite," said Felicity. What Mr Merton was saying was completely plausible, but he was also perhaps aware that whatever disagreement he'd had with Mr Shakerley had been overheard through the door. This might have been an attempt to quell any suspicions that could arise as a result.

Yet this wasn't the first clash between them, was it? On the stage before the prize-giving ceremony, it had sounded as though Mr Merton and Mr Shakerley disagreed about the choice of Best in Show winner.

"But I'm still here and happy to talk." Mr Merton gave a little chuckle. "If that's of any use to you."

Alex nodded. "Of course, Mr Merton." It was a shame to miss out on speaking to Mr Shakerley, but it was probably best to speak to the two flower show judges separately.

"Wonderful." Mr Merton knitted thick fingers and pressed his hands on the glossy table. "Lady Felicity, may I say that you did quite an excellent job as judge and prize-giver at the festival? Mr Etty as well, of course. Are you back to reporting now? I'd rather assumed you were building up your reputation as a sleuth."

"Oh, I'm not investigating anything at the moment, Mr Merton," assured Felicity a little loudly, in case there was a policeman in the corridor to overhear. "I'm simply assisting Mr Cooper with his reporting."

"Ah," said Mr Merton, his eyes sparkling. "Splendid. Splendid. So tell me. How might I assist today, Mr Cooper? I was very glad to see you quoted me in yesterday morning's edition about what an awful tragedy the whole situation is." The flower show judge pulled at his waxed moustache. "I mean, I was very pleased to help with bringing the story to your readers."

Alex had his notebook ready. "I'll come straight to the point, Mr Merton. There have been questions raised about the Best in Show prize—"

Closing his eyes, Mr Merton held up a solemn hand.

Alex stopped, a frown on his face.

"Mr Cooper, I know exactly what you're talking about. I've heard this chatter, too. I completely understand why you're here today at our association asking this question. The question being, of course, given all that has happened, does Lord Anthony Templeton keep the title of Best in Show for his Rosa 'Red Vixen'? Am I right, Mr Cooper? Is that indeed your question?"

"That's correct," said Alex, his tone taut. He preferred to be in control of his interviews.

"No doubt you've already heard Colonel Bolt's take on the situation."

"I have," confirmed Alex, his pencil poised.

"Then I can only echo what our association president has to say on the matter."

Alex's broad shoulders sagged slightly. "It's what Colonel Bolt said you would say, Mr Merton."

Alex needed an angle on the story no other paper would have, but his attempts were floundering. Was it so unusual, however, that the representatives of the association had aligned upon the response they would give to the press? It was a sensible approach to a sensitive situation.

But might there have been more they agreed upon, such as doing away with the disruptive and disrespectful Best in Show winner?

Considering the risks involved, it was hard to see how the British Rose Association stood to benefit from conspiring to end Anthony Templeton's life. A murder plot would have put the reputation of British rose breeding in an even more precarious situation.

"But I will add this." Mr Merton paused dramatically, a finger held in the air. "The roses presented by Lord Anthony Templeton and his Champs Verts Nursery were of exceptional quality. Truly exceptional. If Mr Shakerley were still here, a difficult man though he occasionally can be, he would surely agree with me on this point. Not that my assertions need to be externally adjudicated. I was a flower breeder myself for many years, and I've been a professional show judge for many more. I gave up my own breeding activities to dedicate myself to the profession, for the judging of flower shows is an area of expertise in itself. I judge blooms of all types, but roses are my passion. There is no other flower with such beauty and resonance as the rose."

Felicity raised a subtle eyebrow at Alex. There had to be a way of getting something worthwhile out of Mr Merton.

Alex nodded. Another approach was needed.

"May I put a question to you, Mr Merton?" Felicity tipped her head. "To satisfy my curiosity."

"Naturally, your ladyship," said the show judge. "I'm all ears."

"What did you think of Lord Anthony Templeton? Personally, I mean. Had you met him before his appearance at Bickleford Rose Festival?"

"I knew *of* him, your ladyship." Mr Merton shifted in his seat. "We all knew of him. Anyone who knows roses knows the Templetons, knows they had a son who abandoned the family early on. Otherwise, Lady Leonora wouldn't have inherited the business and be where she is today." He pinched at the tip of his moustache. "Why the young Anthony Templeton left home when he did was not a common topic of discussion, although I believe we can draw conclusions based on what we saw of his behaviour and attitudes during the prize-giving ceremony."

Remembering her run-in with Anthony Templeton behind the marquees, Felicity couldn't help but agree. Her facial expression, however, remained neutral.

Mr Merton lowered his brow, lines puckering on his forehead. "But there's something you must understand, your ladyship. A man's character has no bearing on his blooms. The very nicest and deserving of men might get nothing at all while the unpleasant, disrespectful fellows get every accolade under the sun. Rose breeding is not a personality contest. It's about the plants. The plants and nothing more."

Alex scribbled in his notebook. Might Mr Merton's frankness about his disapproval of Anthony Templeton's character help elevate his story?

"Why do you suppose Lord Anthony Templeton chose this year to make his return to British rose breeding?" continued Felicity.

Mr Merton gave a lengthy sigh. "We all heard his speech. I thought it was a joke to begin with, but then I realised the fellow was serious. I think it's safe to say his reasons were rather personal." The show judge didn't seem to be one for supposition.

With a glance towards Alex, Felicity forged onwards. "During the rose festival itself, after the prize ceremony, forgive my curiosity, but may I ask where you went?"

"Where did I go?" Mr Merton laughed a little. "I went nowhere. I remained at the show."

"You didn't attend Mr Shakerley's presentation, as I understand it," continued Felicity gently, recalling Mrs Winterpole's testimony. "I'm simply interested to know what you might have seen that could have a bearing on what happened."

The show judge chuckled. "I thought you said you weren't sleuthing, your ladyship?"

Felicity blinked as though shy. "Oh, my apologies, Mr Merton. I promise you, I'm not. It's just such a puzzle, isn't it? What might have happened that led to... Well, you know."

Mr Merton frowned. "I shall be honest with you, your ladyship, and this isn't for the papers, Mr Cooper—"

Alex dropped his notebook and pencil into his lap and held up his hands.

"—but I've hardly given the puzzle, as you call it, any thought. That a fellow could annoy someone to the point they walloped him in the head doesn't surprise me, but nor does it interest me to fathom out the whys and wherefores."

Felicity tipped her head innocently. "So you couldn't help the police with any information when they asked you for your testimony?"

Concern rippled over Mr Merton's features, but he maintained his composure. "Well, not really, no. I was round and about. Looking at the various stands, talking to guests and to breeders. But I didn't see or hear anything useful to the investigation. Like I said, the whole thing is a mystery to me."

Felicity nodded. "Thank you for your honesty, Mr Merton." But had Mr Merton been entirely forthcoming? Anthony Templeton had certainly irked the show judge on some level. Had it been enough to prompt him to violence?

There was a knock at the door. The pince-nezed secretary reappeared. "Telephone call for Lady Felicity."

Alex looked at Felicity quizzically as she rose from her seat, suppressing a sigh of frustration.

She knew who it was on the telephone. There was no point in putting it off.

Chapter Fifteen

Felicity's brother Jasper had given up on trying to discourage Felicity's interest in and skill for solving crimes. Nor did he object to Felicity spending time with his old war pal, Alex. He preferred that over her getting into trouble alone.

But as the extremely well-connected editor of the Westcountry's most-read newspaper, there was little that escaped Jasper's attention, even if he was away on business in Scotland. Exactly how he'd traced his sister's precise whereabouts, Felicity would never know. As her brother was fond of saying, a good journalist never betrays his sources.

The rose association's secretary respectfully left Felicity alone in his cosy yet rather cramped office, the surface of the secretary's leather-topped desk offering room for little more than a compact typewriter and a candlestick telephone. The telephone's receiver lay on the desk, glinting in the sunlight from a narrow window overlooking the courtyard garden.

Felicity had, of course, expected a reaction from Jasper at some point. He'd most likely begin with something along the lines of, "Will you please get those blasted magazine articles finished?" But with their grandmother sworn to secrecy, Felicity hadn't imagined her brother capable of hunting her down on Day One of her investigation into Anthony Templeton's demise.

As Felicity lowered herself onto the worn velvet cushion of the secretary's office chair, she silently ran through the lines she and Alex had already used with Chief Inspector Luscombe. Felicity was simply assisting Alex, not reporting or investigating herself. She was putting the needs of the Western Daily News first and would return to writing her magazine articles as soon as was possible. Of course, she had no intention of disappointing the London-based editor with whom Jasper had struck a hard-won syndication deal that not only benefitted the Quicks but also everyone who worked for the Western Daily News.

As Felicity picked up the mouthpiece and lifted the receiver to her ear, she immediately realised the rehearsal had been for nothing.

Yap! Yap! Yap!

"Felicity? Felicity, dear? Can you hear me?"

Yap! Yap!

"Pip, please! You simply must quieten down!"

"Grandmama?" Felicity had never heard Pip bark so bossily. "Is everything all right?"

"Oh, Felicity. I do so hope you can hear me. Only Master Pip will not take no for an answer. He's already had a plate of sausages this morning, and I gave him half a scone when I had elevenses. He thinks he's due more, but I shan't ring for a servant just to bring him food he doesn't need to eat."

Felicity pressed her forehead into her hand. There was no point in trying yet again to explain to Lady Henrietta how giving into a dog's demands rarely led to good behaviour.

Yap! Yap!

"Pip, please!"

Pip could be heard growling with frustration. Why Lady Henrietta had suddenly stopped complying with his requests made no sense to his doggy mind. His poor conduct was the crescendo effect of many weeks of pandering to the terrier.

"Tell him to sit." Felicity raised her voice above the clamour on the line.

"What's that, dear?"

"I said, tell him to sit."

Lady Henrietta's voice moved away from the receiver. "Master Pip, would you please sit down?"

The yapping continued.

Felicity shook her head.

Her grandmother returned to the receiver. "He's not listening, dear. I simply don't know what to do."

"Tell him: 'sit'. Just one word. Say it loudly and firmly. 'Sit'."

There was a doubtful pause while the yapping continued. "Very well. Master Pip, sit!"

The yapping stopped.

"Ha! He's sitting down. Would you believe it?"

"Actually, I would," said Felicity, her head still in her hand. It had been one of the first commands Felicity had taught the Yorkie, although she was also to blame for the current state of Pip's behaviour. When leaving Pip in Lady Henrietta's care, she'd not been precise enough in her instructions on how to care for him.

"Now tell him: 'good boy'."

"Good boy!" parroted Lady Henrietta.

"Now, leave him like that. And when we're finished talking, if he's still sitting nicely, you can reward him with a charcoal biscuit. There's a pot of them near the umbrella stand by the front door."

"Charcoal?" There was disgust in Lady Henrietta's voice.

"They're good for dogs. Unlike cakes, I'm sorry to say. And Pip likes them even if we don't." At least Felicity hoped he still did, after all the rich food he'd grown used to with Lady Henrietta.

"Good boy, Pip," cooed the dowager.

Felicity let out a sigh. "Is that why you called me? For help with Pip?"

"No. Of course not." Lady Henrietta's tone was forthright. "I'm telephoning for something far more important. Why isn't Percy in this morning's edition of the Western Daily News?"

Felicity frowned. How was this her issue to solve? Was she not doing enough for her grandmother? "Shouldn't you be putting this question to Jasper? He's the editor-in-chief."

"Yes, but your brother's off on his travels and always so busy, and I feel quite dreadful. Really quite awful. I promised young Percy I would help him, and what have I done? With my reputation besmirched, I can't take him to the Historical Garden Appreciation Society next week, can I? I'd hoped I might profile him at the fundraiser for the war widows and orphans. It's the biggest event in the philanthropic year, but if I'm cut out of that..." Lady Henrietta attempted to hide a sniff. "Well, I'm no use to anyone anymore."

"Grandmama, that's simply not true." Felicity hated to hear her grandmother upset.

"It's actually Pamela I keep thinking about." Lady Henrietta's voice was wobbling. "He looks so much like her, you know."

Pamela Colhayne, Percy's mother, had been a dear friend of Lady Henrietta's. They'd led quite different lives but had much in common when it came to gardening. Pamela had been an ally of Felicity's grandmother at various plant-related societies and events until illness slowed her down, then took her away.

"She was gone too soon," said Lady Henrietta quietly. "Gone far too soon."

The pain in her grandmother's voice tugged at Felicity's heart. "I shall ask Alex if we can interview Percy."

"Oh, my dear. You're an angel." Lady Henrietta sounded relieved. "Will the interview take place today?"

"I can't promise anything," said Felicity, using much the same tone she used to curb Pip's enthusiasm. "Alex has an awful lot to report on, you know." And he was already accommodating Felicity's investigation into his schedule.

"Well, whenever he has the time would be wonderful. The sooner the better, of course, but please do thank Mr Cooper enormously on my behalf. And just one more thing. Are Mrs Winterpole and Mrs Broughton in the garden looking after the roses?"

Felicity's chest squeezed.

She peeked a glance out of the little office's slender window. The two women were still in the courtyard, tending to the shrubs. They even seemed to be laughing together.

Was it the moment for a white lie?

Chapter Sixteen

It was with haste that Felicity and Alex made their departure from the British Rose Association's headquarters. Alex had allowed his schedule to be adjusted yet again, and with no time for a sit-down lunch, Felicity nipped to the bakery just along Chagstock's sunny high street because she didn't want either of them going hungry. The beef and vegetable filling of the pasties she purchased was warm and succulent and the enclosing pastry buttery and flaky.

"One of my favourite things about Devon," said Alex, dusting the crumbs from his jacket before climbing into the Alvis.

"Do they not sell pasties in London?" she asked as she slid behind the steering wheel.

"Can't say I saw them before I moved down here." Alex quirked an eyebrow mischievously. "Perhaps we could start a business. A stall at Covent Garden."

Felicity smiled as she guided the Alvis into the afternoon traffic. The idea of herself and Alex running some kind of bakery was, of course, ridiculous. Neither of them knew the first thing about pastry or ovens. But thinking about sharing a future together filled her with warmth.

"Splendid idea," she said. "What could possibly go wrong?"

Leaving Chagstock and the British Rose Association behind, hedgerows, trees, and fields began flying by, all brilliant green under a bright blue sky.

"Will Percy have an opinion on what should happen to the prize for Best in Show, do you think?" Though open to supporting Felicity's grandmother by fitting in a visit to Percy Colhayne, Alex remained focused on securing a unique angle for his reporting.

Felicity sighed. "It would surprise me if Percy had much of an opinion on anything. He's quite the woolgatherer."

"Your grandmother's rather invested in him, though, isn't she? I realise I perhaps don't know Lady Henrietta terribly well, but she doesn't strike me as the sort who has time for daydreamers."

Felicity gripped the steering wheel. "I'm afraid my grandmother sees only her dear friend Pamela whenever she looks at Percy. But then my grandmother has enough to worry about at the moment without fretting over Percy's suitability as a nurseryman."

Felicity had taken the plunge on the telephone at the rose association headquarters. She'd informed Lady Henrietta that Mrs Winterpole and Mrs Broughton were both present in the courtyard garden. The pause on the line after the delivery of the news had been painful. Clearing her throat, Lady Henrietta had said she was pleased the roses were being looked after, but then the call ended rather abruptly, with the dowager saying Pip had become fidgety and needed attending to.

"You can't protect your grandmother from everything," said Alex gently. "Not only is it impossible, but I think your grandmother would be rather peeved at being mollycoddled."

As much as Alex knew how to rile Felicity, he also knew how to reassure her. "Are you positive you don't mind dropping by to see Percy?"

Alex smoothed a hand over his dark blond hair as the Alvis continued to hurtle along hedge-lined lanes. "If I can help Lady Henrietta and still get my pieces turned in on time, then I'm all for it. She's the grandmother of my employer, after all." He smiled. "And of an extremely dear friend."

Felicity felt a tingle in her belly as she fixed her eyes on the road.

She had no wish to rush anything with Alex. She enjoyed their working relationship as much as she valued his friendship. Yet it thrilled her to her core to hear him refer to her as 'an extremely dear friend'. And how much he cared about Lady Henrietta was enormously touching.

Ought they announce their fondness for one another publicly somehow, or at least to family and friends? What exactly would they say? The thought of it made Felicity's chest tighten slightly. She wasn't one for attention.

"Talking to Percy won't bring your case any further, will it?" asked Alex, plucking an errant pasty crumb from his lapel.

Felicity took a deep breath. Her investigation was the most pressing matter for the moment. "According to Mrs Winterpole, Percy was at Mr Shakerley's presentation. I could ask him to confirm her testimony of who else was there."

"Do you have a reason not to trust Mrs Winterpole's evidence?" asked Alex.

Felicity raised an eyebrow. "We must always have at least two sources before reporting something as truth," she said, repeating one of the core tenets of good journalism.

Alex smiled. "There'll always be a reporter in there somewhere."

Felicity ignored the needling about the direction of her career. "For whom do we have alibis so far?" To avoid appearing to be too active an investigator, Felicity hadn't used her notebook during the interviews, knowing Alex could be relied upon to get everything down.

He flicked through the pages of his notebook. "Colonel Bolt and the association's secretary were in the organiser's tent, counting the ticket takings. Mrs Winterpole, Mr Shakerley, Percy, and Edna Dingle were all at Mr Shakerley's presentation." He flicked through a couple more pages. "Mrs Broughton said she was at Percy's stand. Can we trust that?"

Felicity nodded energetically. "Even my grandmother is more convincing as a killer than Mrs Broughton."

"Mr Merton by his own account was off by himself," continued Alex. "Clive Dingle is so far unaccounted for, as are the victim's two assistants. What about the other celebrity judge?"

"Mr Etty? We could talk to him in case he saw anything, but I hadn't considered him a suspect. What was there in Anthony Templeton's speech that could have triggered a music-hall singer into action?"

Felicity manoeuvred the Alvis across a little stone bridge over a gushing river, the narrow crossing suitable for horses but less accommodating of modern motors.

Alex gave a grim little frown. "But then you've already made your mind up, haven't you?"

Felicity glanced sharply at Alex. "Made my mind up?"

"You still think it was Leonora Templeton's gardener. You're just waiting to find the evidence to confirm it. Yet you saw them leaving the show grounds yourself."

It was annoying when Alex read Felicity's thoughts, although oddly, he wasn't entirely accurate on this occasion.

The church bells had rung the hour not long before Leonora, Havelock, and the dogs passed Felicity and her grandmother on their way towards Bickleford village. There hadn't been much of a window for the deadly deed, but it wasn't impossible.

Yet Felicity had done her best to move her thoughts along from the burly gardener. It wasn't helpful to become narrowly focused too early in an investigation.

Felicity sat up straighter, both hands firmly on the steering wheel. "Opportunity is one thing, but what about motive? Havelock may be protective of Leonora, but Mr Merton gave up a career in rose breeding to dedicate himself to judging. Anthony Templeton made a mockery of the Bickleford Rose Festival and, by extension, of Mr Merton."

"But how would violently doing away with the winner of the Best in Show improve the rose association's standing?"

Felicity braked as a pointy-eared red squirrel hopped across the road, its long fluffy tail bobbing as it ran. "The deed wasn't premeditated, though, was it? The police are looking at it as a passionate act. And before you say it, I know everyone had a reason to be thoroughly angry with Anthony after the shocking speech he gave, but who was most affected? Who had the deepest reason to take offence at his very presence at the show?"

Alex chuckled. "You're talking about Leonora again, aren't you?"

Felicity fumed silently as she pressed gently on the accelerator pedal. She hadn't been thinking about Leonora specifically, but Alex had a point. If Felicity could just talk to Leonora, she would get a far better understanding of Lord Anthony Templeton and of the whole situation. The whole case.

"I have to help my grandmother," said Felicity. "Even if I fail to come up with a breakthrough before the police, I can't sit by and—"

Screech!

Felicity stepped hard on the brake. The Alvis came to a sudden halt.

Chapter Seventeen

"What the..."

Felicity peered through the windscreen with shock and confusion at the tall pile of terracotta pots that stood in the middle of the road. She'd brought her two-seater Alvis to a stop about twenty yards from the leaning terracotta tower, despite coming upon the obstacle on a rather tight bend.

"Bravo," said Alex, already alighting from the motor and advancing towards the pots. He was about to dismantle the tower when something caught his eye at the side of the road. "I say."

Felicity approached the curious scene, following Alex's gaze to a gap in the tall, dense hedgerow at the side of the road. A carved wooden sign hanging on the white-painted gate read: *THE DEN.*

The terracotta pots might have caused a rather nasty accident, but if they hadn't been in the road, they might have whizzed past their destination.

"How long do we have?" asked Felicity.

Alex checked his wristwatch. "Not long enough."

Felicity gave a firm nod. She knew what she had to ask.

The Den was a squat cottage with cob walls and a thatched roof. The humble and slightly unkempt dwelling was typical of the Devonshire countryside, but its gardens weren't. They were very special indeed.

Separated by narrow slate paths and thin strips of lawn, generous borders were stuffed full of blooms. Bright pink hollyhocks and vibrant blue delphiniums swayed gently in the breeze. The silvery leaves of lavender and sweet peas dangling from trellises filled the air with sweetness, as purple campanula crept along the ground, softening the paths.

The focus of the attention was, of course, the rose bushes, their dark green foliage providing the perfect foil for the delicate pinks, soft whites, and velvety red of the perfumed flowers.

"Oh," said Percy by way of greeting as he emerged from the cottage and into the garden. He had the air of a dishevelled artist in a baggy pair of corduroys, a battered set of braces, and a billowing linen shirt. His sun-kissed hair kept catching in the breeze as he stared confusedly at the pots Felicity and Alex were carrying. "Lady Henrietta telephoned to say you'd be coming, your ladyship, but she didn't mention you'd be bringing anything with you. Here. Let me."

"We found them in the road," clarified Felicity as Percy took over the pile of pots Felicity had been carrying.

"In the road?" Percy's green eyes widened. "Goodness. Of course. I had a delivery for the greenhouses earlier this morning. Must have forgotten to bring them in."

I told you he was a daydreamer.

Felicity pulled a face at Alex as they followed Percy through the cottage's garden, past a wall of beech hedging, and onto a stretch of land containing neat rows of roses in precisely cut beds. Beside the beds were several small glass houses.

"Would you like the tour?" offered Percy brightly, as he and Alex settled the pots beside one of the greenhouses.

Felicity looked at Alex. It was his time they were using.

"If it's short," he said.

Percy nodded eagerly. "Lady Henrietta told me how busy you are and how grateful I should be. And I am, you know, grateful."

He smiled in his disarming, boyish way. There was something of the lost baby deer about Percy. Is that how Lady Henrietta had felt compelled to spend so much of her energy on the lad?

To give him his due, however, the tour Percy gave was indeed to the point and rather brief.

"This all used to be my mother's," he explained, gesturing to the cottage and its land as he picked a path between rows of carefully maintained rose bushes, the surrounding ground thickly mulched with straw.

Felicity had met Pamela Colhayne at Bradley Court on a few occasions. Lady Henrietta was incredibly upset when she died of a short, devastating illness while Percy was away at the front.

"I suppose you learned your skills from your mother," said Felicity, touching a fingertip to a pale pink bloom. It had been in the competition for Best in Show, hadn't it? The edges of the ruffled satin-like petals were a darker shade of pink than the rest of the flower. The effect was quite striking.

Percy looked over his shoulder, his hands in the pockets of his baggy trousers. "My mother tried to teach me about plants when I was just a boy, but I had little interest. My focus was painting. Portraits, mainly, although after the war, I found myself unable to continue. Found myself not able to do much of anything."

Alex ceased writing in his notebook. He looked sombre.

It was best not to push too directly for the wartime accounts of those who survived the trenches. Having been at the front himself, Alex knew this, too. The stories from those years could be difficult tales to tell and were best told only when the teller was ready.

In any case, Felicity knew much of Percy's story from her grandmother.

By the time news of his mother's passing reached him, Percy was already in a field hospital, thoroughly numb and barely functioning. A terrible case of shell shock, by all accounts.

"You never went back to painting?" asked Felicity as they advanced for a look around the greenhouses.

Percy shook his head as he quickly checked the trays of cuttings lined up neatly on wooden shelves. His approach to breeding and propagation was surprisingly orderly. The heat under the sparkling glass of the greenhouse was a little stifling.

"I was sent to convalesce near Noyon. The hospital had a flower garden, and I found solace there. I suppose the plants reminded me of my mother, although I could hardly think about her at the time. I could hardly think of anything, really. It was all rather too much."

Alex lifted the brim of his homburg with the end of his pencil. "Did they send you back to the front?"

Percy took up a watering can. "The armistice was signed before they discharged me from hospital." He sprinkled water onto the trays of cuttings. It trickled onto the gravel beneath the benches. "But I couldn't face coming back to Blighty. I worked at a botanical garden in Amiens for a couple of years. Only came back here in 1920." Percy gazed up at Felicity and Alex as he set the watering can down. His eyes were sorrowful, yet he wore a peaceful smile. "Took me an awful long time to come to terms with things. I'm still coming to terms even now."

Lady Henrietta had ensured Pamela Colhayne's garden was looked after in Percy's absence. She did so in memory of her friend, as it wasn't clear if Percy would ever return. But when he came back, and Lady Henrietta saw how skilled Percy was with his mother's roses — thanks to his time in Noyon and Amiens, no doubt — Lady Henrietta felt she had to invest in Percy as well.

From the neat efficiency of the greenhouses, Felicity could see it now, too. She'd perhaps judged Percy rather too harshly. "You seem to be doing an awfully good job of it," she said encouragingly. "All things considered."

Alex nodded in agreement as he continued to write in his notebook.

In a normal year, with his boyish handsomeness and his moving story of triumph in the face of strife, Percy would have been the star of Bickleford Rose Festival. If he'd won Best in Show, how far might he have gone?

A man of a different character might have been outraged or

embittered by what had happened at that year's flower show, his limelight having been well and truly stolen.

Percy, however, seemed reflective. Even sanguine.

He ran his fingers through the papery petals of a stand of pink poppies as they returned to the slate pathways of the cottage garden.

"If your mother had been here for this year's rose festival, what do you think she would have made of it?" Alex's question was bold, but he refused to compromise his readers' expectations for a unique perspective.

Percy sighed deeply. "I think she'd be proud of me for having done what I could, but I think ultimately she'd be sad. Sad that things turned out the way they did."

"Sad about what, exactly?" pressed Alex.

Percy winced. "Mother abhorred violence of any kind. She was practically angry with me when I got my call up. She wanted me to run away, hide somewhere abroad, and of course, part of me wanted to." Percy stared out towards the edges of the garden, his eyes haunted. "But of course I didn't."

Alex nodded stiffly. He'd done his duty alongside Felicity's brother, Jasper, and they'd formed a strong bond. But his experiences at war had been far from purely edifying, as the scar on Alex's forehead attested.

They came to a stop beside a large, fragrant laurel bush, which offered pleasant shade across a faded table and chairs with patches of rust.

Felicity turned down Percy's offer of a pot of tea and biscuits. Alex's work schedule couldn't be compromised further. She had her own magazine articles to work on, of course, but she could stay up into the night with a candle and work on those. There weren't daily deadlines like at the newspaper.

"Just one more question," said Alex, "if I may?"

Percy pressed his hands into his pockets. "Please."

"What do you think ought to happen to the prize for Best in Show?"

"The silver plate?" Percy looked confused. "Don't the police have it?"

"I mean the title," clarified Alex. "Given everything that has occurred, do you believe Lord Anthony Templeton ought to remain the winner? Or should this year's Best in Show go to someone else?"

Percy's eyebrows drew together as he gazed across the sea of nodding flowers that stretched out before the cottage. "I can't say I've thought about it. I'm at peace with the fact I didn't win, if that's what you mean." He smiled at Alex. "I found peace with that before the festival even started."

Given how certain Lady Henrietta had been about Percy's chances for Best in Show and what Felicity had now witnessed in his garden, it was a curious comment.

Felicity cocked her head. "May I ask why?"

Percy pushed his hands deeper into his pockets. "Being a successful rose breeder is about more than just the roses. You need a certain head for it. Be commercially savvy or business-minded or whatever it's called." He frowned a little. "I tried telling your grandmother, your ladyship. She said business acumen was a skill I could pick up along the way, but deep down, I always knew it wasn't for me. I'm not a salesman, your ladyship. I could never be one."

Alex set his pencil to rest on his notebook. This wasn't at all what Lady Henrietta would want to read about her protégé in the next edition of the Western Daily News.

"What about getting someone to help you?" suggested Felicity, the instinct to protect her grandmother kicking in, although the situation was already quite hopeless. There was indeed no one less like a salesman than Percy.

Percy smiled sadly. "I suppose I could. If it were up to Lady Henrietta, then I would. And who would I be to stop her? She's been so kind to me. But I'm not sure I would enjoy that kind of life. Running a business. It's not what I want. I see that now."

Felicity swallowed. "Does my grandmother know how you feel?"

"I have tried to tell her, your ladyship. Like I said, she seems convinced the urge and necessary skills will come to me when the time is right. I'd be happy to sell the odd plant here and there, perhaps do some gardening for others. But I don't think I'm built to run a nursery. Not commercially."

Felicity glanced at Alex. He looked dismayed. Lady Henrietta had already so much to deal with. Yet she mustn't be mollycoddled. The dowager indeed detested that.

"Please, Percy. You must try to be clearer with my grandmother. She needs to understand how you feel. Shall I speak to her on your behalf?"

Percy pushed a hand through his hair. He seemed unsettled. He said nothing.

"There will be other projects into which she can pour her energy," continued Felicity.

Percy nodded. He looked sad. "I suppose we were both thinking about my mother. Trying to do the best by her. I do so hope I haven't disappointed her. She adored roses. This was all hers." He looked towards the greenhouses. "Only she never made it to the rose festival."

"I know, Percy." Despite the sunshine warming the back of her cardigan, Felicity felt a brief chill. "My grandmother was so awfully fond of your mother." If Lady Henrietta was to pull through this whole ordeal, Felicity would have to redouble her efforts.

"I say," she began. "You attended Mr Shakerley's presentation, didn't you?"

Percy seemed a little dazed by the sharp change in topic.

"At the flower show, I mean," added Felicity.

"Y-yes, I did. As far as I recall."

"May I ask who else you saw there?"

Percy thought for a moment. He smiled playfully. "Are you conducting an investigation?"

Felicity exchanged glances with Alex. Might it help Percy be more mindful of his interactions with Lady Henrietta if he understood the pressure the dowager was under?

"Of a kind," admitted Felicity. She explained the situation her grandmother found herself in, and how Felicity wished to do what she could to help bring the case to a quick conclusion.

"Naturally, I shall hand anything I find over to the police," she concluded. "But the net they've cast is extremely wide. I'm hoping I can help narrow things down. As quickly as possible."

Percy drew his eyebrows together. "They can't seriously consider your grandmother a suspect. Can they?"

"She's not at the top of the police's list," assured Alex.

"But the lack of clarity is fuelling speculation," explained Felicity.

"Goodness." Percy ran a hand through his hair, his brow still creased. "If there's anything I can do."

Felicity nodded. "Just be gentle with her. And honest."

A blackbird landed in the laurel bush, eyed Felicity, Alex, and Percy suspiciously, then flew away chirruping.

"Do you remember who else was at Mr Shakerley's presentation?" asked Alex. The deadline for the evening edition wasn't far away.

Percy looked thoughtful. "The tent was rather full."

"Whoever you can remember would be helpful," added Felicity reassuringly.

"Mr Shakerley was there, of course," began Percy. "And one of the association's volunteers was doing the time keeping." That would have been Mrs Winterpole. "Mrs Dingle was in the front row. One of Anthony Templeton's, um... One of his assistants was there as well."

Mrs Winterpole had mentioned none of the Champs Verts assistants. Had her testimony been not entirely reliable?

"Which one?" asked Felicity.

Chapter Eighteen

Felicity didn't object when Alex said he had to get back to Exeter to submit his stories. She had no desire to keep him from his work. After dropping Alex off at the newspaper's Exeter headquarters, Felicity reflected on the first day of her investigation as fork-tailed swallows swooped and danced before the Alvis on the run over to Bradley Court.

Percy Colhayne had noticed Anthony Templeton's male assistant at Mr Shakerley's presentation. Percy's testimony didn't exactly contradict Mrs Winterpole's, but neither did it add up. Mrs Winterpole had seen no one from Champs Verts Nursery at the talk.

It was too soon to draw conclusions about the case, but the gathering of evidence was already proving more difficult than imagined. In vowing to investigate, had Felicity over-estimated her abilities and under-estimated those of the police?

Her sense of usefulness was somewhat restored upon arrival back at home, where Felicity found Lady Henrietta struggling to control Pip's demands for shortbread tails during afternoon tea. Felicity guided her grandmother in instructing the wayward Yorkie to sit and also to lift a paw, after which he was rewarded not with treats from the tea table but with a charcoal biscuit from the jar in the hall.

"Upon my word," exclaimed Lady Henrietta as the little dog followed her commands.

"Consistency is key," assured Felicity, who provided further distraction for her grandmother in the form of piquet before dinner and cribbage afterwards, in the cosy sunken leather armchairs of Bradley Court's salon.

Lady Henrietta's mood wasn't exactly jolly, but then neither was she morose. If she'd received further letters uninviting her from events, then she didn't wish to share them with Felicity, and Felicity didn't ask. There was little to gain from focusing on one's problems, and Felicity was already doing what she could to help the situation.

Lady Henrietta moved her peg along the cribbage board. "Did you and Mr Cooper learn anything of interest today, dear?" She'd waited rather a while to ask and made it sound awfully casual.

"Not yet," answered Felicity, keen to prevent her grandmother from participating even vicariously in the collection of testimonies and the associated deliberations. It was less about protecting Lady Henrietta from the details and more that Felicity needed to remain focussed.

Felicity laid a card down. "Did you know Anthony Templeton's parents very well?" she asked, pegging her points.

Lady Henrietta squinted at her cards. "We were acquainted with one another, mainly through the British Rose Association. They were awfully active, of course. The Templeton family established the organisation generations ago."

Felicity recalled the large oil painting of the Templeton ancestor staring down at all who arrived in the entrance hall of the rose association headquarters.

"But we weren't close," said the dowager, her eyes still on her cards. "I didn't know them awfully well."

Pip let out a loud snore from Lady Henrietta's lap, almost waking himself up.

"What were they like?" asked Felicity.

"Polite. Serious. Utterly dedicated to their roses." Lady Henrietta set down her card. "A run of four, dear."

"Did you meet Anthony before his disappearance?"

Lady Henrietta frowned as she moved her peg. "Once or twice."

"What was he like?"

"Like many young men at that age. Rather too full of himself."

"And Leonora, what was she like?"

"Oh, quite the opposite. Withdrawn. Studious. Awfully quiet."

The contrasting impression created by the two siblings persisted into adulthood.

Felicity attempted to study her hand and select a card, but she was distracted. "Do you have any inkling why Anthony left Templeton Manor when he did?"

The topic had been discussed *ad nauseam* in the papers, but up till now it was all speculation, the man himself being unavailable to explain his motives and Leonora still in hiding from the press.

Felicity felt restless with the need for real details. "I mean, was there much chatter about it at the time?"

The dowager folded her hand together. "It wasn't the sort of thing one discussed. I'd always assumed it was the boy's brashness clashing with the more subtle sensibilities of his parents. It's not entirely unheard of for a young man to leave the nest as soon as he reaches maturity, although it's, of course, unfortunate when it happens. And in the case of the Templetons, I suppose they'd assumed Anthony would take over the family business, so that would have been an extra blow. Do you wish to continue playing, dear, or shall we retire for the night?"

Felicity snapped her attention back to the cards and continued the game with gusto. Her grandmother needed a distraction, and rousing her competitive spirit did the trick. Lady Henrietta triumphed, reaching one-hundred-and-twenty-one with Felicity just two points behind her.

It was only after her grandmother had gone to bed, buoyed by her win, that Felicity found the envelope tucked behind a porcelain figurine on the mantelpiece of the salon. It was from the Young Women's Support Society.

...regret to inform you that your presentation on techniques for abundant flowerbeds has been placed on hold indefinitely...

Felicity's stomach clenched. It was admirable that her grandmother was putting on such a brave face, but something had to be done.

By candlelight in her bedroom, Pip already snoring on the bed, Felicity typed out several pages of lacklustre copy for the Gentlewoman's Gazette. It was difficult to immerse herself in the affair at Liverton Ladies' Academy. Though it had occurred only recently, the matter was thoroughly resolved and Felicity's mind was focused on the present.

What had really happened at Bickleford Rose Festival?

The pieces of the jigsaw were still so scattered that it made it hard for Felicity to sleep, like a child the night before a birthday party, so keen was she to return to the puzzle.

The same buzz had Felicity out of bed early and waiting in her motor, the cool freshness of the morning biting at her shoulders through her belted cardigan when Alex arrived at Bradley Court in his Model T.

"I thought you said no rush?" Alex looked bemused as he climbed into the Alvis' passenger seat. "Aha," he said, his nose leading him to bacon sandwiches and a flask of tea in a basket in the footwell.

Gravel crunched under the two-seater's tyres as Felicity sped away. "Help yourself. And I didn't want to rush you, but that doesn't mean we can dillydally."

Their first stop meant a drive hugging the edge of the moors, along steep wooded valleys and through a ford, which was rather high as it had rained the night before. The surrounding greenery smelled fresh and glowed brightly in the damp.

Felicity had read Alex's coverage while waiting for him in the Alvis. He'd continued to focus on what might happen to the prize for Best in Show, added a few updates from the police, and also a short article about Percy at home.

Thankfully, he hadn't included Percy's talk of dropping out of the rose breeding scene. Lady Henrietta ought to hear it from Percy himself first, which was why Felicity hadn't brought the matter up with her.

"I tried Templeton Manor again," Alex reported between bites of a bacon sandwich. "No joy."

Felicity slowed the motor to roll through another stream of water crossing the road's surface. "I don't think we'll ever get to the bottom of things without speaking to Leonora."

"So you can wear her down over her alibi for her gardener?"

Felicity shot Alex a glare.

He raised an eyebrow at her.

"No," she said firmly, returning her eyes to the road, although her thoughts returned frequently to the disagreement she'd overheard between the victim and Havelock, like a tongue worrying a bothersome tooth. "I wish to understand Anthony Templeton better. That's my priority now. A chat with those assistants of his would be quite helpful, too."

"On that subject, I have good news." Alex shook open his notebook, his bacon sandwich still in his other hand. "Madame Blanche Ernault and Monsieur Jacques Gobillot will be returning to Bickleford. And guess which newspaper has secured an exclusive interview with the pair?"

Felicity turned to see Alex's grin. "It's no wonder Jasper was so keen to bring you down to Devon," she said. "Today?"

Alex nodded. "Promising to buy them lunch seemed to swing it."

Felicity quirked an eyebrow. It was an important reminder not to overlook the simplest of tactics.

"I've had less luck with Shakerley, however. I reached him by telephone at his private residence. Told me he's busy."

"Busy with what?" As the accounts given so far varied, Felicity wished to hear Mr Shakerley's version of who was at his presentation. His view of the audience would have been unrivalled.

"No idea. He hung up on me."

Felicity frowned. "If he hadn't been on stage in view of everyone during the window in which Anthony Templeton was killed, I'd say he's behaving rather suspiciously, don't you think?"

"He strikes me as the sort of chap whose behaviour is flummoxing at the best of times."

A large painted sign came into view on the road ahead.

Felicity brought the Alvis to a gentle halt. "I hope our next interviewees prove less perplexing."

Chapter Nineteen

The Alvis was the first vehicle to arrive on the gravel provided for the motors of visitors to the nursery. There remained a chill in the air. Felicity tugged the belt of her cardigan tight over her pale-grey cotton day dress and firmed the position of her bead-trimmed beret on her head. Alex fastened the button on his suit jacket as they followed a sign painted in red pointing to a gate in a row of neat white fencing set before beech hedging, the faintly pleated leaves sparkling with droplets of last night's rain.

Beyond the hedge, the nursery came into full view. Rows of tables were covered in pots, with larger containers on the ground. Many of the plants were roses, mainly the simpler sort with a smaller number of petals and not much fragrance, but there were also bedding plants, perennials, and even evergreen shrubs for sale.

Beyond the rows of plants were several medium-sized greenhouses, sturdy, practical, and glimmering in the morning sunshine. Tucked off in the distance was a rickety old barn that appeared to have been transformed into a dwelling. A chattering of starlings lifted off from the branches of a nearby elm and into the blue of the sky. The faint tang of smoke hung in the air.

"Where is everyone?" asked Felicity.

Alex frowned as he looked in his notebook. "They said to stop by this morning." He tapped a page with his pencil. "We're within their opening hours."

"There." Felicity pointed to a greenhouse in the distance.

Silhouetted against the sunshine, two figures were moving about within the glass building.

As Felicity and Alex approached, the figures became recognisable.

In a shirt patched at the elbows and rough woollen trousers, Mr Clive Dingle was tall and wiry, his thinning red-blond hair tucked under a worn brown cap. Mrs Edna Dingle was much smaller, and her shapeless corduroy pinafore had also seen better days. She, too, wore a flat cap, her grey-blonde hair pulled back in a tight bun underneath. It was an unusual choice for a woman but perhaps well suited to countless hours spent outdoors.

Edna was pushing a broom, and Clive was putting items into a bucket. They were perhaps nearing fifty, but there was a sense of industry and proud practicality to the couple. While they perhaps lacked the creativity and flourish of some of the other rose breeders, the Dingles could apparently be relied upon for sturdy plants with good resistance to weather, disease, and pests.

Upon arrival in the greenhouse's doorway, however, Felicity gasped.

The floor was strewn with broken pots, spilt soil, and damaged plants. Several panels of the greenhouse's glass had also been smashed. Trowels, dibbers, and plant labels were strewn over the ground. The smell of compost and broken stems filled the air.

As Clive bent to pick up another sherd, Edna twisted towards Felicity. Her eyes were red, the tears barely dry on her cheeks. Clive looked up angrily, but his face became conflicted when he saw Felicity and Alex in the doorway. At the far end of the greenhouse, a brindle greyhound with a mostly white muzzle lay shivering on a blanket under an empty table.

"Have we come at a bad time?" asked Alex.

Edna threw a panicked look at Clive.

"What happened?" asked Felicity.

Edna sniffed. "I'm so sorry." She brought her wrist to her nose.

"Do excuse me." She left the greenhouse and hurried towards the converted barn. On trembling legs, the greyhound rose and went after her, its thin tail low.

Felicity felt the urge to follow. "Will Mrs Dingle be all right?" she asked of Clive.

Clive swallowed and nodded. "She's had rather a shock. That's all. We both have." He set his bucket of broken pot pieces and glass on the ground. "To come out this morning and find the place like this." He cast a pitiful gaze over the greenhouse.

"Someone did this to you?" asked Alex, pulling out his notebook.

Clive frowned. "I know we said for you to come by whenever you liked, Mr Cooper, but I'm not sure this is something for the papers."

Alex paused. "May I ask why not?"

"Well, I..." Clive looked troubled. "I don't suppose we've quite come to understand the matter ourselves yet."

"Why would someone do this to you?" said Felicity, looking around at the damage. She knew little about the price of plants, but several older roses had been destroyed, as well as countless younger specimens. The cost of the damage may have been considerable. "Who would do such a thing?"

Clive shook his head. He gave a little smile, the lines in his face deepening further. "I suppose we ought to be grateful it was just our greenhouse and that we weren't targeted ourselves. Seems like rose breeding's not the safe, quiet activity it used to be."

Felicity exchanged looks with Alex. Could the same person who did for Anthony Templeton now be targeting the Dingles? The approach was completely different, and a deadly bludgeoning was far more serious than the destruction of plants. The attack on the greenhouse looked frenzied, however, rather than systematic. Emotions had perhaps been running high in both situations.

"Why would someone do this?" Felicity was desperate to understand what on earth was going on.

Clive adjusted his cap. Though still early in the day, the sunlight coming into the greenhouse was rather warm. "I wish I knew, your ladyship. Perhaps it was just local lads having a bit of fun."

"The next village is how far away, Mr Dingle?" enquired Alex.

Clive sighed. There was a defeated sort of sadness to him. "You're quite right, Mr Cooper. I suppose it's a little too far for that." He went to pick up his bucket.

Felicity stepped forward. "What I'm about to say may sound rather odd, Mr Dingle, but you might wish to leave matters as they are and not clear up any further."

Clive frowned. He relinquished his bucket, his hand trembling a little. He stood up straight. "I'm not sure I follow, your ladyship."

"The police can do quite wonderful things with fingerprints these days," said Felicity.

Clive's eyes widened. "Oh, I doubt we need to bother the police about this. I'm sure they have enough to deal with, after what happened in Bickleford and all. We need to have the place cleaned up before any customers come by."

"Would you not like whoever did this to face justice?" said Felicity. "What about if they were to strike again?" She stopped short of mentioning a potential link with what happened to Anthony Templeton. The thought had likely crossed the Dingles' minds. Edna already seemed upset enough.

Clive put his hands on his hips. "I take your point, your ladyship, and I shall think about it. But can we please keep this to ourselves for now? I should like to talk to Edna before taking any further action."

Felicity looked to Alex to respond to Clive's request for privacy. He was the reporter on the scene. Not her.

Alex nodded. "Of course. May I ask you a few questions unrelated to the wrecking of your greenhouse?"

Clive gave a small nod. "Go ahead, Mr Cooper." He sounded weary. "Now is as good a time as any, and I suppose more coverage in your newspaper will do us good. Certainly couldn't do us any harm at this point."

"Is everything all right with the business?" asked Alex, clearly intrigued by Clive's comments. "Aside from what's happened in here, I mean."

"No, not that. It's just..." Clive sighed heavily. "Please, what was it you wanted to ask? About the Bickleford Rose Festival, was it?"

Alex brought matters back on track, asking Clive about what ought to happen to the Best in Show prize.

"Not only considering Anthony Templeton's passing," said Alex, "but also given what he said during his acceptance speech." He flicked through his notebook. "'It's all you breeders imagining this whole charade means something.' Those were his words."

Alex quoting Anthony seemed to leave Clive unmoved. "A prize isn't about the man's character or his background or his situation," he said. "It's about his plants. The quality of the rose that won him the prize hasn't changed due to anything the fellow said or what happened to him, has it?"

Alex persisted. "Do you not think it would be fairer for the rose association to offer the prize to someone else?"

Clive wiped a hand over his mouth. His fingers were still shaking. "Edna and I have never had a Best in Show, and we've been entering the competition for many years. Too many to count. We're accustomed to the disappointment." He gave a weak smile. "But there's always a rose that's been better than ours. And there's always next year. That's what we say to one another. There's always next year."

Clive's combination of optimism and stoicism was heartrending. Would the Dingles ever win Best in Show, or would their roses always be too sturdy and predictable?

Alex glanced up at Felicity as he wrote in his notebook. It was her turn.

"Had you met Lord Anthony Templeton prior to the flower show, Mr Dingle?" asked Felicity. "Or 'Mr Fox', as he also went by?"

Clive adjusted his cap, his smile gone. "I knew of him, your ladyship. We all did, Templetons being what they are among us rose breeders. Can't say I knew his lordship personally, though. Certainly never expected him to return the way he did."

Mrs Winterpole and Percy had both seen Edna Dingle at Mr Shakerley's presentation. They hadn't seen Clive, but what would have been his motive for doing away with Anthony Templeton? There was a sense of defeat to the man, an acceptance that the Dingles would never be the stars of the show. It was hard to imagine Clive picking up a weapon in anger. At least not to defend his reputation.

"Might you be able to guess at why he lashed out as he did in his acceptance speech?" asked Felicity.

Clive shook his head, his mouth a straight line. "Your guess is as good as mine, your ladyship. I dare say Lady Leonora Templeton would be your best chance of getting an understanding of the fellow."

Felicity nodded. Leonora was indeed an important and glaringly absent part of the puzzle.

"Could you perhaps share with us what you witnessed around the time of Lord Anthony Templeton's passing?" asked Felicity, softening her approach to investigating Clive's alibi. From the tremble still in his hands, the destruction in his greenhouse had already been quite the blow that morning. "I'm sure you know that the police have narrowed the window to between two o'clock and a quarter past on the day of the flower show."

Clive looked thoughtful. He seemed not at all irritated by being asked such a question by someone other than the police. "I'm afraid I don't have much to share on that point. I was with Edna at Mr Shakerley's presentation."

Felicity smiled to cover her surprise — and her disappointment. The witness testimonies she'd gathered so far were turning out to be rather unreliable or, at best, incomplete. Her investigation was already faltering.

"Thank you, Mr Dingle," said Felicity. "Might it be possible to have a word with your wife?"

Chapter Twenty

Edna was easy to spot among the neat rows of wooden tables covered in orderly lines of bright pink potted roses. She was dead-heading and removing damaged leaves from the plants, her gestures sharp and forceful. The greyhound was curled by her feet, the buckle on its thick leather collar glinting in the sunshine. The dog watched Felicity's approach with big inquisitive eyes but didn't lift its head. There was still a whiff of smoke in the air.

"Mrs Dingle?" Felicity was enormously grateful to Alex for the opportunity to speak to Edna alone. He'd stayed with Clive for a tour of the nursery, mirroring the coverage he'd given to Percy the day before, because the Western Daily News couldn't be seen to be inclined in favour of one rose breeder or another.

Edna looked up nervously as Felicity approached. Her cheeks were still flushed and strands of grey-blonde hair had escaped her cap. The handles of a set of secateurs protruded from the voluminous pockets of her corduroy pinafore.

"I don't want to talk to the papers," she said before Felicity came to a stop.

It had indeed been for the best that Alex remained with Clive.

Felicity spoke gently. "I'm not reporting for the paper. I only wish to check with you that you will call the police about the damage done to your greenhouse."

Edna blinked up at Felicity. She looked confused.

Felicity held her gaze. The idea of the damage at the Dingles' nursery going unreported was unsettling. The police needed all the leads they could get, and while Felicity could puzzle her way through a case, she couldn't dust for fingerprints at a crime scene.

"Your husband didn't seem convinced it would be worth the police's time, but I assure you, the Devon County Constabulary will take any report you make seriously. Especially considering what happened at the rose festival."

Edna continued to stare. She gave a vague nod. "I'll talk to Clive." She returned her attention to the rose in the terracotta pot on the table before her, pulling away yellowed leaves with thick-knuckled hands. The plant's blooms shivered with each movement, the petals glowing an ethereal pink in the sunshine.

Given the shock of the damage to the greenhouse, Edna couldn't be pushed too hard. Yet despite a solid alibi of being at Mr Shakerley's presentation — both Mrs Winterpole and Percy having attested to her presence — there were still other things Felicity wished to discuss with her.

"Your roses are beautiful, Mrs Dingle."

Edna glanced up from her work. "Thank you, your ladyship." She pulled the secateurs from her pocket.

"How did you come to run a nursery?"

Edna smiled tightly. "That'll be my Clive, your ladyship. I just went along with things."

"Breeding plants was Mr Dingle's trade before it was yours?"

Edna snipped at a faded bloom. "His father was a groundskeeper. Clive followed in his footsteps. I was a kitchen maid. Knew nothing about flowers or gardens or anything like that."

"You do now, though, don't you?"

"I suppose you could say that." Edna continued to snip, her movements short and pointed. "He had a talent for roses, Clive did. Worked for some of the best around. Got to the point there was nothing he didn't know about them. It made sense for him to set up on his own."

Felicity looked across the nursery. Alex was following Clive between the greenhouses.

"You must be very proud of what you've built here together," she said.

The greyhound's ears twitched.

Edna drew in a shaky breath. "Of course, your ladyship."

Felicity paused, allowing the silence between them to breathe for a moment. Sparrows twittered in a nearby hedge. The Dingles' roses didn't have a heavy scent, but their perfume could still be detected in the air.

Felicity looked towards the ruined greenhouse. "Who would seek to harm you like that?" she asked delicately. "To damage your property and your business?"

Edna froze, secateurs at the neck of a fading bloom. "We've hurt no one. All we've done is work hard. All our lives, we've worked so hard." She brought a knuckle to the corner of her eye. "Please excuse me, your ladyship." She was crying.

The greyhound lifted its head, its elegant muzzle extending in Edna's direction.

"There's no need to apologise." Felicity tugged a handkerchief from her cardigan pocket and offered it to Edna. "Please."

Gingerly, Edna took it.

"I'm the one who should apologise," Felicity continued. "For arriving at your nursery at such an inopportune moment. It saddens me to see what's happened to you and your husband. If there's anything I can do—"

"There isn't," said Edna, cutting Felicity off as she dabbed her eyes. "Thank you, your ladyship."

Felicity paused before speaking again. "It's all been a bit much, hasn't it? The pressure of the show is already so much to handle. There was the drama at the prize giving, and then... Well, we're all aware of the terrible thing that happened next."

Edna stiffened. She dropped Felicity's handkerchief onto the table, picked up her secateurs, and moved onto the next plant. It was highly possible she wished Felicity would leave her in peace but dared not say so.

"I suppose it's got everyone wondering," continued Felicity carefully. "But I should very much like to know who did it and why."

"Clive and I were at Mr Shakerley's presentation," said Edna with a sharp snip of her secateurs. "So we wouldn't know, your ladyship."

Felicity had indeed wished for Edna's corroboration of Clive's alibi, and there it was. Felicity had hardly pushed at all.

"I told the police already," continued Edna, shuffling along to the next plant. "We saw nothing, and we know nothing about it."

Was there a chance Edna was covering for her husband? Just because neither Percy nor Mrs Winterpole remembered seeing him, it didn't mean he wasn't there. Yet there was something about Edna's eagerness to present both her own and her husband's alibis that pricked Felicity's curiosity.

"Did you know Lord Anthony Templeton at all?" asked Felicity.

Thunk.

Edna slammed her hand and her secateurs onto the table.

Felicity felt a pang of guilt. She'd irked Edna, and the woman was already upset. The sabotage of a greenhouse wasn't a trifling matter. Yes, Felicity wished to address Lady Henrietta's suffering, but was the dowager's pain more acute than the Dingles'?

"My apologies," said Felicity. "You've been through quite—"

"If you want to know about *him*—" The word was spoken with distaste. "—you should speak to his sister."

Felicity's stomach twisted a little. Leonora. It all came back to Leonora.

"You're absolutely right, Mrs Dingle. I should very much like to speak to Lady Leonora, only I've not had much luck in obtaining an audience."

Edna fixed Felicity with a steady glare. "I can tell you where to find her, your ladyship."

Chapter Twenty-One

Crickets chirped in the tall grass. Oxeye daisies and red campion nodded in the breeze. The jagged, ivy-clad remains of buildings built from hand-hewn granite reached towards the blue of the sky.

Edna Dingle's directions had been excellent, but the ruined monastery had still been hard to find. Plundered for even the stones in its walls after Henry VIII's command for dissolution, the monastic enclosure had almost disappeared back into the natural surroundings.

For rose breeders, however, this location was firmly on the map.

Felicity and Alex stood side by side in the shadows of the woodland at the edge of the site. Thankfully, there'd been time enough before their lunch appointment in Bickleford for what would hopefully be an extremely worthwhile detour.

Among the tall grass and crumbling walls, a figure dressed in wide trousers, a billowing shirt, and a battered straw hat was bending over in the sunshine. From the plait of dark hair between her shoulder blades and the elegance of her long limbs as she tugged aside the grass, it had to be Lady Leonora Templeton.

Felicity felt a flutter of excitement. She'd been dying to speak to Leonora. Surely she understood Anthony better than anyone. And on the walk from the Alvis to the ruins, there'd been no sign of Havelock or the Jack Russells.

"Go without me," hissed Alex.

Felicity frowned at him. "But your scoop?"

Alex shook his head. "I doubt she's keen to speak to either of us. If we both appear, we might frighten her off altogether. You have a better chance of gaining her trust."

Sending Felicity in alone seemed like a selfless gesture, but Alex was also being pragmatic. If she could win Leonora over, Alex stood to benefit, which motivated Felicity all the more.

"Very well."

Sweeping an errant curl back under her beret, Felicity stepped out from the shade of the trees and began wading through the long grass.

Absorbed in her work, Leonora didn't look up immediately. When she noticed Felicity's approach, she didn't appear surprised. She put a hand on her hip and waited, her secateurs dangling in her fingers. She wore an amused but dry smile.

"You found me then."

Felicity hadn't expected Leonora to be so relaxed about her presence. "You're rather difficult to pin down."

"Well, you are Britain's foremost lady detective, are you not?"

Felicity raised an eyebrow. This was language from the Gentlewoman's Gazette. Language that Felicity had objected to — she didn't know of any other lady detectives, let alone her being foremost amongst them — and that Jasper had insisted was to be expected if Felicity's serialised exploits were to be a success.

But was Leonora making fun of her? Felicity had only spoken to her briefly and rather formally at the flower show. She hadn't been able to get a proper measure of her character.

"I wouldn't put it like that, exactly," clarified Felicity.

Between the overgrown grass and the stone ruins, there were roses blooming in basic tones of white and red, like the colours on a deck of cards. The petal arrangements were also simple, but the blooms were pretty and very sweet smelling.

At Leonora's feet was a bucket of water. In it were plant cuttings.

Leonora followed Felicity's gaze and looked down at her bucket. "The monks were excellent rose growers. And breeders, on occasion. They liked them for their medicinal qualities, mainly. Amazing how hundreds of years later, they're still here. No sign of the monks, though."

"These aren't Templeton roses, are they?" Felicity wasn't entirely comfortable recognising the different rose types, but from what she knew of the Templeton varieties, they were rather more complex and subtle than the monastery's blooms.

Leonora snapped her secateurs closed. "This is a hobby. The rose market, the clients of today, they're looking for something else. Not these thorny old dears." She affectionately tapped a big white bloom, which nodded as though on a spring. "You didn't come all the way out here to speak to me about flowers, though, did you?"

There was to be no dancing around topics, and Felicity was more than happy to come to the point. "I was hoping to speak to you about your brother."

"Of course. Everyone does." Leonora adjusted the brim of her straw hat, tucking strands of her dark hair behind her ears. "I do hate to disappoint, and it goes without saying that I wish nothing I tell you to be quoted in any publication, but there's something you really must understand. My brother left when I was still a child. I had no contact with him after that. I was as surprised as anyone to see him in Bickleford. So did I know my brother? Through the eyes of a child, I knew him as a young man. A lot can change in twenty years, but does a leopard change its spots?"

Leonora's tone wasn't unfriendly, but her blue-green gaze was severe. Did she feel remorse at what had happened to Lord Anthony Templeton? If Leonora was sad, she didn't wear the emotion openly.

Felicity had to stick to the questions she really wanted to ask. Leonora was so difficult to read, it felt as though their time together were balanced on a knife's edge. "Why did your brother leave home?"

"Let me ask you a question, if I may." Leonora slid her secateurs into her trouser pocket. "What is a comfortable home?"

Felicity gave a little frown. She was feeling rather too warm out in the sunshine. "Do you mean in terms of furnishings? Or something else?"

"Allow me to put it another way," said Leonora. "Imagine a grand, luxurious house, providing every comfort and amenity one could desire. I suppose such a situation is easy for you to call to mind."

Felicity didn't react. Where was Leonora going with this?

"Is wealth and physical comfort all one needs to blossom?" Leonora blinked enquiringly at Felicity.

"Well," she began. If Leonora intended to set Felicity off-balance, she was succeeding. "I suppose not."

"There's much one can never understand about a person," continued Leonora, "even your very nearest loved ones. One can never truly walk in another man's shoes." Leonora's expression was stony. She was talking about her brother, wasn't she?

Felicity couldn't risk asking Leonora to stop speaking in riddles. If Felicity mis-stepped, Leonora could vanish back into obscurity, never to be interviewed again. Yet it was awfully hard to judge where to tread next. Was Felicity building a rapport with Leonora, or was the famed rose breeder simply playing games with her?

A breeze rustled the dense leaves of the ivy covering the remains of a nearby wall.

"Might you know why your brother came back to rose breeding?" asked Felicity. "Or could you hazard a guess?"

Leonora folded her arms over her linen shirt. "I didn't know him as well as you or the police perhaps hope I did. But I can tell you that Anthony has my respect. His roses cannot be argued with."

It was the same observation Felicity had heard from practically everyone. Anthony Templeton's roses clearly deserved their prize.

"To put that level of endeavour into something simply out of spite—" Leonora broke off suddenly. Had she caught herself saying too much? "It's a tremendous amount of work to produce roses of such a standard." She bent down for her bucket. Leonora was preparing to leave.

Felicity couldn't let the situation slip from her grasp. "Spite towards who? Why?"

Straightening, Leonora set her bucket into the crook of her elbow, the water sloshing against the sides. "At me. At the world. Who can say? I didn't know my brother. Who did?"

"Someone knew him well enough to want to hurt him."

Leonora's face changed. For a moment, there was pain in her expression. "If I knew who'd done for him, I'd already have informed the police and the case would be closed." She began clearing a path for herself through the high grass, separating the blades with elegant sweeps of her hand.

"Have you been the target of any acts of violence yourself?" The change in topic was sharp, but Felicity had to use what little time she had left with Leonora to the best effect.

Leonora's mouth fell open for a second. "Violence against myself?"

"Has anyone tried to attack you or your property?" The smashed greenhouse at the Dingles nursery was at the forefront of Felicity's mind. It couldn't be a coincidence, could it?

"No," said Leonora firmly. "Why do you ask?" Her eyes flicked away.

Leonora had heard it before Felicity did. The sound of dogs barking.

Where was Alex?

Felicity scanned the tree line, but the shadows and the glare from the sun made it impossible to see into the woods.

Felicity dashed to keep up with Leonora as she forged through the grass.

"Does your gardener, Mr Havelock, take care of security for you?" ventured Felicity.

Something like anger flickered across Leonora's features. Had Felicity gone too far?

The barking grew louder.

Emerging from the long grass, Leonora began striding towards the trees, the water in her bucket sloshing.

"Was your brother jealous of you?" Felicity struggled to keep up with Leonora's stride. "Is that why he wanted to hurt you? Is that why he came back?" Her questions were becoming sloppy, but she had to keep trying.

Leonora stopped and twisted towards Felicity. "Jealous? Of me?" She sounded sad. "Please." She stalked off.

Raised voices added to the barking. Men shouting.

Alex.

Felicity hesitated, then hurried towards the noise. Ought she have gone when she first heard the dogs barking? Had she ruined her chances with Leonora by pushing too hard? She'd done her best to think on her feet and ask the important questions, but had she done enough?

Confronting Leonora about the possibility of her gardener's guilt had been out of the question, but there'd been something in her reaction when Felicity had mentioned Havelock, hadn't there?

Felicity stopped.

The burly gardener in question had stepped out from the tree line and into the sunshine. He had the two Jack Russells on leads. Their barking seemed more out of general excitement than aggression, but when Havelock laid eyes on Felicity, his brow lowered. He looked like an angry bear, preparing itself to come crashing towards her.

But when Alex appeared from the trees, completely unharmed, Felicity's heart lifted. He was chasing after Havelock, his notepad in his hand. His mouth was moving, but his words couldn't be overheard above the barking.

Havelock stormed towards Leonora, and she bent to pet the dogs. They quietened and took to growling and gambolling with one another, tongues lolling.

Felicity and Alex were reunited at the edge of the long grass. The chase was over. Their chances gone. They looked at one another, their cheeks red. Alex's eyes shone with expectation.

"How did it go?" he asked, as Felicity watched Leonora and Havelock leave the monastery clearing, the gardener firing angry glares over his shoulder at the interlopers.

Felicity felt heavy with regret. "I'm afraid I may not have handled matters as well as I could have."

At the edge of the trees, Leonora stopped and turned. "If you could find out who did it, Lady Felicity, I'd be grateful," she said, her voice raised to carry across the distance. "I have more faith in you than in the police somehow."

Chapter Twenty-Two

Despite the detour to speak to Leonora, Felicity and Alex were still just about on time for their lunch appointment. Tearing along twisting, hedge-lined lanes while maintaining proper control of the Alvis didn't allow Felicity to indulge in careful reflection on the winding discussion she'd had with Leonora.

One thing came back to Felicity, however.

Leonora's face had grown pale during Anthony's Best in Show speech. She'd put her hand on Havelock's arm to prevent him from reacting.

Her brother had hurt her, but Leonora didn't want him punished. And with Havelock seemingly obsessed with protecting Leonora, it made it harder to imagine him as Anthony's murderer, even if — despite Alex's best efforts — the gardener remained determined not to provide comment to anyone.

But if Havelock didn't do it, then who did?

Passing the yellow marks in the grass from the flower show marquees at the edge of Bickleford village, Felicity brought the Alvis to a gentle stop alongside a neatly pointed stone wall topped with frothy white lobelia.

Alex straightened and positioned his hat on his head as he

alighted from the motor. “This had better be good. There’s more than just your grandmother counting on you to get the job done now.”

Tightening the belt of her cardigan, Felicity gave Alex a glare. *I have more faith in you than in the police somehow.* Those had been Leonora’s parting words, but on the other side of the wall was a bustling tea garden attached to a popular tea room, with who knew how many people capable of overhearing Felicity and Alex’s discussion.

“I’m not investigating, remember?” she hissed, as they approached the garden’s wrought-iron gate. “Not officially.”

The white-clothed tables were nearly all full. The towers of scones and sandwiches and polite chatter in the sunshine felt like a different world compared to the drama and scandal that had rocked the rose festival just days before. Lord Anthony Templeton’s assistants, however, were nowhere to be seen.

Taking a table under a parasol, Felicity and Alex ordered a round of sandwiches and a pot of tea each. The setting was pleasant and the weather comfortably warm, yet Felicity felt an itch of discomfort. She had a strong desire to get on with things. Did it indeed make a difference that Leonora was now counting on her, too?

“Any chance we got the time wrong?” said Felicity between bites of salmon triangles.

Alex shook his head. “I got the message from Beatrice herself.” Miss Beatrice Pearce was Jasper’s extremely reliable secretary. “She read it to me twice, and Beatrice doesn’t make mistakes.” Alex smiled as he said this. It was a line Jasper used when less reliable journalists than Alex came to him with excuses about missed deadlines.

“A ruse, then?” suggested Felicity, eyeing the road beyond the garden gate for any sign of the assistants. “A fake appointment?”

Alex frowned, the scar on his forehead creasing deeply. “How would that benefit them? If they miss this, I’ll start telephoning them twice a day instead of just the once.”

“It’ll be more than telephone calls,” said Felicity, her hopes for the encounter riding high after gleaning not a great amount of information about Anthony from Leonora. "We'll show up on their doorstep."

"And I thought I was the aggressive one," smiled Alex.

Felicity wanted to reach across the table and take his hand, as much to steady herself as out of affection for him. They were certain about their feelings for one another, but a brief gaze full of longing was the most they could get away with in public. At least until they had announced that they were officially courting.

"Monsieur Cooper?"

A pale-skinned woman in a well-tailored green jacket had approached from behind. She was around fifty, with painted eyebrows and dark, deep-set eyes. A small toque topped her complicated chignon.

It was Anthony Templeton's female assistant.

"M-Madame Ernault?" Alex rose to his feet. It was unusual to hear him flustered, but then Felicity and Alex had clearly been rather too busy gazing at one another to notice the woman's approach.

"Blanche Ernault." The woman introduced herself to Felicity with a firm handshake and a thick French accent. "I believe we met at the rose festival."

"Indeed, we did." Felicity had not forgotten the confrontation between her grandmother and Anthony Templeton and Blanche's efforts to separate them.

"And this is Monsieur Jacques Gobillot," added Blanche.

The young man with straw-blond hair stepped forward to shake hands with Felicity and Alex. Felicity recognised Jacques from the flower show. He had on typical gardener's attire, namely loose corduroy trousers and a roomy and worn linen shirt topped with a sun-bleached brown jacket and a checked flat cap. His face was tanned and deeply lined, despite him being not much older than perhaps thirty. The skin of his hands felt as rough as a tree trunk.

"*Enchanté*," Jacques mumbled as he and Felicity shook hands, his eyes darting in an uncertain manner.

"Lady Felicity is assisting me with my reporting." Alex was careful to specify this as part of the introductions.

Felicity smiled politely. Playing second fiddle to Alex in this particular encounter would be a challenge. Blanche and Jacques surely knew Anthony better than anyone else who'd been at the flower show. Percy had said Jacques was at Mr Shakerley's presentation, but so far Blanche had no known alibi.

After sitting down in the parasol's shade, the assistants' attention went straight to the menu, which they discussed quietly in French, Blanche regarding the options with something between disappointment and disdain. The bustle of the flower show had perhaps created the impression of Bickleford as a more cosmopolitan location for a luncheon than it actually was.

A waitress in a black-and-white uniform took the order from a defeated-sounding Blanche for two rounds of ham sandwiches, two pots of coffee, and a single jug of cream.

As the waitress returned to the kitchen, Alex readied his notebook. "Let's get started." He had, after all, offered the pair lunch in return for an interview.

"You must understand, Monsieur Cooper," began Blanche before Alex could ask his first question. "We are very busy with the affairs left behind by Monsieur Fox." The assistants apparently knew Anthony by the pseudonym under which he entered the rose competition. "We have barely any time. But we agreed to meet with you because we do not want the wrong impression to become the story."

Felicity kept her expression neutral. If there was any 'wrong impression' left behind by the deceased rose breeder, Anthony had created it through his behaviour at the flower show.

"By 'Monsieur Fox', you are referring to Lord Anthony Templeton?" clarified Alex.

Blanche's forehead wrinkled for a moment. "Yes, yes. That is right. I have always known him as Fox. Monsieur Tony Fox. I did not know of any Anthony Templeton. Not until the police spoke to us."

Going by another name had no doubt helped Anthony to disappear and remain hidden over the years. Why had he so desperately not wanted to be found?

"When was it you first met Monsieur Fox?" asked Alex.

Blanche's face softened with fondness. "Oh, many years ago. Too many to count. Since long before the war. He was new to France and needed guidance."

"Where did you meet him?"

"We had the same employer. I was a housekeeper. He was a tutor of English."

Tutor wasn't the lowliest of positions in a household, but if Blanche's account was true, Anthony had given up a great deal to find his freedom on the continent.

"Where was this?"

"In Paris. *Seizième arrondissement.* We changed employer together a few times. Then Monsieur Fox found his way on his own. I went with him. I have worked for him ever since."

"What kind of work did he do after leaving his post as a tutor?" asked Alex.

A little smile passed over Blanche's painted lips. "All sorts, Monsieur Cooper. He did all sorts of things. And whatever Monsieur Fox needed doing, I would do it."

It was a vague answer but also slightly salacious in tone. It made Felicity shiver.

"Could you provide more details about what kept your employer busy all these years?" Alex had looked into Anthony's period in France, but the information was patchy.

Blanche looked at her lap for a moment. "He was employed by some of the most important households in the country."

"Doing what?"

"Advising."

"On roses?"

Jacques glanced at Blanche.

The Frenchwoman gave a little shrug. "Among other things." Either Blanche was being deliberately evasive, or she perhaps didn't know as much about her employer as she claimed.

"And you, Mr Gobillot." Alex's tone was calm and matter-of-fact. It wasn't yet clear how trustworthy he perceived his interviewees to be. "How did you come to know Monsieur Fox?"

"Monsieur Gobillot joined us only a couple of years ago." Blanche continued to talk as Jacques lit a cigarette, his gaze wandering over the other patrons of the tea garden.

"He is dedicated to the matters of the plants—" Blanche nodded towards her colleague. "—and I look after everything else."

"*Plus maintenant.*"

Blanche span towards Jacques, her eyes widening.

Not anymore. Felicity's French was far from fluent, but she'd understood what the gardener had said.

Jacques returned Blanche's stare, wincing against the smoke of his cigarette. "The master is dead, so we have no work. No pay."

Felicity lifted an eyebrow. That perhaps explained how the offer of lunch had enticed the assistants to the interview.

Blanche's nostrils flared. "I have work to do, even if Monsieur Gobillot does not." She returned her gaze to Alex. "There is much to be arranged, even if Monsieur Fox is no longer here."

"Like what?" asked Alex.

Blanche missed a couple of beats before responding. "There are many... Many plants at Champs Verts." Her posture stiffened as she spoke. "They cannot simply be thrown away."

Jacques turned to Blanche and said something in French. She responded sternly. Felicity couldn't follow everything, but she was sure she heard money mentioned a few times.

"There's been some discussion of what ought to happen to the Best in Show prize," said Alex.

While the topic of money was a thread upon which Felicity wished to tug, Alex was right to steer the conversation away from a potential falling out between the two assistants. The interview couldn't end before the coffee and sandwiches arrived.

"Based on what was said in the acceptance speech and what happened subsequently, it's been suggested the prize ought to be withdrawn," added Alex.

Blanche's mouth fell open. "It's not possible."

Jacques continued to smoke. He looked amused.

"The rose association hasn't yet decided how to proceed,"

continued Alex. "What would your reaction be if they were to take back the prize for Best in Show presented to your employer?"

"I would not accept it," said Blanche. "I would not accept it at all. He won. Where in the rules does it say that death makes it meaningless? No. No. Not acceptable."

"Lord Anthony Templeton's demise aside, what he said in his speech was unprecedented." Alex flicked through his notebook. "He called the Bickleford Rose Festival a 'charade'. He promised the crowd 'a new way of doing things'."

Blanche blinked as though hearing the words for the first time, yet she'd been in the audience at the prize-giving.

The Frenchwoman lowered her painted eyebrows. "You know, Monsieur Cooper, in England, there is a problem with emotion. Here, a man cannot have or show feelings. He must always have a straight back and a serious face. Maybe one day you are angry or happy or sad. No one would know. You always appear the same."

Alex smiled a little. The observation was valid.

"A man like Monsieur Fox," continued Blanche, "who has spent more time in my country than in yours, is unafraid of emotion. If he is angry, he will show it. If he is happy, he will display it. Do you then judge a man for all time based on the emotion of one day?"

As Alex scribbled in his notebook, Felicity spoke up. "What about the person who swung the silver plate at your employer? If that person was angry or upset at the time, should that person be allowed to walk free and not be judged?"

Blanche sat stiffly. The look she gave Felicity burned with something fierce.

Tapping the ash off his cigarette, Jacques continued to gaze across the garden.

Alex quirked an eyebrow, expressing both amusement and mild reproach at Felicity's comment.

The arrival of the ham sandwiches and coffee was a welcome distraction. The atmosphere calmed as Blanche and Jacques poured their coffees and sampled the sandwiches.

Alex looked down at his notebook. "From what you've told me, Mr Fox wasn't always involved with roses."

"No," said Blanche. "I mean, not always as part of his work. But roses were always very dear to him."

Felicity came in with a question. "When did he get back into breeding? Was it after he stopped working as a tutor?"

Blanche looked at Jacques, but the gardener's attention was on his sandwiches.

The Frenchwoman drew her eyebrows together. "Oh, not so very long ago. A few years, perhaps."

"What prompted him to enter this year's Bickleford Rose Festival?" asked Alex.

Blanche sighed. "Family. He always had his family in his thoughts. Always."

His sandwich plate quickly emptied, Jacques lit another cigarette and looked across the tea garden. He seemed to have no interest in participating in the interview or listening to Blanche.

"In what sense?" pressed Alex. "Was he seeking revenge on his family for some reason?"

"Revenge?" Blanche's eyes widened. She looked stunned. "What makes you say that? Monsieur Fox adored his family. He returned to roses out of love for them. When he was looking at his roses, he would say, 'If only my father could see this.'"

Felicity suppressed a frown. Didn't Blanche's assertions go against what Leonora had shared in her riddle-like way about Anthony's early years at Templeton Manor? The Frenchwoman's claims certainly didn't match the spirit of his acceptance speech. Anthony had targeted his family alongside the association, hadn't he?

Alex tapped his pencil on his notebook. "I suppose there could be different sentiments behind such words."

Blanche looked momentarily confused.

Jacques continued to pay no attention to the conversation. It was unfortunate that they couldn't speak to the two assistants separately. They might receive another account from Jacques.

"Did you both attend Mr Shakerley's presentation at the flower show?" ventured Felicity. With Blanche something of an unreliable witness for Anthony's motives and background, a change of topic was worth a shot.

Blanche straightened. "I did not."

Jacques flicked his attention back to the table under the parasol. "I did." So he had been listening. "A very interesting event for anyone who cares even a little about roses."

Affront flickered over Blanche's features, but she said nothing.

"May I ask who you saw at the talk?" enquired Felicity.

Jacques exhaled a plume of smoke. "Monsieur Shakerley, of course."

"Who else?" pursued Alex.

Jacques shrugged. "I don't know the names."

"You know the other rose breeders, don't you?" suggested Felicity.

The gardener dragged on his cigarette. "The young fellow. He was there. The one with the old lady helping him." Felicity took this to mean Percy, although her grandmother wouldn't appreciate being known as 'the old lady helping him'. "The couple, too. They grow more than just roses."

"Clive and Edna Dingle?" Felicity perhaps spoke too hastily.

"The man and the woman, yes."

Felicity fired an excited glance towards Alex. It was significant that Clive Dingle's own wife wasn't his only alibi. The pool of suspects was growing smaller.

"And where were you, Madame Ernault, when your employer met his end?" asked Alex.

Blanche huffed out a sigh. "Monsieur Cooper, you telephone multiple times wanting to meet with me, and then you treat me like a criminal? I worked with Monsieur Fox for so many years. I am more dedicated to him than anyone."

Felicity stepped in. "Forgive us, Madame Ernault. The question was perhaps expressed clumsily. No one considers you to be a criminal."

Alex glared a little at Felicity. There had indeed been nothing clumsy about his questioning. It had simply been too direct.

"What we should like to know is," continued Felicity in a soothing tone, "did you witness anything of note? Anything that might help answer the mystery of what happened to Monsieur Fox?"

Blanche tipped her chin upwards. "I was talking to clients. Liaising with customers. I am still doing this. I take the business of the nursery seriously." She fired a look at Jacques. "As much as I can. Monsieur Fox wished for a legacy for his roses. For himself and his roses. I am doing my best to help secure that by ensuring the Champs Verts customers get the plants they ordered at the flower show. If the roses he bred can live on, then Monsieur Fox might live on with them."

Felicity nodded with understanding. Anthony Templeton's worthiness aside, it was an honourable goal. Yet the assistants' discussions about money and their enthusiasm for a paid lunch perhaps hinted at other reasons for Blanche's keenness to keep the business going.

"It's why I'm talking to you now," Blanche continued. "Talking to the newspaper. To raise the profile further, so that people know the roses are still for sale. So that Monsieur Fox can continue to be remembered."

Felicity nodded her understanding as a theory flashed through her mind. Might Blanche have done away with Anthony with the plan to collect her employer's earnings? If so, to what extent was Jacques involved?

"After you've arranged for Mr Fox's stock of roses to be sold, what will you do next?" Felicity looked at both Blanche and Jacques.

"I cannot say," replied Blanche. "There is so much to arrange. Who knows how long it will take? I'm here to see things through to the end."

Jacques shrugged. "Monsieur Fox was my employer. I need money to live." He looked at Blanche. "Now I have no income."

Blanche stared back at Jacques. The frustration between them was more than an undercurrent. Had Anthony's death sparked disagreement between the two assistants, or had they never seen eye to eye? Perhaps there wasn't as much money to be made off the business as they'd expected.

"I should like to visit the nursery, if I may," said Alex, sensing the situation between the assistants needed to be diffused once again. "Do a write up on Champs Verts for the paper. That should help you with sales."

Jacques nodded vaguely. "Of course. Any time."

Blanche lifted her chin. "Not yet, Monsieur Cooper. I should like to see what you write about Monsieur Fox first, based on our discussion here today. Much has been written about him these past days, not all of it pleasant."

Jacques looked annoyed, his brow drawn low. He spoke to Blanche in French. She responded, also in French. Their tones grew heated. Customers at the other tables in the tea garden stared.

"Now, now," said Alex, but the assistants paid him no heed.

Felicity had to concentrate hard to understand what was being said, so rapid was the exchange.

Bang!

Jacques slammed a fist on the tea table.

Blanche recoiled with shock.

"*Je me moque de cela,*" said Jacques angrily. "*Je veux mon argent.*"

I don't care, Jacques had said. *I want my money*.

Chapter Twenty-Three

Despite their bickering, Blanche and Jacques had little choice but to leave the tea garden together. They had an appointment at the British Rose Association to discuss the future of the rose varieties developed by Anthony Templeton. Blanche nodded but said nothing when Alex requested he be kept abreast of any developments regarding Anthony's roses.

"Funny pair," said Alex, settling the bill with the waitress as the French assistants continued arguing on their way out of the tea garden.

Felicity watched through the gate as they set off in a small goods van driven by Jacques, both their faces displaying severe discontent.

"Not murderers, though," she said in hushed tones after the waitress had left the table.

Alex narrowed his eyes. "Can you say that for certain?"

"Not entirely. You heard them arguing about money, though, didn't you?"

Alex's French was better than Felicity's. "Anthony's demise seems to have put them at a disadvantage."

Felicity nodded. "And if they had wanted to do away with him, why do the deed at the flower show?" Felicity gazed out across the families and couples enjoying cake and tea in the sunshine. "They could have done away with him quietly at his nursery in a far less suspicious manner than a bludgeoning. Perhaps even made it look natural."

Alex flicked through his notebook. "This is a passionate crime, though, isn't it? Maybe Blanche had enough of Anthony for whatever reason, even if she's regretting it now."

There were indeed no solid conclusions to be drawn. Not yet.

"Where to next?" asked Felicity.

Alex gestured with his pencil. "The telephone booth on the green. I've got to call my stories in for the evening edition. Maybe Beatrice will have another appointment for me. I mean us."

Felicity nodded eagerly. She was thankful for the access to witnesses Alex provided. "Anything I can do to help?"

Alex blinked in the sunshine, which was creeping under the parasol. "There's something I've been considering."

"Tell me."

"Elliot Etty. The other celebrity judge. I've been hounding his agent for a quote, but apparently, he's on a steamer to America."

"No." A flush of warmth raced through Felicity's chest. "He can't be."

Alex winced a little. "He was already booked in for a tour over there. The police gave him a special dispensation to leave the country."

Felicity said nothing. She pressed her lips together. She was determined to maintain her composure.

"I didn't realise the news would upset you," continued Alex. "I'd have informed you sooner otherwise."

"The police told everyone to stay put until after the investigation," blurted Felicity, "but because he's a famous singer he's allowed to—" She stopped mid-sentence, aware her voice was growing in volume.

Given everything Lady Henrietta was going through, the exception made for Mr Etty caused Felicity to seethe. Personally, however, she bore the music-hall singer no ill will, and getting angry solved nothing.

Felicity cleared her throat and smoothed the skirt of her dress. "What have you been considering?" she asked Alex in a gentler tone.

He rubbed his jaw. "I was thinking about sending him a telegram to—"

"Absolutely. We should absolutely do that." Felicity was on her feet. "I'll go to the post office right away. Had you a question or two for him in mind?"

Alex also stood up. "I hadn't yet planned what I might—"

"Don't worry, I'll think of something to ask him." Felicity was already halfway towards the garden gate. There was no way an innocent like her grandmother should be dogged by uncertainty while others roamed free and continued their business as normal.

Felicity glanced over her shoulder. "Where shall I meet you?"

Alex looked equal parts flummoxed and amused by Felicity's sudden enthusiasm as he followed her through the gate. "The medieval rose garden?"

Bickleford's medieval rose garden was the reason the unassuming Devonshire village was home to Britain's most important annual flower show.

A young princess established a rose garden at Bickleford in the Fourteenth Century, where she could seek privacy and solace from the political machinations that went with her marriage to one of the king's most trusted advisors. Besides medicinal plant collections at monasteries, the princess' garden was one of the earliest in England to be dedicated to roses, and it thrived for many generations.

During the English Civil War, the grand house attached to the garden was destroyed by the Parliamentarians. The rose garden lay in ruins for over a century until what remained of its roses was rediscovered by Lady Philomena Templeton in the Eighteenth Century. Not only did Lady Philomena revive the garden, she established the British Rose Association and forever linked the Templeton name to English rose breeding.

The British Rose Association continued to care for Lady Philomena's garden, which was hidden away down a path between a pair of unassuming cottages, all trace of the grand house erased from the land. Its layout was the same as it had been in the Fourteenth Century, a criss-cross of paths with seating at the edges. The collection of traditional rose varieties, with their open petals and wild habits, had been augmented by the addition of more recently developed varieties suitable for cutting. Dense herbaceous planting gave the paths and benches a sense of seclusion.

Lady Philomena would no doubt have been proud to see the continuation of her efforts in the medieval garden. But what might she have made of the drama surrounding Lord Anthony Templeton's reappearance and sudden demise?

Selecting a bench under a pergola dripping with tiny white roses and enveloped in delicious scent, Felicity pondered the matter with calm inquisitiveness. The sending of the telegram to Mr Etty had relaxed her. It didn't matter if he responded to the barrage of questions Felicity had relayed to the telegraphist in Bickleford's post office. The music-hall singer shouldn't be allowed to escape the hullaballoo of the investigation while others were unwittingly caught up in it.

As she was alone in the garden, Felicity might have closed her eyes in the sunshine, but she felt restless. Was she getting closer to resolving the mystery surrounding Anthony's downfall? It was hard to tell.

The sabotage at the Dingles' nursery felt significant. Leonora's empathy for her brother had been somewhat of a surprise, and all was clearly not well between the French assistants. While some of Felicity and Alex's interviewees had solid alibis for the time of Anthony's death, others did not.

But who had a motive?

Had Blanche lashed out at her employer but was now failing to make the money she'd hoped for? Had Clive Dingle, with his initially shaky alibi and decades of hard work unrewarded, swung the silver plate? Could professional show judge Mr Merton have resorted to violence to defend the rose association's honour and with it his own reputation?

Alex appeared at the garden's entrance. Felicity stood and waved to him.

"Who, in your view, is our top suspect?" Felicity asked before he'd sat down.

Taking off his homburg, Alex smoothed a hand over his dark blond hair. "And there was me imagining we might have a bit of quiet time alone together, our focus on nothing but each other."

Felicity drew in her chin. Her cheeks became warm. "Really?"

Alex smiled. "Of course not." He leaned back on the bench and surveyed the nodding blooms. "I know what you're like when you're onto something." He looked back at her. "And I wouldn't want to miss it for the world."

Felicity smiled. Alex had managed to both chastise and flatter her. The way he made her feel was rarely straightforward, but it was indeed not the moment for sweet nothings.

"What about Blanche?" she suggested. "You took a disliking to her, didn't you?"

"Not a disliking, exactly. When speaking in French, she had a very condescending tone. Quite disrespectful towards Jacques."

"We don't know that he didn't deserve to be spoken to like that. The fellow seemed obsessed with money."

Alex looked down at the hat in his lap. "When one doesn't have much of it, it can become rather an obsession."

Felicity nodded. Like anyone, she had blind spots. She was grateful for Alex's gentle correction. "Jacques can't be a suspect, anyway. Not directly. He was at Mr Shakerley's presentation."

"Who are we left with?"

"Mr Merton. Blanche Ernault. Clive Dingle's alibi seemed unreliable at first."

Alex pulled out his notebook and flicked past a few pages. "You don't believe Edna and Jacques saying they saw him at the presentation?"

"It's not as convincing as everyone having seen Edna and Percy, is it?"

Alex tapped his pencil on his notebook. "Anyone else?"

Felicity sighed. "I would like to still say Havelock, but I have the firm impression the man would do anything to keep Leonora happy, and her brother's passing hasn't brought her contentment of any kind."

"So Merton or Blanche. Perhaps Clive Dingle," repeated Alex. "Not Elliot Etty?"

Felicity shook her head. "Not for our purposes. I'm sure the police are looking into all the visitors and staff who were at the event, but the speech had to be the catalyst. The timing. The upset it caused. The swift violence of the reaction."

"So not Blanche, then." Alex was quick. The assistants were indeed not targeted in the speech.

Felicity propped her chin on her fist and looked out across the dense planting. "And as we already discussed, Blanche would have had ample opportunity alone with Anthony, away from Bickleford. Why take the risk at the show?"

A gentle breeze brought with it a wave of perfume from the roses covering the pergola. A wood pigeon glided between the trees, perched on a branch, and began cooing.

"Clive Dingle, then," said Felicity. "Made jealous by Anthony's sudden success."

Alex's forehead creased. "I can understand why you might doubt Edna's alibi for her husband, but why would Jacques lie about seeing Clive at the presentation?"

Felicity eyed her companion. She sometimes enjoyed it when Alex challenged her. At other times, it was incredibly hard work.

"Fine," she said. "That leaves Mr Merton. What's his motive? Judging flower shows is his career, but he said himself he believed Anthony's speech to be some kind of joke initially. He wasn't as shocked as some."

"He took what Anthony was saying seriously eventually, though, didn't he?" From the press area, Alex had an excellent view of the stage. Like Felicity, he'd have seen Mr Merton's expression change.

Felicity tapped a finger to her chin. "And when he realised Anthony's jibes at the flower show and the association weren't a form of fun..." She trailed off. Her own grandmother had been wounded by the disrespect displayed in Anthony's speech — enough to confront the man — but Lady Henrietta's reputation didn't depend on the rose association and its competition. Not like the show judge's did.

"I wouldn't object to another interview with Mr Merton," continued Felicity, "but it's not for me to decide."

Alex nodded thoughtfully. "We could invite him into town for tea. I'd rather not visit Merton at home if we're considering him a murder suspect."

"Naturally," agreed Felicity. One always had to be careful.

"Anything else?"

"What about your reporting?"

"I'm keen for a quote from Mr Shakerley, but he's playing rather hard to get. Got to the stage where he won't even answer the telephone, but I'll get him somehow." Alex smiled. "For the rest, I can fit it in between whatever you want to look into next."

It was wonderful to count on Alex, but he was also accustomed to snatching a scoop by sticking close to Felicity. It was a well-balanced arrangement.

"I wouldn't mind going back to the Dingles," said Felicity. "I should like to ensure they tell the police about the damage to their property. My grandmother certainly wasn't involved and will have the entire staff at Bradley Court as witnesses to prove it. So if the police can link the sabotage to what happened to Anthony Templeton—"

"How might the destruction at the Dingles' nursery be linked to Anthony's death?" As an interrogator, Alex was even-handed. His most difficult questions weren't reserved only for his newspaper sources.

Felicity sat up straighter, adjusting her beret. "I need to think about it." And fast, if any difference was to be made to Lady

Henrietta. Who knew how many more rejections she might have received that day already?

Alex took Felicity's hand, his familiar warmth engulfing her palm.

Felicity's worries melted into the background.

"I'm sorry," he said, his dark blue eyes earnest. "I don't want to pressure you. It's only your second day investigating. You can't expect to have all the answers, but you're making progress."

Felicity squeezed his hand. "Thanks to you."

Alex shook his head. "I'm just writing things up. You're actually figuring it out."

"I'd prefer it if you didn't denigrate the honourable profession of journalism with such over-simplification," she said, although her words rang a little hollow considering her still-unfinished pieces for the Gentlewoman's Gazette. "We're a team, aren't we?"

"Of that, there's no doubt. Back to the Dingles?"

Still holding hands, they stood up from the bench. With the flowers, the sunshine, the warmth from Alex's hand, and his encouraging words, Felicity felt far away from her investigation, even though she was right in the middle of it. It was almost as if she were floating.

Alex gazed at her as they walked along the narrow gravel path, bees and butterflies dancing from one flower border to another. Felicity looked up at him, her stomach lifting like a balloon. They came to a natural stop in the shade of a cherry tree with weeping branches through which a vigorous rose climbed, its yellow flowers buzzing with hover flies.

"Do you worry about what it might be like if we didn't work together?" The words slipped out of Felicity's mouth almost without thinking. She barely second guessed anything she said to Alex now. She'd grown to enjoy great freedom of expression with him, despite not getting on at first.

Alex gave a little frown. He was surprised but not fazed by the question. "Would you like us to stop working together?"

"No, but when a woman marries, she has to give up—" Felicity halted mid-sentence. A flush rose in her cheeks. While she didn't feel the need to censor herself in front of Alex, this was surely too much. They'd known one another for just a year. They weren't officially courting, whatever that meant in this day and age. It was far, far too soon to be talking about marriage.

Wasn't it?

Alex gazed down at her, both her hands in his.

Felicity's pulse quickened.

She swallowed. "I didn't mean to say that. Not exactly."

Alex's smile was kind but also amused. "I don't believe you were asking for my reassurance, and I don't dare assume that what I'm about to say is comforting to you, but I would like to clarify that I don't believe that a woman should give up any activity she enjoys or benefits from simply because she is married."

Felicity's legs turned to jelly for a moment. "It is enormously reassuring to hear you say that. Even though I knew deep down that I could expect nothing less."

"And," continued Alex, his grip on Felicity's hands still gentle but firm, "knowing you now as I do, I can't imagine any change in status, whether that's unmarried to married, living at home with your family to living elsewhere, having no children to becoming a mother—"

Felicity's knees were feeling positively weak.

"—no such change could curb your drive — against which I honestly believe you are powerless — to investigate matters of wrongdoing and restore normality and justice to the world."

Felicity's voice escaped her like a sigh. "Oh."

She'd done her best to calm her ideas about where things might go with Alex. They were both committed to their careers, and neither wished to jeopardise the relatively smooth working relationship they now enjoyed.

Alex rubbed a thumb over the back of her hand. "Or am I mistaken?"

Felicity's heart thumped. "I..."

Despite being serious about taking things slowly, Felicity had often imagined what it might be like to kiss Alex. Or to have him kiss her. How would it work exactly?

Alex continued to look down at her with his calm, blue gaze. He was never nervous, yet Felicity detected in him something like apprehension.

Was he waiting for a sign? Should she let him know to go ahead?

Then she saw it.

Over Alex's shoulder, beyond the tree. Shining in the sunlight.

The polished leather of a gentleman's shoe.

Felicity dropped Alex's hands and stepped back. She drew a hand to her mouth.

"What is it?" Alex looked alarmed. "What did I say? Whatever it was, I take it back, unreservedly."

"Not you," said Felicity. Her throat felt tight. The lightness in her stomach had been replaced by a lead weight, but still she surged forward, towards the shoe, which was still attached to the foot of a man who was lying on his back half hidden behind a large rose shrub with red blooms in a patch of white geraniums.

Felicity gasped.

Alex was right behind her. "What the deuce..."

It was Mr Merton. The flower show judge lay unresponsive on his back among the geraniums.

Chapter Twenty-Four

"There's simply not a chance in the world Lady Henrietta has anything to do with any of this."

The interior of Bickleford's tea room had been taken over by the Devon County Constabulary. Felicity was seated at a round table with a lace table cloth. In the chair opposite her was a very stern-looking Chief Inspector Luscombe.

The tea room's proprietor had done a wonderful job of accommodating the sudden influx of policemen and witnesses, but the plate of once-warm scones at the centre of the table had now thoroughly cooled.

"I'm quite certain my grandmother has been at home at Bradley Court this whole time." Coming upon Mr Merton in the medieval rose garden had been a shock, but Felicity had quickly come to regard it as a rather grim opportunity. "You can ask any member of our household staff for an alibi."

The inspector eyed Felicity carefully but said nothing.

Felicity and Alex had given their statements about what they'd seen in the rose garden. Alex had then interviewed Chief Inspector Luscombe as part of the scoop. Although not as dramatic as initially thought, the discovery of Mr Merton among the geraniums was still enormous news.

The flower show judge had been lying unconscious. He'd received a blow to the back of his head, the cause of which had yet to be identified. Mr Merton had been sped to the Royal Devon and Exeter to receive whatever treatment he needed as well as a full examination for the police's purposes. An officer had been posted at the hospital to take note of anything Mr Merton might say when he regained consciousness.

Having provided their statements, Alex headed into the village to interview policemen and Bickleford locals to flesh out a story for the next edition after a dramatic stop-press announcing more to follow. Felicity, meanwhile, had a different goal.

Chief Inspector Luscombe had agreed to a private audience with her, as long as Felicity kept it brief. Although if the chief inspector continued to refuse to say anything at all, the meeting threatened to drag on.

"Can't you declare that Lady Henrietta is now certainly not a person of interest?" pressed Felicity.

In normal circumstances, it might be assumed that Mr Merton had an unfortunate fall and knocked himself unconscious. In light of Anthony Templeton's passing and the sabotage at the Dingles nursery, however, the injury to the flower show judge's head had to be considered a crime. It would have been wholly against the odds if it turned out not to be.

"Lady Felicity, while I have witnessed your abilities as an investigator in the past and found your skills in that area to be quite adequate—"

Felicity quirked an eyebrow. This was high praise from the policeman.

"—we cannot, at this stage, know for certain that the same perpetrator was present at both scenes. And unlike amateur investigators, at the constabulary, we don't deal in half-truths and gut feelings."

"Are you saying Mr Merton's injury was accidental?" needled Felicity.

The chief inspector frowned. "I'm saying we can't know anything for sure. Not yet."

"But criminal activity is surely the assumption you're working under," continued Felicity. "Why send one of your men to the hospital otherwise?"

The policeman's jaw tightened. "We do our utmost not to work under assumptions," clarified Chief Inspector Luscombe. "You, of all people, must understand that, your ladyship."

Felicity bit her lip. "Did you receive a report of vandalism today? Perhaps even sabotage?"

The policeman blinked. "Sabotage?"

The Dingles hadn't reported it. At least, not yet.

It wasn't Felicity's incident to hand over to the police, but it was only right that the chief inspector be informed. Especially now that it was perhaps more by luck than intention that Mr Merton's life hadn't ended in Bickleford's medieval garden.

"I was at the Dingles' nursery this morning," began Felicity.

"I thought you said you weren't investigating, your ladyship."

The chief inspector squeezed this comment in rather pointedly, but Felicity wouldn't be distracted by the question of her role. There was far too much on the line now that the killer had attempted to strike again.

"One of the Dingles' greenhouses and its contents had been smashed," continued Felicity. "Rather badly."

Chief Inspector Luscombe raised his brow. He perhaps wouldn't say it to Felicity, but this was clearly a development that would have bearing on the police's investigation.

"Mr Cooper saw it, too," said Felicity, "in case you require more than just my word. We can share with you the couple's account of how they discovered the damage. Mr Cooper made notes."

The policeman remained quiet. Chief Inspector Luscombe wasn't a pompous or egotistical man, but it was never pleasant to be one step behind. He couldn't be angry at Felicity, however. The onus to report was not on her. If anyone could be blamed for keeping the information from the police, it would have been the Dingles.

"So, given everything that's happened, the chances of Mr Merton having had an accident seem slim, don't you think?" continued Felicity. "And I'm certain my grandmother has solid alibis for both the sabotage at the Dingles' nursery and whatever happened in the medieval rose garden." Felicity stopped short of saying that a woman of Lady Henrietta's seniority and stature could hardly be considered capable of such actions. If word ever got back to the dowager about such assertions, then Felicity would be in trouble.

Chief Inspector Luscombe stared steadily at Felicity. "We don't make announcements about who the wrong doer isn't, your ladyship. We find the culprit and announce the arrest. That's how it works. You know that."

Felicity considered an appeal to the policeman based on Lady Henrietta's suffering, but it was unlikely to land. The chief inspector no doubt came regularly into contact with people much worse-off than a dowager countess who'd been uninvited to afternoon teas and demonstrations of floral arrangements.

She had to take a different approach.

"There are only two people who weren't at Mr Shakerley's presentation," said Felicity, "and who don't have a continuous alibi for the period in which Lord Anthony Templeton met his end. Is that not so?"

Felicity's cards were now on the table. Yes, she'd been investigating. Coming clean to Chief Inspector Luscombe was a bold move, but considering what Felicity herself had witnessed that day, it was the moment to be bold. This had to be stopped.

The policeman shook his head slowly. "I should have known you wouldn't leave it alone."

Felicity sat up straighter. The chief inspector's response implied Felicity's view on the alibis was correct. "One of the two is Mr Ronald Merton, who now lies unconscious at the hospital. The other is Madame Blanche Ernault, who was here in Bickleford shortly before Mr Merton was found."

Chief Inspector Luscombe narrowed his intelligent, wary eyes. "I told you that this is a delicate investigation, and that we don't need extra hands. I thought you'd understood me, your ladyship."

"Allow me to suggest a scenario, Chief Inspector," continued Felicity, lowering her voice so that the other policemen and tea room staff wouldn't be able to hear. "Following Lord Anthony Templeton's speech, Mr Ronald Merton took offence on behalf of his expertise and the rose breeding community in general. In a fit of anger, he strikes out at the Best in Show winner. Devastated by her master's death, Madame Blanche Ernault, through her passionate dedication to Lord Anthony Templeton, unravels the mystery before any of us and seeks revenge on Mr Merton this very afternoon."

Admittedly, Blanche's lack of a verifiable alibi at the flower show had no bearing on this scenario, and conjuring up emotion-fuelled encounters with nothing close to hard evidence wasn't usually Felicity's style. But the attack on Mr Merton had to be the turning point. Even if Felicity couldn't solve the increasingly complicated case, she must at least get her grandmother out of harm's way.

Chief Inspector Luscombe knitted his long fingers together. "Lady Felicity, your efforts are admirable. And believe me when I say I understand your situation. But let us please be clear. When is it that we, as the Devon County Constabulary, have named your grandmother as a person of interest in this enquiry?"

Felicity drew in her chin. "You haven't. But—"

The policeman cut her off. "And when, your ladyship, does the constabulary ever communicate about ruling out people from our enquiry who we've never named as suspects?"

Felicity turned the question over in her mind for a moment. "Well, never. But—"

The chief inspector leaned forward. "I have a lot of respect for you, your ladyship, and for your grandmother. I know what you want me to do, but I'm afraid I can't do it. If we made a public declaration of your grandmother's innocence, we'd have queues up and down Exeter's high street with people asking us to do the same for them, for every case where there's been even an ounce of confusion over who the real criminal was. And we can't have that. We have to treat everyone the same. We're all equal in the eyes of the law. No matter our backgrounds. No exceptions."

Felicity's temperature rose. "That's not exactly true, though. Is it, Chief Inspector?"

The policeman's eyebrows drew low, his expression dark. "Are you calling me a liar, your ladyship?"

"Mr Elliot Etty. He was at the flower show when the murder occurred. He's surely a valuable witness. Perhaps even a suspect." Felicity was being facetious to make her point. "Where is he now?"

The policeman's mouth gaped for a moment. "Mr Etty has a strong chain of alibis for the time that—"

"I do realise he's not a suspect, Chief Inspector. Certainly no more than my grandmother. But you asked even Mr Cooper and myself not to travel while the investigation was ongoing. That's hardly treating everyone the same, is it?"

Colour appeared in the policeman's cheeks. It was the first time Felicity had seen him so out of sorts.

"Your ladyship, you simply don't know the half of it. A tour like Mr Etty's employs a great number of—"

Felicity held up a hand. "It's quite all right, Chief Inspector Luscombe. I don't need to know the details. I completely understand." Felicity stood up from the little table. "We're all equal in the eyes of the law. Especially high flying entertainers with an immense public profile. I wish you a good day."

Felicity's blood was still boiling as she marched through the tea room and out into the village. It wasn't polite to end the conversation in that way, but Felicity had been on the edge of saying more things she might later regret.

Perhaps she herself had crossed a line by using her access to the police to try to get relief for Lady Henrietta. But that's what families did, wasn't it? They strove to take care of one another. Surely that was forgivable.

Yet it had been foolish to imagine the discovery of Mr Merton on his back in the flowerbed would fix Lady Henrietta's situation. Would talk start swirling about Felicity's grandmother being responsible for smashing up a greenhouse and coshing the flower show judge on the head? It was too ridiculous to think about, and Felicity knew the police were truly doing everything they could to solve matters.

But it wasn't right to give someone special treatment simply because he was famous. And Felicity wouldn't allow herself to be handled as a problem to be neutralised through tea and talking.

His notebook still in his hand, Alex was leaving the telephone box on Bickleford's green. As Felicity stalked towards him, clouds pulled over the sun and there was a chill on the grass-scented breeze.

Alex pushed the brim of his hat up with the tip of his pencil. "The talk with Luscombe didn't go well, then."

"I'm going to do," began Felicity before coming to a stop, "whatever I can to resolve this whole mess of a situation cleanly and quickly. My grandmother deserves better than this. Leonora, too. Everyone does."

"It went worse than 'not well' with Luscombe, then. How about a quick game?" Alex tapped his pencil on his notebook. "Care to guess who's waiting at the newspaper's headquarters, desperate to speak to us?"

Chapter Twenty-Five

As Felicity and Alex entered the little office off the bustling main newsroom of the Western Daily News' headquarters, Mr Lucas Shakerley leapt out of his chair. He had on a dark green suit with a mustard bow tie and a pair of spectacles settled crookedly on his nose.

"You must put a stop to it. This can't continue." Mr Shakerley's voice shook with outrage, although it wasn't immediately clear with whom or what he was angry.

"Let's keep things calm, if you don't mind, Mr Shakerley," suggested Alex firmly as he seated himself beside Felicity at the highly polished desk that took up most of the little room that was mainly used for interviews.

"Calm?" Mr Shakerley's hands gripped the chair's wooden armrests as he lowered himself back into his seat. "How can I be expected to remain calm?"

Alex kept a wary gaze on the rose expert as he stood momentarily to close the room's only window, the clatter of the trams along Exeter's high street doing little to bring peace to the situation.

"It must have been very shocking to learn about what happened to Mr Merton," suggested Felicity gently. She was still full of fire after her encounter with Chief Inspector Luscombe, but that didn't mean she couldn't appear cool. She was now more ready to solve the case than ever.

Mr Shakerley held up a hand. "You misunderstand me. You misunderstand me completely."

"We're very keen to understand you," said Alex, already sounding mildly impatient. "We came directly from Bickleford at your request." He was generous to omit that Alex's own appeals to Mr Shakerley for a quote had gone unanswered. "Please, tell us why you wish to speak to us."

Mr Shakerley adjusted his spectacles and took a steadying breath. "As I'm sure you are well aware, my book on the history of English rose breeding will be published next week."

Felicity threw Alex a questioning look. He gave a little shake of his head. They knew Mr Shakerley had a book coming out, but they hadn't been aware of its publication date.

"It's the culmination of many years of work," continued the rose expert. "I have written books before, but you cannot imagine how I have dedicated myself to this tome. It brings English rose breeding out of the shadows and into the Twentieth Century. I've done my best to establish once and for all why England as much as France or even China can be considered one of the great centres of the development of the rose. And this announcement could now be completely eclipsed." He spoke rapidly, his voice going high at the end. Mr Shakerley was evidently very upset.

"We shall, of course, mention your book in the newspaper," said Alex, his expression a little strained.

The rose expert put a hand to his chest, his shoulders collapsing with relief. "Oh, thank goodness. Thank goodness."

Felicity raised a disbelieving eyebrow. "Is that why you called this meeting with Mr Cooper so urgently? To ensure your book made the papers?"

"No, no." The force of his head shaking rendered Mr Shakerley's spectacles crooked once more. "Goodness me. I wouldn't dare be so presumptuous. I wanted to speak to a journalist because the police won't listen to me, and because I cannot have the rebirth of English rose breeding overshadowed by the foolish actions of my idiotic colleagues."

"I see," said Felicity, sitting forward in her chair. This was quickly becoming interesting.

"What have you tried to communicate to the police that has gone ignored?" asked Alex with a hint of scepticism. It was out of character for Chief Inspector Luscombe and his men to disregard even a scrap of evidence.

Mr Shakerley closed his eyes, clutched the wooden armrests of his chair, and took a deep breath. "First, I wish to clarify, just as I have clarified to the fine gentlemen of the Devon County Constabulary, that I have no recollection whatever of who was at my presentation on the day of Lord Anthony Templeton's fatal accident."

Felicity blinked. Naturally, she'd had this question lined up for the rose expert. Was Mr Shakerley being truthful on this point, or was it a topic he wished to avoid? With his distinct interests and a talent for deep focus, it was plausible that the rose expert had little regard for his surroundings.

"You don't remember anyone at all?" pressed Felicity.

Mr Shakerley's sigh carried an edge of frustration. "There was a volunteer from the association seated directly before me in the audience. She was fiddling with some kind of clock that caused rather a distraction."

"Mrs Winterpole?" suggested Felicity.

Mr Shakerley winced apologetically. "I'm awfully sorry, but unless it's a plant, I'm not terribly good with names. I don't remember anyone else."

Felicity nodded. The matter had to be left there.

Alex's jaw was taut with anticipation. "What is it you've brought us here to say?" he repeated with a thin veneer of patience.

Mr Shakerley took another deep breath. He straightened his spectacles. "I wish to distance myself most severely from the British Rose Association. Particularly concerning their practices in the area of show judging."

Alex looked up from his notebook. His eyes were wide and

shining. Now, this was news. It was also an unexpected development in the investigation.

"I wish to make a public statement on the matter," continued the rose expert. "In the newspaper."

Was there something rotten at the heart of the rose association?

"Could you explain your reasoning?" asked Felicity.

Mr Shakerley placed his hands together and brought his fingers to his lips. "This is exactly what I tried and sadly failed to communicate to the police. What is going wrong in society when it's only journalists who can be counted on to listen without judgement and attempt to truly understand the whole story?"

Felicity and Alex gave one another a knowing look. This always had been the role of a journalist. Reporting the truth was a tenet that the Western Daily News did its best to uphold.

"We're here to listen to your story, Mr Shakerley," said Alex encouragingly but also slightly urgently, his fingers no doubt already itching for his typewriter.

"The whole story, if you please," added Felicity with gentle encouragement. Her investigation was at a crucial stage. It was no time for skipping important details.

Mr Shakerley sat a little straighter on the other side of the polished desk. "We've had disagreements in the past. It's in the nature of judging. One doesn't stroll around throwing rosettes about willy-nilly. That's not how judging works. The scoring system is rigorous, and every decision is a battle between opinions. I've bitten my tongue before. Frequently, in fact, but this year was particularly difficult. And now, considering Mr Merton's... Considering his unfortunate situation, I feel it's time I let my feelings be heard." Mr Shakerley gave a brief nod to reinforce the point.

A frisson of excitement passed through Felicity. This could be big.

"Mr Shakerley," she began, before Alex could cut in with harsher words urging the rose expert to come to the point as quickly as possible. "May I say that it's deeply appreciated that you're sharing your feelings on this matter?" Mr Shakerley perhaps came across as a little pompous, but by talking to Felicity and Alex, he was stepping outside familiar territory. He needed encouragement.

Alex glanced at Felicity. He was doing his utmost to keep his impatience in check, but he was clearly champing at the bit to get Mr Shakerley's statement into the paper.

Felicity laid a gentle hand on the polished desk. "Please tell us. What are your feelings, exactly?"

Mr Shakerley eyed Felicity carefully. "Just to be clear, I do not condemn the association in its entirety. The colonel and his volunteers do good work in many areas."

Felicity nodded. "I quite understand."

"It's only the system used for judging flower shows like Bickleford Rose Festival and the associated chain of decision making from which I wish to distance myself."

"Very well," said Felicity. "My colleague, Mr Cooper, is making very precise notes about your wishes so that your words can be accurately relayed in the paper."

Alex peered up from his notebook with a strained smile. It was difficult to rein in his wolf-like interviewing instincts, but kid gloves were needed for an interviewee like Mr Shakerley.

"And what is it about the judging in particular that you disagree with?" asked Felicity.

"Well," said the rose expert, his eyes widening behind his spectacles. "All of it."

Felicity tilted her head slightly. "All of it?"

"Yes." Mr Shakerley nodded adamantly. "All of it."

"Then why come to us now?" Alex could hold back no longer. "You've been judging Bickleford for a fair few years. Why is it this year in particular you feel compelled to stand up and voice your displeasure?"

Felicity would have asked the same question albeit worded rather differently. "Has there indeed been a trigger for your decision to come forward?" she added calmly, attempting to downplay the accusatory nature of Alex's enquiry.

Mr Shakerley's bottom lip trembled. "Has the possibility not occurred to you," he began quietly, as though afraid of being overheard, "that someone might have wished to punish not only the winner but also the judge—" He swallowed. "—or perhaps the judges who chose the winner?"

Felicity drew her eyebrows together. It wasn't a motive she'd yet considered. "Do you fear for your life, Mr Shakerley?"

"A little." His voice was a squeak. "I must admit."

"And that's why you wish to distance yourself from the rose association?" Alex sounded irritated. "To save yourself?" If there was no genuine disagreement between Mr Shakerley and the rose association, it was less of a coup for the Western Daily News.

"No, no. You misunderstand me. I disagree with the association. I really do."

"You don't think Lord Anthony Templeton should have won the Best in Show prize?" Alex was getting stuck in.

The rose expert screwed his eyes shut. He looked like he might cry. As determined and thorough as Chief Inspector Luscombe's men could be, it was possible to see how interactions between Mr Shakerley and the police had ground to a halt with little to show for it.

"It's all right, Mr Shakerley," reassured Felicity while simultaneously firing a glare of warning at Alex. "Take your time and tell us what you'd like us to know."

Mr Shakerley opened one eye and peered at Felicity. "The roses from Champs Verts Nursery were all of impeccable quality. You must understand that I've never questioned the quality."

Felicity nodded. "We understand. Don't we, Mr Cooper?"

Alex looked at Felicity. He gave a stiff little nod.

"If there was no discussion over the quality of the Champs Verts blooms," recapped Felicity, "what were the disagreements between yourself and the association regarding this year's prize?"

Mr Shakerley's lip trembled. "Shall I try to explain?"

Felicity nodded patiently. "Please do."

The interviewee cleared his throat. "When a rose of outstanding beauty and strength is developed, it becomes father to an untold number of children across generations, let alone the countless duplicates of itself that would naturally also be created."

Felicity listened intently. Alex wrote rapidly in his notebook. It was of utmost importance that Mr Shakerley felt his concerns were being treated seriously.

The rose expert continued. "Such a rose can far outlive the breeder responsible for creating it. Perhaps it's the rose's scent, or its ability to withstand harsh weather, or a new petal count. Something will inspire breeders for generations to continue experimenting with that rose, creating more varieties. More children, if you will. All the rose's children are different, yet all bear characteristics that — sometimes imperceptibly, at least to the untrained eye — create a connection with that original father plant."

"I see," said Felicity.

Mr Shakerley adjusted his spectacles. "Such a father plant might come along once a century, but its effects could be felt for many more years than that."

Alex glanced up at Felicity from his notebook. *And where might this be going, do you suppose?* his expression seemed to say.

Felicity shot a look back at him. *Patience. We're getting somewhere.*

"Do go on," she said to Mr Shakerley.

"In judging the Bickleford Rose Festival, I'm asked to provide my expert opinion as a historian. I'm the historian not just of the association but of all rose breeding in Britain, if you will. Unofficially, of course. Our great universities have yet to recognise horticulture as an area worthy of the highest academic qualifications."

"Yet this year was different?" offered Felicity, attempting to keep the expert gently on track.

Mr Shakerley looked uneasy. "This is where it gets difficult. If I said to you spiral phyllotaxis, would you know what that meant?"

Felicity had to be honest. "Not immediately, no."

Alex looked up from his notebook. "Spell that for me, please?"

The rose expert complied with the request. "What about reticulate venation?"

Felicity shook her head. Alex was also stumped.

"Might you be able to recognise pearlisation in a flower bud?"

"No," said Felicity, "but I'm sure I might—"

Mr Shakerley waved a hand. "Please. I've made a mistake by trying to explain. I wish simply to state that I'm distancing myself from the judging practices." He stood up, his chair scraping noisily on the wooden floor. "And I do not wish to become the next victim." His voice trembled. "That is all."

Felicity stood up, too. "Mr Shakerley, please. We sincerely wish to understand your disagreement with the rose association. Might you tell us what these terms mean?"

"No, no. I've said too much." He began for the door.

Alex rose from his seat. "But your book, Mr Shakerley. Don't you wish to promote your book?"

The words had no effect on the frightened rose expert. Mr Shakerley reached for the door handle.

"So your disagreement with the association was not about the quality of the Champs Verts blooms," said Felicity, "but about their provenance?"

Mr Shakerley halted, his hand still on the door handle. He turned towards Felicity. His eyes were wide behind his glasses, both fear and passion burning in his gaze. "They employ me to give my expert view on the historical context. The generations. It's a view no one else can bring to the situation, not Mr Merton, not Colonel Bolt, not any of the dedicated volunteers. But this year they disregarded me completely."

"That must have been quite galling," said Felicity, her skin prickling. A crucial piece of information was almost within grasp. "Would you be able to share with us the view you provided to the rose association that they ignored?"

Mr Shakerley blinked. "But I told you already."

Felicity glanced at Alex. He looked as confused as she felt.

"You did?" she asked.

Mr Shakerley nodded. "Spiral phyllotaxis. Reticulate venation. Pearlisation in the flower bud."

Felicity attempted a grateful smile, but it faltered. “I’m awfully sorry, but I still don’t understand.”

Mr Shakerley adjusted his spectacles. “It wasn’t declared in the paperwork, yet I could see it, as clear as day. The Champs Verts roses were all Templetons. They were Templeton roses through and through.”

Chapter Twenty-Six

A deposit from a flock of geese on the roof of Felicity's Alvis had to be dealt with promptly, lest it permanently damage the sparkling white coachwork. Alex's inconspicuous Model T was, therefore, the chariot of choice for the following morning's outing.

Thankful for the warmth of her periwinkle-blue twill jacket, Felicity snuggled down into the passenger seat as Alex guided the Ford past fields of silvery green barley that danced in the wind as white clouds rolled overhead.

"Your grandmother seems to be bearing up well, all things considered."

Alex had joined Felicity and Lady Henrietta on the terrace where they were enjoying a slightly chilly *al fresco* breakfast in the morning sunshine.

Felicity frowned a little. "She's rather too good at putting on a brave face. She hasn't left Bradley Court for days, and the only visitors she's seen have been Mrs Broughton and our local vicar."

"She seemed pleased with my piece on Percy," said Alex, which was an understatement. Lady Henrietta had always been a fan of Alex's reporting, but she'd been effusive in her praise for this particular article.

Felicity sighed. "I just wish he'd tell her the truth about his lack of interest in becoming a professional rose breeder. Although I suppose it's the least of the perfidy we face." The revelation they were heading towards had the potential to be more explosive than any reaction from Lady Henrietta.

Alex shifted down a gear to navigate a steep climb. "How do you feel about what your grandmother said about us?" he asked, changing the subject.

Felicity smiled. "That the discovery of bodies and the unravelling of their messy ends are the glue that binds us together, you mean?"

Alex flashed Felicity an amused grin. "Not that, although I suppose she has a point." He brought his gaze back to the road. "Lady Henrietta described us as 'courting', didn't she? Or did I mishear her?"

Felicity's heart gave a little leap. Her grandmother had indeed said it, but it had been so fleeting and had felt so natural that Felicity had hardly taken note. Yet to have someone beyond just Felicity and Alex recognise the seriousness of their bond was to take things to quite another level, wasn't it?

"Is there any harm to announcing ourselves as a courting couple?" said Felicity, her pulse quickening.

"Quite the opposite." Alex beamed at Felicity. "I dare say it might be good for us."

Felicity gripped his hand on the steering wheel for a moment. Alex was inordinately handsome when he smiled.

His smile quickly disappeared, however. "Something's been troubling me."

"Oh?" Felicity's insides quivered a little. It had all been going so smoothly between them.

Alex rubbed his temple. "This whole 'father rose' thing Shakerley was waxing on about. I can't quite fathom it."

Felicity's shoulders dropped with relief. "He made it sound rather more complicated than it actually is," she assured. Getting the information out of Mr Shakerley had been something of an ordeal, but tracking down the origins of Lord Anthony Templeton's roses was surely key to unravelling the man's demise.

Alex slowed to allow a shepherd and two Border Collies to cross the road. The shepherd lifted his crook in thanks.

"The Champs Verts roses were linkable to Templeton roses," said Alex. "But only in a manner that an expert like Shakerley could notice. Is that it?"

"Not just linkable," said Felicity. "They were from the same family. They'd been bred for several generations — plant generations, that is — to resemble quite something else, but the fundamentals were still there."

"But why is it an issue?" said Alex as the Model T picked up speed past high hedgerows. "Shakerley said himself that 'father' roses have lots of 'children'."

"The paperwork," said Felicity. "To enter a rose into the annals at the rose association, certain forms must be completed. It sounds like Anthony Templeton or one of his assistants did this, otherwise they wouldn't have been able to enter the competition. But they failed to mention the true origins of the roses."

"According to Shakerley." Alex studied the road as it twisted along the hillside. "Bit odd that no one else agreed with him, isn't it? Also rather convenient that he's the only specialist with enough knowledge to make the call."

"But what would Mr Shakerley's motivation be for spreading lies about a competition entrant?" said Felicity. "Is he not rather exposing himself by making these claims? What happened to Mr Merton clearly frightened him."

Alex lowered his brow. "Did you see the front page this morning?"

"Of course." *Rose Judge Calls Foul On Competition* was the front page headline of that morning's Western Daily News. It was Alex's write-up of the interview with Mr Shakerley, but a reporter rarely had the final say in the headline.

"Hardly keeping a low profile, is it?" Alex had been very clear about the level of interest the story was likely to attract, but Mr

Shakerley had insisted he wanted to go ahead with distancing himself from the rose association.

"Perhaps he's torn between his principles and his personal safety?"

Alex continued to look doubtful. "If Shakerley is such a revered expert, why would the rose association just ride roughshod over him?"

The Model T slowed as it drew up outside the gates. The lodge keeper appeared from his little house. Instead of coming to ask what Felicity and Alex's business was, he went straight to the gates and opened them.

With a wave to the lodge keeper, Alex rolled the Model T forward.

"Perhaps we're about to find out," suggested Felicity.

Chapter Twenty-Seven

Only a glimpse of the pale limestone Palladian symmetry of Templeton Manor was possible. A footman waiting on the forecourt of the main house directed Felicity and Alex and the Model T to continue even deeper into the estate. Upon rounding the drive's final bend, the sight that met them was dazzling.

Thousands of glass panes between elegant spans of white-painted ironwork glinted in the sunlight. Ornate finials and cresting along the roof marked the design as Victorian. As tall and as long as a row of cottages, the Templeton family's Rosarium was a cathedral to rose breeding.

The interior was warm but not uncomfortably so. The mammoth greenhouse was fitted with thoroughly modern ventilation and heating systems. A path of York stone slabs running through the Rosarium's centre had been dampened, and the stone glistened as the water evaporated in the sun. Roses of all shades cascaded from pots and climbing frames and exploded from beds. Their honeyed, musky scent was heady.

A corner of the Rosarium looked like a laboratory, with brilliant white work tops and all manner of tools neatly laid out. In a broderie anglaise blouse and a sturdy olive-green linen skirt, Leonora stood at one of the work tops grafting cuttings, her hands moving with the grace and speed of someone with decades of experience.

Havelock was there, too, of course. There was no escaping the man. In a white linen shirt, black braces, and moleskin trousers, he was at the bench behind Leonora, repotting plants, his big hands easily scooping soil into terracotta pots.

Havelock ceased his work and watched Felicity and Alex as they approached. Leonora didn't look up from her cuttings, her fingers working almost mechanically, the plait of her long dark hair shifting rhythmically on her shoulder with her movements.

A growl came from under Havelock's work bench. The two Jack Russells were there, lying on a battered corduroy jacket, teeth bared at the new arrivals.

"Flossie. Daisy." Havelock kept his gaze on Felicity and Alex, his voice itself something of a growl. His words had little effect on the dogs, one of whom snarled.

"Girls," said Leonora brusquely, without breaking the flow of her movements or her concentration on her work.

The dogs' eyes and ears flicked to their mistress, and their growling stopped. One of them whimpered apologetically.

Felicity stood slightly ahead of Alex. She had telephoned Templeton Manor to arrange the meeting. She hadn't needed to say what it was about. Without hesitation, the butler had offered Felicity an appointment for the following morning. Was Leonora expecting an update on the investigation into her brother's untimely demise? Felicity couldn't offer answers, but she hadn't come to Templeton Manor empty handed.

Leonora arrived at the end of the row of pots before her on the bench. "There." She folded her knife away and dropped it into the pocket of her skirt. The tips of her fingers were rough, the nails worn down by her work. "Lady Felicity." She stepped out from behind the work top. "To what do we owe this pleasure?"

Felicity smiled politely. At the abandoned monastery, she'd won Leonora's trust, perhaps even her respect, yet Felicity couldn't quite fathom how she'd done it. Might she build on it further?

"You said nothing about the newspaperman." Havelock spoke before Felicity had a chance. He was apparently aware of everything Felicity had discussed with the butler on the telephone the evening before.

Havelock glared at Alex. "There won't be any comment for the paper."

In his brown two-buttoned suit, Alex looked every inch the professional. Maintaining a polite aloofness, he answered Havelock's stare with a raise of his brow.

"I'm terribly sorry." Felicity looked from Havelock to Leonora. "Is Mr Cooper not welcome?"

Alex held up his palms. "I'm here only to accompany Lady Felicity. I shan't put anything in the paper unless you want me to."

Leonora looked thoughtful. She'd not seemed to doubt Alex's presence until Havelock raised the issue. "I should indeed perhaps prefer it if Mr Cooper leaves us."

Felicity nodded tightly. "Very well. May I request your gardener leave us also?"

Havelock furrowed his brow. He was about to speak, but Leonora cut him off.

"Touché." Leonora seemed amused. She turned to Havelock. "What will it be?"

The gardener glared at Alex, then grunted.

Alex allowed a glimmer of amusement to pass across his calm, chiselled features.

The men would stay.

Slowly, the dogs rose from their bed and trundled towards Felicity and Alex. Their eyes were lowered, but their noses twitched rapidly.

"Now." Leonora put a hand on her hip. "What is it you've come to tell me? You made it sound rather urgent. Found out who did for my brother, have you?"

Leonora's tone was light. Her eyes glinted with something like mischief. She was difficult to read, but Felicity had devised a plan for how to handle their discussion, and she was determined to stick to it.

"Your brother entered Bickleford Rose Festival with Templeton roses." Felicity came straight to the point. "It's how he won Best in Show."

Leonora's face fell. She looked deeply troubled. After a glance towards Havelock, her composure was regained.

"Well," she said. "That's quite some news indeed."

"Were you aware of this?" asked Felicity.

"I was not."

"Did you see the Champs Verts roses?"

"I did."

"But you didn't recognise them as originating from Templeton stock."

Leonora's eyes narrowed slightly. "Who's making this claim?"

"Mr Lucas Shakerley," clarified Felicity.

Some of the colour left Leonora's cheeks. Havelock's expression darkened. Mr Shakerley's opinion was clearly well-regarded in the Templeton household.

"Mr Shakerley said as much to the newspaper, your ladyship," added Alex tactfully. "We ran with it in this morning's edition. Not to pressure you into saying anything to the paper yourself, but just so that you're aware of the situation."

Havelock folded his thick arms over his barrel chest. He continued to watch Felicity and Alex as though angry at them for even being there.

Leonora put a hand to her throat. "Thank you for informing me."

"Might you know how your brother achieved this?" Felicity's voice was calm and clear.

The Jack Russells had arrived at Felicity's and Alex's feet. Felicity paid them no mind as they began sniffing around their ankles. Alex peered down warily at the dogs.

Leonora did her best to maintain her composure. "I could offer a guess or two, but do I know for certain how he did it?" Her voice shook a little. "I'm afraid I do not."

Felicity kept her tone neutral. "Mr Shakerley explained how the roses must have been bred through many iterations. That's how they developed a different appearance while maintaining subtle yet significant qualities of the original Templetons."

"Quite," said Leonora, a little coolly. Felicity wasn't telling the rose breeder anything she couldn't work out herself.

"Your brother then failed to mention this in the flower show paperwork."

Leonora folded her arms over her blouse. "Hmm." The situation seemed to perplex her.

"When your brother left home all those years ago," said Felicity, "did he take any roses with him?"

"He left with the clothes on his back. Nothing more."

Havelock's glare skipped to Leonora for the briefest of moments. She bowed her head a little.

"He took no scrap of any plant material with him?" pressed Felicity. If she could unravel how Anthony Templeton had achieved the deception, it would surely lead to further understanding of the whole flower show plot, including Anthony's end.

Leonora watched the dogs at Alex's ankles. "There was a period in which Anthony used to come back. Or at least, we assumed it was him. He would snap stems to make bouquets. Occasionally, he'd take a whole plant. My parents tightened security—" Leonora glanced at Havelock. "—but that was many years ago. We've never had problems since."

Felicity cocked her head. So Anthony didn't depart for France directly after leaving home. "Is it possible one of the plants he took all those years ago—"

Leonora's laughter cut Felicity short. "There's simply no way my brother could keep a rose going for decades. That he kept any plant alive long enough to transport it from Dorset or wherever he had his nursery to Bickleford is already incredible enough, although I suppose he had other people doing the work for him." Leonora looked down at her roughened fingertips. "Anthony wilfully ignored anything my father wished to teach him." She no longer sounded amused.

Blanche Ernault had said Anthony had returned to roses out of love for his family. *If only my father could see this*, the French assistant had heard him say. How did that match up with ignoring his father's teachings about rose breeding? Having turned his back on his family, did Anthony truly wish to make amends somehow?

"Might your brother have stolen plants from you more recently?" suggested Felicity, casting her gaze over the vast floral contents of the Rosarium. "It must be difficult to keep every corner of your nursery under surveillance."

"Not a chance," snarled Havelock, sounding even more intensely annoyed than usual. Anthony was certainly one of his least favourite subjects. "Flossie!" he bellowed.

While Alex was busy side-stepping one wet nose, the other dog had attempted to take hold of his bootlace.

Surprised by Havelock's chastisement, the Jack Russell withdrew.

"Thanks," said Alex a little reluctantly.

Havelock grunted.

"As I understand it," said Felicity, continuing to address Leonora, "the provenance of your brother's roses is an avenue the police have yet to investigate." Although that could change now that Mr Shakerley had been to the newspaper with his story. "So if you wish for me to continue looking into your brother's demise, I should appreciate any input you have on this matter."

Leonora shook her head. "I told you, this comes as a surprise to me. I wasn't aware he'd used our roses." There was a hint of sadness in her voice.

Felicity took a step towards Leonora. "I believe you, but I need to understand. Why would he do this? Why would he use Templeton roses and not declare it?"

Leonora lifted her chin. "I suppose he has the right. He is Lord Templeton, after all. They took everything else away from him, but one can't take away a man's title."

Felicity tucked her chin. "Who took what away from him?"

Leonora pressed her lips together. She eyed Alex. Had it been a mistake not to allow him to be dismissed? Was his presence as a journalist stifling the discussion?

"Please," said Felicity. "If you can help me understand, we might get to the bottom of things. You must have heard about what happened to Mr Merton. Did you hear about the Dingles?"

Leonora nodded. "News travels."

"So, what on earth is this all about?" pleaded Felicity. "Why was your brother even at Bickleford?"

A cool breeze swept in through the vents of the gigantic greenhouse.

Leonora hugged herself. "He deserved his win. He deserved to have something good happen to him. Yes, he's behaved badly. But perhaps you would, too, if you'd experienced what we went through."

In a flash, Havelock was at Leonora's side. He put a hand on her shoulder.

Leonora laid her hand atop her gardener's.

It was a gesture of such empathy and tenderness but also an unusual sight, especially from the gruff, burly Havelock. Felicity had no judgement to pass, however. Everyone needed a supporter in life. The openness of the gesture was also a testament to how far Felicity had gained Leonora's trust.

"How was your brother badly behaved?" asked Felicity gently.

"That is something I will not speak about." Leonora's answer was sharp. "Especially now he's no longer with us."

The desire to honour one's family, even if they weren't the best of people, could be extremely strong.

A different tack was needed.

"What was it you and your brother went through, if I may ask?"

Leonora sniffed and straightened. "As much as I respect your need for information, I will not lay it all bare. There's a need for privacy in certain arenas, but I will say this. Our parents weren't the easiest of people. Our father in particular." Leonora glared at Felicity. "You saw my brother, didn't you? After what had happened to him?"

Felicity hesitated before nodding. She couldn't forget the collapsed lemonade bottles, the hessian sacks, and what lay underneath.

Leonora's gaze was intense. "You saw the scar on his cheek?"

"Y-yes," said Felicity.

Leonora's nostrils flared. "I witnessed my father give Anthony that scar. He suffered far more than I ever did, and goodness knows, we both suffered. I couldn't be angry at him for abandoning me. I fantasised about doing the same. About escaping."

Felicity could barely imagine witnessing such abuse, let alone experiencing it. "I'm truly sorry to hear that."

Leonora averted her gaze. "I wasn't surprised when Anthony didn't return, even after our parents passed. But then he never felt bound by the limits of acceptable behaviour." Leonora sniffed and lifted her chin. "I was surprised and hurt by what he said in his speech, but honestly, I was pleased to see him win. And if he did it with our father's roses, so much the better."

Tears threatened in the corners of Leonora's eyes. From the pocket of his moleskin trousers, Havelock offered a crisp checked handkerchief, which Leonora accepted and brought to her face.

"I understand." Felicity had pushed Leonora to her limit. She'd posed all her questions, and Leonora had answered them with unexpected frankness. But in terms of clues towards a solution for the flower show plot, where did it leave them?

Alex coaxed a couple of short comments for the paper from Leonora, reassuring her she could read them before publication. Havelock continued to regard Alex with suspicion. He was Leonora's protector, and she relied upon him to an even deeper extent than first imagined.

The hulking gardener offered to accompany Felicity and Alex to their motor. Thankfully, it was only a short distance, so they could politely decline the offer. Leonora needed Havelock by her side more than Felicity or Alex did.

In leaving the Rosarium, they passed a small office area with a desk, a pencil pot, and a shelf full of ledgers. There were even a few faded photographs hanging up on the hoarding that separated the desk from the rest of the greenhouse.

Felicity lingered for a closer look.

Men in flat caps worked on freshly dug borders. A pair of Jack

Russells very similar to Flossie and Daisy sat obediently on a wall between floral urns. A group of gardening staff posed in lines arranged according to height. At the centre, a young Leonora, her hair in ringlets, was seated between what must have been her parents.

Felicity squinted. The father looked stern. The mother appeared cold. There was no sign of Anthony, but something else caught her eye.

"Alex." She pressed a finger to the glass of a framed print. "Look."

Chapter Twenty-Eight

"Blast it!"

It was unusual for Alex to utter an oath, but he had every reason.

The goods van that almost ran him and Felicity off the road had come from behind at tremendous speed. The errant vehicle had cut sharply in front of the Ford and gone careening around the bend ahead.

To avoid a collision, Alex had swerved, branches from the hedge that lined the narrow lane clattering against the Model T's bodywork.

"You did well," assured Felicity, relaxing her grip on the wood of the dashboard. The danger had passed. "Haven't we seen that van before?"

"There are so many of the popular models about," said Alex, regaining his composure. He gave the steering wheel a grateful pat. "This old girl's ubiquitous to the point of boredom. Can be handy when one doesn't wish to be noticed."

When they arrived at their destination and found the same goods van parked at a hasty angle in the spot that Felicity's Alvis had taken the last time they had visited the Dingles, Felicity's pulse quickened.

Alex frowned. "Looks like you were right."

"Goodness," muttered Felicity. Were they too late?

Alex didn't stop the Model T. The motor rolled past the nursery's parking area.

Felicity twisted in her seat to watch the Dingles nursery gliding into the distance. "We must stop. We have to."

Alex drew the Model T to a halt a little further along the lane, the engine still running. He turned to Felicity, his forehead creased. "I'm sorry I dismissed your claim to have recognised the van. Otherwise we'd have already discussed what to do. It's Blanche and Jacques, isn't it?"

Felicity nodded. "It's the same colour and model as I saw outside the tea garden in Bickleford."

"Why do you suppose they're here to see the Dingles?"

Felicity hadn't got that far in her workings. She only imagined arriving at the Dingles and gently probing about why the couple hadn't reported the sabotage of their greenhouse to the police. At least, that's what Felicity had planned as her innocent pretext for returning to the nursery.

But that plan was now out of the window. The situation had already been risky. It was perhaps now dangerous.

"We can't just keep driving," insisted Felicity. "We have to do something."

"We can stop further up and find a telephone," suggested Alex. "Inform the police."

"But what if we're too late?" Felicity turned in her seat and gazed back down the lane towards the Dingle nursery. "A smashed up greenhouse is one thing. What if someone gets hurt? We're not near a town. It'll take the police a while to get out here." Felicity shifted to face Alex. Her heart was pounding. "What if Blanche and Jacques attacked Mr Merton? What if the Dingles are next on their list? If no one interrupts them this time, they may well finish the job."

Alex studied Felicity for a moment, his uneasiness at what she'd said obvious in his expression. He turned the ignition key, and the motor fell silent.

Felicity opened the passenger door.

Alex put a hand on her forearm. "Stay behind me, all right?"

Felicity nodded. "We have to move fast."

Felicity and Alex used the goods van for cover as they crept closer to the Dingles nursery. While trotting back down the lane — Felicity thankful for her choice of a jacket and skirt with room for movement and a pair of sensible Oxfords — they'd discussed and decided on a plan.

They would get as close as they could without being seen. Then, depending on what they heard and saw, they would step in, but only if it was safe to do so. Otherwise, they would retreat and seek help.

Felicity mildly disagreed with this last point. It was never fully safe to engage with people responsible for murder or even attempted murder. There was no time for squabbling, however. Something simply had to be done.

Felicity and Alex crouched beside the van's bonnet and sneaked glances at the nursery's entrance gate. In the distance, several voices could be heard, but the words couldn't be discerned. Her heartbeat quickening, Felicity's mind raced through the scenarios.

If Anthony's assistants had attacked Mr Merton, was it in retribution for what Mr Merton had done to Anthony? Did they believe Mr Merton to be the killer? Did the Dingles also somehow have a hand in Anthony's demise?

Edna and Clive had apparently both been at Mr Shakerley's presentation, so they can't have been directly involved. Jacques had even confirmed Clive's presence at the talk.

So why would the French assistants target the Dingles?

What if Blanche and Jacques were responsible for their master's demise? Blanche had the opportunity during the crucial window at the flower show, but why target Mr Merton as well? And now the Dingles?

There was some devilish plot holding everything together, but Felicity couldn't quite grasp it, although that didn't much matter now. Further violence had to be prevented.

Alex made a gesture for Felicity to stay low and follow him. They moved quietly across the gravel and approached the nursery's gate, which they found unlatched. Alex pushed it silently open, and they took up position beside a section of hedging just inside the entrance. Remaining stock still, there was only the twittering of the sparrows in the hedge and Felicity's own nervous breathing disrupting her ability to listen.

The voices were closer now. Men's voices. Raised and angry.

After looking himself, Alex shifted position so that Felicity could slowly peek around the hedge, her cloche pulled tightly to her curls to reduce her profile.

The Dingles stood beside one of the undamaged greenhouses. Clive had positioned himself in front of Edna, the greyhound trembling behind her.

Jacques was there, his cap in his fist, his straw-blond hair protruding at all angles, his gestures aggressive.

There was no sign of Blanche.

"I need the money now," shouted the Frenchman. "Right away. Do you not understand?"

"I told you, we don't have money," bellowed Clive. "We were left with nothing. Like you. Like everyone."

Smash!

Jacques kicked a pot through the greenhouse door. Glass shards flew. Edna shrieked.

"Clive," she pleaded. "This has to stop."

"You're lying!" Jacques sounded wild, the whites of his eyes clearly visible. "I know you're lying to me. You have money. He gave you money. I know it."

"You need to leave." Clive took a step towards Jacques. With shaking hands, he lifted a large garden spade into the air.

"No," cried Edna. "Clive, please!"

"Now," said Clive firmly to Jacques, the spade's shining edge trembling above him.

Edna clutched at her pinafore skirt, her knuckles white. She was in a panic.

"All right." Jacques held up his hands and scurried backwards. "I just want my money. *Flûte*. There is no time."

"Leave," growled Clive. "Now."

"Please." Edna was now addressing Jacques. "Just go."

His palms still raised, Jacques continued a slow retreat. He was heading towards where Felicity and Alex were hiding.

Felicity shot Alex a look of concern, but he was already gesturing for her to follow him. Slowly and quietly, they eased backwards as Jacques' footsteps drew nearer.

Clank!

Felicity hadn't seen the garden fork with the thick metal handle resting against the hedge. When it fell to the ground, it did so with rather a din.

Felicity froze. The twittering of the sparrows ceased.

Jacques' footsteps stopped.

Alex put a hand on Felicity's wrist and a finger to his lips.

"*Mais qu'est-ce que c'est que ça?*"

They remained absolutely still as the footsteps on the path resumed, slower this time.

Felicity swallowed. She stood up.

As Jacques rounded the hedge, their eyes met.

Alex was between them before anything further could happen, but the blond Frenchman didn't look angry. He looked confused. He looked scared.

A commotion at the front of the nursery distracted his attention. Tyres crunching on gravel. More footsteps. Running.

"*Bon sang!*" Jacques fled back towards the greenhouse. Past Clive and Edna. He ran fast, arms and legs pumping, dropping his cap as he went.

"He's here. Get him, lads!"

Policemen in uniform poured through the nursery gate as Jacques hopped over a fence behind the greenhouse and disappeared into the field beyond, as nimble as a roe deer. He had a good head start on the policemen and was moving extremely fast.

Alex stood shielding Felicity as a flurry of policemen rushed past them, whistles blowing, truncheons swinging on their belts.

Jacques couldn't have done for Anthony, could he? He'd been at Mr Shakerley's presentation. His need for money was clear, however. Had he demanded cash from Mr Merton, but the discussion got out of hand? The police certainly wanted a rather urgent word with the Frenchman. To put this amount of manpower into an arrest, there was more than just suspicion at play.

But if the assistants had done away with Anthony for his money, why was Jacques asking Mr Merton and the Dingles for cash? And where was Blanche?

Alex turned to Felicity. "You all right?"

"It seems we weren't needed after all," said Felicity, watching as the uniformed policemen struggled over the fence Jacques had so deftly negotiated. Whistles sounded and shouts continued as they dashed into the field after their fugitive.

"This is surely in the running for scoop of the year," said Alex, reaching for his notebook.

"Lady Felicity."

Felicity turned.

His trilby pulled low on his brow, Chief Inspector Luscombe wore a grimace of displeasure. "Why am I not surprised to find you here?"

"Chief Inspector." Felicity straightened. "I see you've got your man, but would you be kind enough to tell us how the whole thing pieces together?"

Alex readied his pencil.

"I'm afraid I haven't been able to work it out," said Felicity, fluttering her eyelashes a little. The policeman wasn't obliged to provide answers, but an appeal to his sense of superiority over an amateur investigator like Felicity might do the trick.

"Piece things together?" said Chief Inspector Luscombe. "I'm afraid it's awfully simple, your ladyship."

Chapter Twenty-Nine

The wind rustled the hedge at the boundary of the Dingles' nursery behind which Felicity and Alex had been hiding. Felicity pulled her twill jacket across her chest as the hem of her periwinkle blue skirt danced against her calves.

Chief Inspector Luscombe continued to gaze sternly at Felicity from under the brim of his trilby, his hands in the pockets of his trench coat.

"You've discovered the explanation for everything to be simple?" Felicity frowned at the chief inspector. The unravelling of Anthony Templeton's murder, Mr Merton's head injury, and now Jacques' confrontation with the Dingles couldn't possibly be simple. Could it?

Beside the greenhouse where Jacques Gobillot had confronted Clive and Edna Dingle, a uniformed officer was speaking to the couple. Jacques and the policemen chasing after him across the green and undulating fields of the Devonshire countryside were no longer in sight, although shouts and whistles could still be heard.

Chief Inspector Luscombe nodded. "That's what I said, your ladyship."

Alex had his notebook poised, but he looked as confused as Felicity felt.

"You came here to arrest Monsieur Jacques Gobillot, didn't you, Chief Inspector?" asked Felicity.

"That's quite obvious," said the policeman dryly. "What's less obvious is what you're doing here, your ladyship."

Felicity ignored the policeman's attempt to divert the conversation. "You wish to arrest Monsieur Gobillot for the attack on Mr Merton, do you not?"

Chief Inspector Luscombe drew in his chin. "What makes you say that?"

Alex gave Felicity a look. *Careful, now.*

But Felicity was beyond playing things too safely. Certainly, as far as the police's opinion of her was concerned.

"Mr Merton did for Lord Anthony Templeton." Felicity hadn't any solid evidence for the assertion, but the policeman apparently had to be goaded into handing over information. "Is that not it?"

Alex had gone from looking confused to rather wary. Was there a risk Felicity might scare off the chief inspector before Alex could get an interview with him?

Or would Felicity help secure the full, exclusive story?

"And the assistants from Champs Verts sought revenge on Mr Merton," continued Felicity. "It's the only explanation, isn't it?"

The policeman sighed. "Your efforts are admirable, your ladyship, but this has nothing to do with Lord Anthony Templeton." He nodded to Alex. "You can put this in your paper if you like."

Alex readied his pencil. "Go ahead, Chief Inspector."

The policeman cleared his throat. "While liaising with the French authorities in the course of our enquiry into the flower show affair, we discovered Monsieur Jacques Gobillot to be wanted for desertion."

"Desertion?" Felicity blinked.

During the war, the punishment for a soldier leaving his post could be severe. In the years since the conflict, attitudes had softened somewhat.

"He's to be arrested for desertion?"

The policeman glowered at Felicity. "It's a serious offence, your ladyship." He returned his attention to Alex. "We were asked by our counterparts in France to bring him in. We collaborated with the police in Dorset to collect Monsieur Gobillot from his residence at Champs Verts Nursery.

"But he saw you coming?" asked Alex.

Chief Inspector Luscombe gave a short, reluctant nod. "The fellow got wind of it somehow. Tried to give us the slip. We chased him over here." The policeman looked in the direction Jacques had fled, the shouting and whistles still carrying on the wind. "I'm sure we'll have him before the day is out. He may be faster than my men, but he doesn't know the land like we do."

Alex nodded as he wrote down the chief inspector's comments.

Felicity still couldn't quite believe it. "So Jacques Gobillot's imminent arrest has nothing to do with what happened to Anthony Templeton? Or to Mr Merton?"

Chief Inspector Luscombe turned wearily towards Felicity. "I've told you my business, your ladyship. Now, why don't you tell me what you're doing here?"

Alex was about to speak up, most likely in Felicity's defence, but Felicity had other plans.

"I'm here to buy a rose," she said confidently.

Alex raised an eyebrow at Felicity.

Chief Inspector Luscombe huffed, amused. "Is it standard rose-buying procedure to park one's motor out of sight when visiting a flower nursery?" Not much escaped the policeman's attention.

Tugging at her jacket, Felicity straightened. She wouldn't be knocked off her stride. "Look around you, Chief Inspector. This is a flower nursery with a speciality in roses. I've come here as a paying client."

Alex was doing an excellent job at hiding his surprise, although he was doing less well at concealing his amusement.

"And you, Mr Cooper." Chief Inspector Luscombe turned his stern, incredulous gaze on Alex. "Am I expected to believe you're here to report on the purchase of a rose?"

Alex's eyebrows shot up. "I like to stay close to Lady Felicity," he said, wasting little time in responding. "There's usually a scoop or two not far away," he added with a smile.

Chief Inspector Luscombe narrowed his eyes. Given what they'd all just witnessed with Jacques, the policeman couldn't argue with Alex's assertion about scoops.

"Now, Chief Inspector," said Felicity, "if you don't mind, I should like to continue with my purchase."

Before the policeman could object, Felicity set off towards the Dingles. They were still being interviewed by a young uniformed officer, his notebook in his hand and his helmet under his arm, though he seemed to be wrapping up.

"So you wouldn't be able to say what prompted Monsieur Gobillot to ask you for money?" asked the young officer.

Clive had planted the edge of his spade in the ground. His red-knuckled fingers still trembled on the handle. "No. Not a clue. Isn't that right, Edna dear?"

Clive's wife stood a little behind him, stroking the smooth head of the elderly greyhound, which leaned into her leg. Both Edna and the dog still looked rather stunned. Understandably so. A fugitive being chased by the police across one's property wasn't a daily occurrence.

Neither was a visit from said fugitive demanding money.

Clive looked at Felicity warily as she approached. Alex was at her side, Chief Inspector Luscombe not far behind them.

"Mr and Mrs Dingle," began Felicity. Halting, she turned to the uniformed officer. "I hope I'm not interrupting?"

The young policeman promptly folded away his notebook and stared at Felicity in something of an awe-struck manner, his jaw hanging a little loose. "Please, your ladyship. Go ahead."

"Constable Graham—" Chief Inspector Luscombe objected, but Felicity spoke over him. She had come to the nursery with a plan, and she would go through with it.

"What a terrible thing to have just happened," said Felicity, returning her attention to the Dingles. "I saw the chase. All those policemen. You must both be quite shocked."

Edna said nothing. She kept stroking the greyhound.

Clive nodded stiffly. "That's right." He continued to eye Felicity cautiously, but Felicity was unafraid. Indeed, she felt emboldened, especially with the police on site.

"Constable Graham." Chief Inspector Luscombe gestured to the young policeman to approach him. "A word."

The constable's gaze lingered on Felicity before he dashed towards his superior.

Felicity ignored the policemen's disagreement. "My timing might now be inopportune, given the events just witnessed," continued Felicity, addressing the Dingles brightly, "but I've come here to make a purchase."

Edna's shoulders sank with relief.

Clive's expression softened. "You'd like to buy a plant, your ladyship?"

"Absolutely." Felicity smiled. "Might I give you the details of what it is I'm looking for, and you can check if you have such a plant in stock?"

Clive looked to Edna. She nodded encouragingly.

"Of course, your ladyship," said Clive. He sounded more relaxed, even friendly. "What is it you're after?"

"It's a very specific sort of rose I'm after. One with spiral phyllotaxis."

Clive's brow lowered a little.

Edna smiled. "That's a very precise request, your ladyship."

"It should also have reticulate venation." After looking the words up to understand them, Felicity had memorised the terms.

Clive frowned deeply. He gripped the handle of his spade. The sudden change in her husband's mood caused Edna to look worried. The greyhound at her side whined.

Was the ruse already working?

Felicity smiled politely. "I would also like the flower to have pearlisation when in bud form. I hope that's not too much to ask."

"That's a very specific list." Clive's jaw tightened. "Very specific."

"Do you not have such a rose, Mr Dingle?"

Clive said nothing. His grip on the spade tightened further.

"Perhaps they're out of stock," suggested Alex gently. He put a hand on Felicity's arm, encouraging her to step backwards.

"Is that correct, Mr Dingle?" said Felicity. "Are you out of stock?"

Clive mumbled something under his breath.

"Clive, please," said Edna.

Chief Inspector Luscombe and the uniformed officer looked up from their discussion.

Felicity maintained Clive's gaze, but the pressure on her arm from Alex's grip continued.

"You know exactly the kind of rose I'm talking about, though." Felicity was onto something. She wouldn't let go. "Don't you, Mr Dingle?"

"Cici!"

The spade swung so close Felicity felt the rush of air on her cheek as Alex tugged her backwards and down. They tumbled to the ground together.

"No!" cried Edna, but it was too late.

Chief Inspector Luscombe and the young constable rushed forward, each taking an arm. The spade clattered to the ground. Restrained, Clive panted like a wild animal. His whole body shook.

Alex offered his sturdy grip and helped Felicity to her feet. The robust twill of her skirt and jacket had perhaps saved her from a bruise or two, although the periwinkle blue was now streaked with patches of red mud.

"Oh, Clive." Edna sobbed. "What have you done? What have you done?"

"Stay back!" commanded the chief inspector as Edna reached for her husband.

The greyhound whimpered, its tail between its legs.

"Are you all right?" asked Alex, his dark blue gaze earnest, his breathing coming hard.

"Thanks to you, I am." Felicity's heart pounded, at Alex's heroics, at the near miss, at the breakthrough in the case.

Clive's head hung limp.

"Now," said Chief Inspector Luscombe, who was also panting a little. "Which one of you—" He looked between Felicity and Clive. "—is going to tell me what's going on?"

"Mr Dingle?" asked Felicity, clutching her elbow, which was throbbing. Perhaps she would have a bruise after all.

Clive's head continued to hang.

"Oh, Clive," sobbed Edna. "What have you done?"

Felicity pulled a starched white handkerchief from her pocket and offered it to Edna. Edna accepted it with some confusion. Felicity was the reason her husband was in his current predicament, wasn't she?

No. Not the reason. The trigger.

"Mr Dingle, would you like me to explain the situation?" offered Felicity. She had no wish to gloat, but Edna ought perhaps to be spared further discomfort, and Felicity was confident she could explain matters succinctly. "At least as far as I understand it."

Clive mumbled something.

The chief inspector bent over to hear his captive better. "What was that, Mr—"

Clive threw his head up. "I did it!"

Chief Inspector Luscombe glanced for a moment in pure wonder at Felicity. His hardened demeanour returned almost instantly.

Felicity stood a little taller, yet there wasn't much satisfaction to be gained from the police being impressed by what she'd achieved. With Clive hanging limp between the policemen, Edna in tears, and the greyhound trembling at her side, the situation was rather sorrowful.

"What did you do, Mr Dingle?" asked the chief inspector.

"You should tell them, Clive." Edna's voice shook. "No point hiding it now. It's too late for any of that."

"Anthony's roses. Those prize-winning plants." Clive spoke through gritted teeth. "They were my roses. Mine."

Alex threw Felicity a look. Despite the incident with the spade, he was rather proud of her. She could tell.

Chief Inspector Luscombe and the uniformed officer exchanged glances.

The chief inspector wore an expression of something close to amazement. "You fathomed this out by yourself, your ladyship?"

"I found evidence proving Mr Dingle used to work at the Templeton estate," said Felicity, recalling the faded photograph hanging in Leonora's greenhouse. "I learned the plants required years of care and attention to develop into the condition they were in when entered into the competition by Lord Anthony Templeton. But I didn't know for certain Mr Dingle was our man."

Chief Inspector Luscombe gave his head a shake. He was doubtlessly struggling to come to terms with everything that had just happened. "Mr Dingle, you're coming with us to Exeter."

Alex had his notebook out. "If I may put a couple of questions to you on the way to the police van?"

Edna was crying, tears rolling down her cheeks, Felicity's handkerchief gripped tightly in her fist.

Felicity felt relief. Her plan had worked. The guilty man was in custody.

It was over, but it felt nothing like victory.

Chapter Thirty

THE NEXT DAY

The sun was shining, the birds were singing, and Lady Henrietta greeted Felicity with a brilliant smile when she arrived at the outdoor seating area of the Cat and Cream, Lower Diddleton's village inn.

The dowager had chosen a prominent table in full view of the pedestrians, motor vehicles, and horse-drawn carts that bustled up and down the village high street. Her wide-brimmed hat and ankle-length dress with beaded detail were in a fetching shade of lavender, which was quite a bold colour for a woman with mainly Victorian fashion sensibilities.

Lady Henrietta stood up and waved at Felicity as she approached the table. Pip trotted beside Felicity's T-strap shoes, the two of them having enjoyed the walk in the sunshine from Bradley Court with lots of sniffs for Pip and thinking time for Felicity.

At breakfast, she'd pored over that morning's papers. The double arrest of Jacques Gobillot and Clive Dingle dominated the news. Alex's eyewitness scoop had made the evening edition the day before and put the Western Daily News well ahead of the pack.

Alex was still busy reporting, keen to keep the News in the lead, but there was no need for Felicity to join him. She'd returned to her typewriter on her rosewood desk, as there was no longer an excuse to avoid finishing her articles for the Gentlewoman's Gazette.

But the scene that played out at the Dingles' nursery just the day before was still vivid in her mind and proved quite a distraction from her writing.

"How was the meeting?" asked Felicity, as she greeted her grandmother with a kiss on the cheek.

"Oh, splendid. Splendid," said Lady Henrietta, still smiling.

The dowager had attended a session with the Lower Diddleton Plant and Floral Society that morning. Being no longer under suspicion, she'd quickly returned to her usual activities. Felicity's intervention had done the trick. Everything was almost back to normal.

"Very glad to hear it," said Felicity, her smile a little forced as she and her grandmother both offered a polite wave to the vicar passing on the other side of the high street.

Perhaps it was the magazine deadline still hanging over her, but Felicity couldn't quite latch into the celebratory mood.

"I've already ordered cake, sandwiches, and tea for us," assured Lady Henrietta as they both took their seats at the little round table.

"Wonderful," said Felicity. It was gratifying to see her grandmother back in fine form.

Without invitation, Pip sprang onto Lady Henrietta's lap and nestled among the layers of beaded chiffon.

Lady Henrietta stroked the Yorkie's silky back. "The plant and floral society is simply buzzing with chatter about that Dingle fellow," said the dowager in low tones.

"I can imagine," said Felicity. The police had yet to reveal the finer details of their investigation into Clive Dingle, but Felicity had heard his confession at the nursery the day before, and that morning's papers confirmed some of the specifics.

Clive had supplied Anthony Templeton with his prize-winning roses. The plants originated with specimens Clive procured decades ago while employed as a gardener by Leonora and Anthony's parents.

At some point, however, Clive and Anthony's arrangement had taken a dark turn.

"It's abundantly clear they had a falling out," said Lady Henrietta, still speaking quietly. "And that Merton fellow was somehow involved, wouldn't you say?"

"Undoubtedly," agreed Felicity, but whether the flower show judge was involved in the plot from the beginning or stumbled on the truth about Clive and Anthony's roses was yet to be determined. Mr Merton was still unconscious and under guard at the Royal Devon and Exeter. "Let's hope he recovers enough to tell his side of the story."

There was a pause in the discussion as a waitress arrived with a wide tray ladened with tea pots, milk jugs, and china cups.

Lady Henrietta waited patiently as the waitress poured the steaming amber liquid.

"Is it true that the French chap had nothing to do with any of it?" she asked after the waitress left the table.

"His arrest wasn't in relation to the flower show plot," said Felicity, lifting her cup and saucer. "But I believe it's yet to be determined whether he was involved."

Jacques Gobillot must have been at least aware of the conspiracy between Clive and Anthony. Why else would he approach the Dingles for money in his desperate attempt to escape the police when they came to arrest him for desertion?

But whether Jacques was actively involved in the plot was unclear. The Frenchman had confirmed Clive's presence at Mr Shakerley's presentation, but had this been a false alibi? Had Edna also lied about her husband being at Mr Shakerley's talk? What was Blanche Ernault's involvement in all of it? Who was responsible for the sabotage of the Dingles' greenhouse?

And how did everything collapse to the point of Clive doing away with Anthony and attempting to do the same to Mr Merton?

Felicity had to be patient. Chief Inspector Luscombe and his men had everything in hand. She would no doubt read about the solutions to the multiple mysteries in the newspapers over the coming days.

"Oh, splendid." Lady Henrietta clapped her hands with glee as another waitress appeared with a tray brimming with sandwiches, scones, and slices.

"Thank you kindly," said the dowager, her eyes sparkling as she perused the snacks, Pip's little black nose rising above the table's edge to take in the mix of rich scents.

Felicity could relax, though, couldn't she? What more was there for her to do?

She smiled at her grandmother. "Hungry work at the society meeting, was it?"

"My dear girl, you may mock me," said Lady Henrietta with a reproachful glare that warmed Felicity's heart. "But until you have as full a social calendar as I do, you cannot imagine the energy required to remain alert in critical meetings such as the one I attended this morning. I also have an appointment with Mrs Broughton and Mrs Winterpole for the fundraiser for the War Widows and Orphans Relief Fund to attend this afternoon. I need sustenance."

Felicity pushed her eyebrows towards the sweatband of her wide-brimmed hat. She was tempted to ask about Percy but bit her tongue. It was a piece of unfinished business upon which the police's investigation had no bearing, but Lady Henrietta had a right to know that her protégé no longer wished to continue as a professional rose breeder. Should bolder steps be taken in encouraging Percy to come clean?

"It's possible Lady Leonora will contribute to the fundraiser this year," added the dowager with more than a hint of pride.

"Oh," said Felicity with surprise. "That's quite the coup."

Leonora's opinions on Clive's confession and arrest had been missing from the papers. Felicity was naturally curious about the reclusive rose breeder's reaction and had considered telephoning Templeton Manor, but it sounded as though Leonora might appear at Bradley Court soon. Felicity could ask her then.

Pip's neck craned to catch an errant dollop of cream from a scone, but Lady Henrietta returned the confection to its plate before the cream could hit her lap.

"Aha," said the dowager, her smiling gaze snapping towards the high street. "There he is."

Chapter Thirty-One

Felicity's heart fluttered.

Alex was alighting from his Model T on the opposite side of Lower Diddleton's high street to the outdoor tables of the Cat and Cream Inn, where Felicity, Lady Henrietta, and Pip were seated.

He waited for a horse and cart stuffed with farm labourers to trundle by before hurrying towards Felicity and her grandmother, his grey homburg clutched on his head, his well-cut three-piece suit emphasising the elegance of his movements.

"Did you invite Alex, Grandmama?" asked Felicity, frowning with amusement. At times, she rather enjoyed her grandmother's meddling

Lady Henrietta didn't answer. She was on her feet with Pip tucked under her arm. She greeted Alex with a kiss on both cheeks.

Alex dealt with the enthusiastic welcome admirably. As he took a seat at the little table ladened with the inn's finest tea, cakes, and sandwiches, he sneaked a concerned look at Felicity. *What's all this about, exactly?*

"So glad you could make it, Mr Cooper," said the dowager, replacing Pip on her lap, the Yorkie's outstretched nose swinging dangerously close to an almond slice. "You have done an excellent job. A truly excellent job."

"Thank you, your ladyship." Again, Alex flashed a worried look at Felicity. He looked as handsome as always, even with the dark patches under his eyes that indicated he'd spent much of the night following up with the police and writing the news for the early edition.

"I'm simply doing my job, you understand," he added, addressing Lady Henrietta.

"My grandmother was extremely pleased to read yesterday evening's edition," explained Felicity.

Seeing the headline *Rose Breeder Arrested In Connection With Flower Show Conspiracy* had inspired Lady Henrietta to attend that morning's plant and floral society meeting. Alex had truly done an excellent job of writing up everything thoroughly and promptly — and without foregrounding Felicity's involvement, as per her preference.

Alex took off his hat. "Aha," he said, the brim tight in his grip. "I, um..." It was unlike him to be stuck for words. "I'm afraid I have little time to spare. I'm rather hard-pressed with deadlines and so forth. I should like to have a word with your granddaughter in private, if I may."

Alex's tone made Felicity uneasy.

The dowager picked up on it, too. She drew in her chin. "What about?"

"Of course." Felicity was already out of her seat and on the move. She didn't want her grandmother's upbeat mood ruined. "I shall be back soon."

"Felicity, sit back down. Mr Cooper, I insist you speak frankly." It was too late. Lady Henrietta was worried. Hopefully unnecessarily.

Alex gave Felicity an apologetic look. She shook her head. They should have known better than an attempt to treat the dowager with kid gloves.

"Whatever you have to share, you may share it with us both," insisted Lady Henrietta. Pip sat alert on her lap, his ears pricked towards Alex.

Alex continued to grip his hat. "Very well." His gaze met Felicity's. "I wanted to stop by and tell you myself."

"Tell me what?" Felicity's chest felt tight.

"It's about the investigation, isn't it?" Lady Henrietta's voice had a wobble to it.

Alex nodded. "Luscombe is tight-lipped, but I have my sources. Clive Dingle's admitted the attack on Ronald Merton."

Felicity raised her eyebrows. In her own version of events, she'd imagined Anthony's assistants to have been responsible for harming Mr Merton. She'd seen them herself in Bickleford at the time of the incident.

"The filthy swine," muttered Lady Henrietta.

"But Clive insists it was an accident."

Felicity narrowed her eyes. "An accident?" Her assumptions were turning out to be rather wrong.

Alex nodded. "I don't yet have all the details, but it sounds like Jacques and Clive have been talking openly to the police. They both say there was some kind of falling out between everyone involved in the flower show con after Anthony was killed."

"Well, that's quite clear," said Lady Henrietta, picking up her scone.

Alex fixed Felicity with a serious gaze. "But Clive Dingle insists he didn't harm Anthony Templeton."

Felicity felt suddenly cold. "Clive says he's not the murderer?"

The dowager paused the lifting of her scone.

"And Jacques is sticking with his alibi for Clive at Mr Shakerley's talk," continued Alex. "Edna, too."

"But Clive confessed," said Felicity. "I heard it myself, as did you."

Alex shook his head. "His confession was for the attack on Mr Merton and for his involvement in the swindle with the roses, but he refuses to take responsibility for the death of Anthony Templeton." Alex looked at Lady Henrietta, his eyes full of regret. "I'm sorry."

Lady Henrietta blinked, confused. She seemed not to have followed all that Alex had said. Her scone once again returned to its plate. Pip whined, frustrated.

"Mr Merton, then?" Felicity asked quickly, before her grandmother had a chance to despair. "Was he part of the con? He could have done for Anthony, couldn't he?"

Alex shook his head. "The police have been extremely thorough in collecting witness statements. They've found a chain of workers from the flower show who all remember seeing Merton waiting outside the back of the first aid tent, looking rather agitated. The timings match up with the period in which Anthony was killed."

"You mean to say—" Lady Henrietta was just cottoning on.

"Blanche Ernault, then?" Felicity was becoming desperate.

Alex looked grave. "Apparently, she wasn't involved or even aware of the swindle. At least Jacques won't confirm it and she won't admit to it. It's not a thoroughly solid alibi, but a few reporters have vouched for speaking to her at the Champs Verts stand around the time of Anthony's death."

The bells of Lower Diddleton's church rang the hour.

Alex placed his hat back on his head. "I'm sorry. I really have to go." He stood up. "I thought you'd want to hear it first, before it reaches the papers."

Felicity nodded. "Thank you," she said rather automatically. She and her grandmother sat in silence as Alex returned to his motor. The blood had drained from Lady Henrietta's cheeks.

It wasn't over. Whoever did for Lord Anthony Templeton was still at large.

"Oh, dear," said the dowager quietly, all trace of her earlier cheer gone from her features. "I've made a fool of myself, haven't I?"

Felicity scooted closer to her grandmother and took her hand. "Absolutely not," she said, sounding confident despite a rising sense of dread.

"I thought I was in the clear," continued Lady Henrietta as Pip, with the best of intentions, tried to lick her face.

Felicity wrestled the Yorkie off her grandmother's lap and stroked him into submission on her own. "You've always been in the clear," said Felicity firmly, though she knew it made little difference to external perceptions on the matter.

"Oh, dear. Oh." Lady Henrietta dropped her head into her hand. "I'm feeling rather queer."

Societal exclusion wasn't the end of the world. Felicity herself knew what it was to rise above negative perceptions. But it pained Felicity to see her grandmother suffer. It pained her greatly.

Felicity squeezed her grandmother's hand. "Let's get you back to Bradley Court," she said, "and settle you down with a nice mug of cocoa."

"Oh, Felicity, dear," said Lady Henrietta. "I don't like to think of you wasting your time looking after me. Shouldn't you be writing your articles?"

"Yes, Grandmama," said Felicity, her decision about what to do next already made. "But there's something I need to work on first."

Chapter Thirty-Two

Felicity's two-seater Alvis could be a little conspicuous, so she parked at the edge of Exeter's city centre and walked the remaining distance to Waterbeer Street in the warm summer air. Opposite the main entrance of the Devon County Constabulary's turreted headquarters, Felicity took up the perusal of rings, necklaces, and bracelets in a jeweller's window on the opposite side of the street.

Wearing a wide picture hat in the same pale mint green as her drop-waisted dress with a lace-overlay, Felicity used the reflection of the window to observe the headquarters' main entrance without her presence being noticed by any of the policemen.

Time passed to the point of Felicity feeling rather peckish, but she couldn't leave her post. She mustn't miss her chance. Indeed, she needed several fortuitous opportunities to align for her plan to work.

Then she saw her.

Edna Dingle, her shoulders hunched, came out through the big swing doors. With her eyes puffy from crying and her cheeks gaunt with worry, she wore a battered cotton blazer in faded brown over her usual pinafore. Her masculine flat cap had been swapped for a simple felt cloche.

Crucially, Edna was alone.

Blinking in the sunshine, Edna stopped outside the police

headquarters and looked up and down the street. Considering the dedication needed to run a flower nursery, Exeter city centre was likely not Edna's usual territory, but Felicity couldn't rush in. She had to bide her time.

Having gathered her bearings, Edna set off with her head down.

Felicity waited before leaving her position outside the jewellers, allowing Edna to be a few yards ahead of her before following on the opposite side of the road.

As expected, Edna crossed the road and joined Felicity's pavement. She was likely heading for a bus stop on the city's main thoroughfare that would take her towards the nursery, where the tired old greyhound was no doubt eagerly awaiting his mistress' return.

Pulling the brim of her hat down to obscure her face, Felicity caught up with Edna before she turned onto the high street.

"Mrs Dingle." Felicity didn't need to raise her voice. She'd edged close enough without being noticed.

Edna twisted, surprised. She attempted to speed away from Felicity, but Felicity kept pace and continued addressing Edna without causing a scene.

"Mrs Dingle, please. I should like to speak to you. I wish to apologise."

Edna hurried onto Goldsmith Street. She was indeed heading for the steady flow of buses on the main thoroughfare.

Felicity uttered a silent oath and sped up. Upon rounding the corner, she came to a sudden halt.

Edna had stopped in the middle of the pavement. She wore a tight, angry frown, her rough hands balled at her sides.

"Mrs Dingle," said Felicity a little breathlessly. "Really. I would like to say I'm sorry."

"Sorry for what, your ladyship?" Edna's words were clipped, but her tone was sad.

"What happened at your nursery yesterday with your husband was my fault."

Edna's jaw tightened. "No. It wasn't." There was no trace of denial in her tone. Had Edna accepted what her husband had done? Did Felicity have a way in?

"Would you be able to explain to me why that is?" continued Felicity. "I do so blame myself for what occurred yesterday. If you have the time to spare to talk to me, I should be awfully grateful. I'm keen to understand matters. Not for the newspaper, of course. It's just I fear I took action without a good grasp of all the facts."

Felicity's appeal was genuine. Would Edna perceive it that way?

Edna glanced over her shoulder towards the buses on the high street. She looked out of place in the city and seemed desperate to get away.

"We could talk in my motor, if you'd like," offered Felicity. "I'd be happy to run you home. Or there's a very comfortable tea house not far from here, if you'd be willing to sit with me."

Edna blinked at Felicity. Was she considering the offer?

Felicity took a step forward. If this first piece didn't fit into place, the rest of her plan would collapse. "Please, Mrs Dingle. Can you help me understand?"

Chapter Thirty-Three

Felicity was a frequent visitor to Lyons tea house. It was the cosiest in all of Exeter and she often went there for tea and a bun with Alex. Despite most of the tables being busy, the friendly staff were happy to find a private booth with shining wood panelling and blue velvet seating in which to settle Felicity and Edna with no delay.

Although there was no one within earshot, Edna continued to look uneasy until a tray of delights arrived at their table. Felicity didn't speak too much as Edna sipped her coffee, only eyeing the sweets at first. Then she nibbled on a biscuit. One biscuit became another, and she soon started on the slices. Whether through her worries about her husband or something else, it was possible Edna hadn't eaten in a while.

"Your husband," began Felicity. "He used to work for the Templetons, didn't he?"

Edna nodded. She washed a bite of petticoat tail down with a sip of coffee. "It was a long time ago, and he wasn't there long. He was young at the time. Young and rather foolish." The hint of a smile flickered over her lips. "We met not long after. He showed me the roses he'd taken when he left the Templetons. I told him to get rid of them, but he never did. They were his pride and joy. He never dared enter them into any competition, in case it was discovered that they came from stolen stock." Edna was evidently not in denial about her husband's guilt when it came to the roses.

Felicity sipped her tea. "He obviously took excellent care of the plants, even if he was wrong to take them. He bred with them, didn't he?"

Edna's smile returned briefly. She averted her eyes. "He was a very talented breeder, your ladyship. Gifted, some might say. But it takes more than that to build a successful nursery. It's not just hard work or even talent that does it."

Felicity tipped her head. "What else is needed?"

Edna poured herself another coffee. "People like a story behind things." She dropped a lump of sugar into the dark liquid. "Or a character. Two hardworking rose growers aren't enough. It has to be someone from the continent or a war veteran or a titled—" Edna stopped. "Apologies, your ladyship."

"No offence taken." Felicity was simply glad Edna was willing to speak to her. "Your husband wasn't in the war?"

Edna frowned. "He couldn't pass the physical exam."

Felicity was surprised. "Mr Dingle looks like a hardy man capable of much physical work." He certainly knew how to wield a spade.

"Oh, that he is, your ladyship."

Felicity might have probed further into what had prevented Clive from becoming a soldier, but she couldn't take for granted that Edna would stay for longer than her cup of coffee lasted.

"How did your husband meet Lord Anthony Templeton?"

Edna stared down at her drink. "He visited us a couple of years ago. He made an appointment claiming to be a client. When he arrived, he soon revealed who he was, and the conversation turned to his intentions to enter the Bickleford Rose Festival and his need for plants." Edna shifted uncomfortably. "When Clive told him we had Templeton stock, he was over the moon."

"Were you involved in the discussions?"

"No, but Clive informed me afterwards."

"What was your advice to him?"

Edna's shoulders tightened. "My Clive has a will of his own, your ladyship."

"But you advised him to steer clear?"

There was a silence. "I didn't like the fellow, but he promised sums of money we could only dream of." Edna stared at her coffee cup. "Looking back, we were foolish, but at the time, how could we have said no?"

Money had been the topic of the heated discussion between Clive and Jacques that Felicity and Alex had overheard at the Dingles' nursery before the police arrived. Had it been the source of the dispute between Clive and Mr Merton in the medieval rose garden? And between Anthony and whoever did away with him?

"Could you tell me how the whole affair worked, Mrs Dingle?"

Edna eyed Felicity warily for a moment. "It was the three of them. Templeton, Merton, and my Clive. Clive supplied the roses. Merton ensured the plants didn't face any difficulty in terms of the judging. And Templeton was there for the glory."

"Mr Merton was in on the scheme?"

Edna nodded. "They needed an insider at the association because they run checks on the nurseries," continued Edna. "Templeton had a nursery, but it would have been clear to anyone visiting he hadn't grown the roses himself."

Felicity shook her head a little. "Anthony Templeton employed a gardener, though, didn't he? What was Monsieur Gobillot's role, then?"

"Oh, he was just caring for the plants and creating more of them for sale from Templeton's nursery. Champs Verts, I think Templeton called it. A French name, isn't it? He lived in France for a fair while, didn't he?"

Felicity nodded. "What about the other assistant?"

"The French woman you mean?" Edna blinked. "I never saw her with the plants, to be honest. Not till the day of the show."

Felicity was trying to hold the threads of the narrative in the correct order. Without a notebook to scribble in, it was difficult, but talking to a witness like Edna without taking notes created less distance. It gave Felicity more access.

"So Anthony Templeton was at the centre of it all, with Mr Dingle and Mr Merton closely involved," summarised Felicity. "You said Anthony offered your husband money. Did he pay Mr Merton, too?"

Edna swallowed. "I know nothing about that, your ladyship. But as soon as Templeton was gone, Merton tried to blackmail us. Said he'd tell the police about the whole arrangement if we didn't pay him."

"Goodness," said Felicity. The injured show judge was proving to be quite a slippery character.

"He wanted money," continued Edna, "but he didn't need it like we did. Nasty, greedy man. He just wanted to spend it on clothes or a motor or wax for his moustache. Clive went to meet him to tell him to leave us alone. He only pushed him. He didn't mean to hurt him. He didn't mean for him to fall over." Tears welled in Edna's eyes. "I've always tried to help my Clive get his temper under control, but he can still lash out sometimes. He's been dealing with so much."

"I'm sure you're an enormous support to your husband," said Felicity soothingly, although it was hard to be entirely convinced that Clive Dingle meant Mr Merton no harm. Being blackmailed could prompt extreme reactions, and Felicity could still recall the gush of air on her cheek from when Clive swung the spade at her.

She gazed calmly at Edna for a moment. "Was it your husband that did the damage to your greenhouse?"

Edna grimaced. She looked to be in pain. "I know it's not right to lie, your ladyship, but Clive was so angry. He didn't mean to do it."

That was one part of the puzzle resolved. The destroyed greenhouse hadn't been sabotaged at all.

"It seems like Anthony Templeton's sudden demise put a number of people in quite desperate situations," said Felicity, doing her best to sound sympathetic. "I hope you don't mind me asking this, but to what extent were you involved yourself in the whole flower show affair?"

Edna shook her head hard. "I wasn't, your ladyship. Not till the end. The day you visited for the first time, I'd thrown all those blasted plants on a bonfire. I suppose I'd known all along what was going on, but I'd tried to ignore it. When Templeton met his end, I knew there'd be trouble. I was trying to erase any trace of it ever having happened. Pointless, really. Trouble always catches up with you, doesn't it?"

"Your actions are understandable," said Felicity gently. "Especially if you had your doubts about it all from the very beginning."

Edna sniffed. "It was so much work and so much risk, and there's no money for anyone now. My goodness, your ladyship, we were so silly. We were counting on Templeton and his money to answer all our prayers. But look at us now." She held out empty palms. "Look what we've got to show for it. Even before the scoundrel passed, there was money he'd promised, and we never saw a penny. Not a single penny. He told us after the show he'd have sales and we'd get a cut. He had a whole business plan. But that's never going to happen now, is it?"

"May I ask why you needed the money so badly?" Felicity spoke carefully. She didn't want Edna walking away yet, but she needed answers.

Edna dabbed at her eyes with the corner of a napkin. "It starts with a tremble in the hands, then it works through the body. It runs in the family, your ladyship. Clive's father was young when he passed from it."

Felicity understood what Edna was talking about. Her stomach felt suddenly heavy with sadness. "I'm so very sorry, Mrs Dingle."

The shaking palsy could ravage a person quickly. Felicity had noticed the tremble in Clive's hands but put it down to nerves and emotion. His illness didn't excuse anything Clive had done, but it explained the desperation with which he'd pursued the illicit money offered by Anthony.

"Was Clive already having difficulty working when Anthony Templeton paid you a visit?"

Edna nodded. "We might only have another season left, and I

can't run the nursery on my own." She sniffed. "The police asked my Clive again and again if he did for Templeton, but why would he? Even with his temper, Clive needed the money he promised us. We needed it."

It was a compelling argument in the defence of not just Clive but also Mr Merton. They were both motivated by money. Why do away with the potential source of it? Especially directly after Anthony had won the Best in Show prize.

Edna rested her head in her hands. "We still need the money, but we'll never see it now, will we?"

As the picture became clearer, Felicity chastised herself a little. She'd jumped too fast into looking at alibis without considering motives. The question still stood — why do away with Anthony?

"Do you have any idea why Anthony Templeton wished so much to win at Bickleford?" asked Felicity. "In his acceptance speech, it sounded as though he had no respect for the rose association, yet he clearly went to a great deal of effort to win Best in Show."

Edna shook her head adamantly. "I couldn't say, your ladyship. I stayed away from the man as much as I could. I wasn't keen on his character."

Felicity had barely known Anthony, but she could sympathise with the sentiment.

"When he gave that speech," continued Edna, "my heart sank. I think it was then that I realised he wasn't serious about making money. He was only interested in humiliation. In dominating and humiliating everyone involved in the show. I asked my Clive, what do we do now? But he wasn't critical of him. He only said, if you'd known his father, Edna, you'd understand it."

"Anthony's father? The late Lord Templeton?"

Edna nodded. "Clive wouldn't say any more on it."

Leonora had alluded to a painful upbringing. There was the con, the promise of money, the stolen and misrepresented roses. But what if that was all a distraction? What if there was something else at the heart of it?

"Mrs Dingle, who do you think did for Anthony Templeton?"

Edna stared down at her coffee. "I know Templeton got people passionate, but I didn't know him or his situation well enough to even guess. All I know for a fact is that my Clive didn't do it. He has a temper, but he's not silly. And that's all I know for certain."

Got people passionate.

Passionate.

That's how the police had described the deadly act that had done for Anthony.

"I'd like to go home now, your ladyship," said Edna.

"Of course," said Felicity.

Felicity tried to insist on taking Edna in her motor, but Edna was adamant about taking the bus. She was grateful for the food and drink at the tea house but perhaps also desperate for a break from Felicity's questioning.

Felicity was thankful for Edna's honesty, in as far as a woman gravely concerned for her ill husband and her own future could be considered fully objective. Gaping holes in the story remained, however, although a plug for the gaps was within reach.

As Felicity swung open the door to the head office of the Western Daily News, she was surprised but also delighted to find Alex on the other side, preparing to leave the building.

"Are you busy?" asked Felicity.

"A classic Lady Felicity greeting," said Alex with a smile. "And from the look in your eyes, it wouldn't matter if I were. Where are we going?"

Felicity had already turned and was striding back out onto Exeter's high street. "We're taking my motor."

Chapter Thirty-Four

The drive to Champs Verts Nursery wasn't a matter of blasting along well-known roads. It was a quest into an adjoining county, where the green hills were often steeper and came more quickly one after the other than those in Devon. The time at which Felicity and Alex had set off from Exeter also meant the run home would be in the dark.

But there was no putting it off. The investigation into Anthony Templeton's demise had dragged on long enough.

Felicity used the drive to fill Alex in on what she'd learned from Edna Dingle. He'd heard similar updates from his police contacts, although not the part about Clive's illness.

Alex winced. "Rather explains his desperate actions."

In anticipation of an approaching incline, Felicity selected a lower gear. "It doesn't excuse them, though."

"Absolutely not." Alex flicked through his notebook. "Although Edna Dingle and Jacques Gobillot won't budge from their claim that Clive was with them at the talk."

"Are the police convinced he's in the clear for Anthony's murder?"

"I'd say so. It's as Edna told you. If the Dingles needed the money from Anthony's roses, how would doing away with the fellow help?"

The Alvis' engine clattered under the strain of the hill.

"Any news on Blanche Ernault?" asked Felicity.

Alex flicked back through his notebook. "The police found a couple more alibis for her. Customers who bought plants from the Champs Verts stand as Mr Shakerley's presentation was getting started."

Felicity sighed. "Which is both a relief and a disappointment."

"A relief because we're not on our way to interview a murderer?"

"And a disappointment for much the same reason."

At the top of the hill, Felicity stopped the Alvis to allow a farmer with a shotgun and a spaniel to cross the road.

Accelerating again, Felicity crunched the gears. She tutted at herself. "If we only look at the alibis," she said, "then everyone is innocent. Havelock. Mr Merton. Clive Dingle." Felicity shot a look at Alex. "What are we missing?"

"Do you doubt the police's methods?"

"Of course not," said Felicity. "If the alibis are studied carefully enough, the answer will be in there somewhere."

Alex smiled. "But you're convinced there's a quicker way of getting to the truth?"

Felicity didn't respond. She wasn't better than the police. She'd made mistakes. Perhaps she was still making them. Because even with the Best in Show swindle laid bare, there was still a huge piece missing from the puzzle.

Why do away with Anthony Templeton?

Although Alex was an expert interpreter of the Bartholomew's half-inch map laid over his lap, Felicity had to bring the Alvis to a standstill so that they could ask a young man on a bicycle for directions. The result was a turn in the road, the two-seater's headlamps nudging into the hedging. They'd driven past the nursery's entrance.

Passing the droop of unkempt beech trees that obscured a recently painted but modest sign announcing that this was indeed the way to Champs Verts Nursery, Felicity guided the Alvis along a winding, mossy drive until a dilapidated Georgian villa came into view.

The window frames were peeling, and the curtains were mainly closed. The door that was perhaps originally black was now a patchy charcoal-grey. A beautiful yet overgrown combination of roses and wisteria scrambled up the off-white facade. Grass pushed up through the gravel before the entrance steps. Beyond the house were rows of boxy, thin-framed greenhouses where maybe an elegant garden once lay.

The decay at Champs Verts wasn't recent. Neither was it aligned with the preened appearance Lord Anthony Templeton had presented at the flower show in his pinstripe suit with a rose in his lapel and an oily smile.

There was much the man had been hiding.

Alex adjusted his homburg and gazed at the house's crumbling facade. "Looks like there's no one home."

Felicity was already climbing the steps. "We have to try," she said, tugging on the doorbell. The handle creaked, and the bell sounded dull, but it was loud enough.

Stepping back, she looked up at the house and sighed. It had been a long drive, and it would be the same again to get back to Devon. Might Blanche have disappeared like Jacques had attempted to? Or perhaps even left with the police's blessing, as in the case of the music-hall singer Mr Etty?

Felicity went back to the doorbell, took the handle, and paused. A sagging, discoloured curtain twitched beside the entrance.

"Madame Ernault?" Felicity raised her voice to speak through the door. "May we speak with you, Madame Ernault?"

There was only the sound of wind through the trees.

Alex joined Felicity at the entrance. He looked intrigued but also concerned. Alex was courageous but preferred not to dash headlong into danger if it could be avoided.

"Madame Ernault, please," continued Felicity, her mouth close to the door. "Everyone knows about the roses. About where they really came from. Perhaps you can supply some context for what happened. To balance out the damage done to your employer's reputation."

Anthony Templeton's standing was on the verge of being unsalvageable, but appealing to Blanche's dedication to her master might work.

The house remained silent.

Alex shook his head.

Felicity wouldn't give up. "You knew 'Monsieur Fox' better than anyone. Can you help us understand him? Perhaps we can help others understand him, too."

Felicity stepped back and watched the windows.

There was no further movement.

"We've done our best," said Alex, who'd given up valuable reporting time for the jaunt to Dorset without complaining.

He reached for Felicity's hand. "Let's go."

Felicity gripped Alex's palm. Her stomach felt tight. She was running out of options. "We had to try," she breathed as she went with Alex towards the motor.

Creak!

Felicity stopped and turned.

The door to the villa had opened.

Chapter Thirty-Five

At the back of the dilapidated villa, French doors in a faded salon opened onto a terrace with weeds blossoming between cracked paving stones. Felicity swept a hand over the wrought iron seat before sitting. Alex tested the sturdiness of his rusting chair before lowering his weight onto it.

The sunshine warming the terrace was soft and golden, but the glass of the nearby greenhouses didn't sparkle like it did at the Dingles'. The structures were purely practical, without the ornate flourish of Leonora's Rosarium, and the arrangement of the plants had less heart to it than Percy's approach.

But the roses were undeniably beautiful.

The blooms were big but didn't droop, their leaves shiny and vibrant green. Their perfume carried subtly through the greenhouse's open vents, but the scent of the flowers was masked somewhat by cigarette smoke.

"I've been watering them."

Blanche was seated on the other side of the rusty terrace table to Felicity and Alex. Between drags on her cigarette, her deep-set eyes flicked to the greenhouses.

"I did not know what else to do."

In a crisply cut dark blue jacket and skirt, a pearl necklace, and an elegant chignon, Blanche held herself upright with grace.

"Without Jacques," she said, "I cannot care for and sell the flowers." She tutted. "Such a foolish boy."

Based on the encounter in the tea garden, it wasn't surprising to hear Blanche speak unkindly about Jacques. There was, however, a hint of regret in her tone. Did she miss his companionship or just his ability to care for the plants?

"You weren't involved with the flowers at all?" asked Felicity.

Alex was writing in his notebook. Though slow to come to the door, Blanche wished to talk to the paper, although Alex had insisted that Felicity take the lead with the questioning. She had, after all, convinced Blanche to open the door.

"I told you already. I told the police, too. That was all for Monsieur Fox—" Blanche continued to use Anthony Templeton's pseudonym. "—and for Jacques to take care of. I knew nothing about this so-called con. I don't know enough about flowers to understand anything."

Felicity nodded. It was natural to distance oneself from wrongdoing. It was so far unclear what the legal repercussions would be for cheating the flower competition. Considering this, could Blanche's testimony be taken at face value? Might it still be useful even if it couldn't?

"You understand the nature of it now, however," suggested Felicity.

Blanche hesitated before nodding. "The police have told me things. I can fill in the gaps myself. I saw Monsieur Merton and Monsieur Dingle here on several occasions." Blanche's painted eyebrows drew together. She looked sad. Perhaps even angry.

"To what extent do you believe Jacques was involved in the con?" asked Felicity. The information perhaps wasn't relevant to unravelling the mystery of Anthony Templeton's demise, but Blanche's answer could help as a bellwether for how seriously her responses could be taken.

The Frenchwoman's forehead creased more deeply. "Jacques was not here for the right reasons. He didn't care about Monsieur Fox. He cared only about the money. But did he know what was really happening?" She lifted her shoulders. "Maybe. The only certain thing is that he was taking care of himself and no one else."

It was a more even-handed response than Felicity had expected. "I'm under the impression," she continued carefully, "that your employer promised several people money that they never received. Might you know anything about that?"

Blanche pulled on her cigarette. "I would not know, your ladyship. I was not here for the money." She lifted her chin with pride. "I am here because I cared for Monsieur Fox. It's why I wish to speak to you. To the newspaper." Her voice trembled. "In his memory."

Blanche seemed less sure of herself than in Bickleford's tea garden. Had the unravelling of the con affected her confidence in Anthony Templeton? Might she say more than she'd previously been willing?

Felicity left a pause before asking, "What do you think drove Monsieur Fox to cheat at the competition?"

"I told you already. The last time we met. He wanted to make his family proud. 'If only my father could see this.' That is what he said"

Felicity recalled Leonora's words. *Our parents weren't the easiest of people. Our father in particular.* Blanche had misunderstood the motivation behind Anthony's words. The assistant didn't have access to the hidden depths of 'Monsieur Fox'.

"Thinking back to the speech your employer gave during the prize ceremony," said Felicity. "The British Rose Association was an institution his father cared a great deal about. It was established by one of the Templeton's ancestors. How would the things Monsieur Fox said that day make his father proud, do you think?"

Blanche paused, smoke lifting from her cigarette. "Monsieur Fox was a man of emotion. If someone is angry one time, does it mean they are always angry?" Even if she'd not been Anthony's confidante, Blanche was clearly extremely loyal.

Felicity gave an understanding smile. "How long were you with Monsieur Fox?"

"More than twenty years."

Alex nodded, impressed.

Felicity raised her eyebrows. "I imagine you saw him through good times and bad."

"Oh, yes. I have been there. I have cleared up the pieces. Many times I have done this."

Felicity cocked her head. "The pieces of what?"

"It is often the same story with a man of such handsomeness and charm, no?"

Felicity fought the urge to wince. Anthony may have been considered handsome, but in terms of charm, he had been severely lacking.

"And what story is that?" she asked.

Blanche struck a match, lit another cigarette, and leaned back in her chair. "He was a breaker of hearts. I cannot tell you how many times." She sounded almost proud. "Sometimes they would come to me in tears. I would say, what did you expect? That you could keep such a man all for yourself?"

Blanche seemed amused, and Felicity continued to smile along, but it was a dark tale. A woman misled and taken advantage of could end up in serious difficulty in the current era, let alone in previous decades.

Was this the reason Anthony had left home all those years ago? Had he been a philanderer even at a young age? Leonora would likely never speak so bluntly about her brother's issues.

Blanche drew on her cigarette. Her face turned serious. "It is as I told the police. My first thought was that a woman did for him. This was the passion Monsieur Fox could create. Such women can become unreasonable."

Felicity's stomach tightened. "Are you aware of such a woman being present at Bickleford Rose Festival?"

Blanche lifted her shoulders. "No, but then I did not watch Monsieur Fox every hour of every day. I didn't keep a record of all his relationships."

"I see," said Felicity, shooting Alex a look of concern. From his frown, she could tell he was thinking the same.

What if Anthony's speech wasn't the trigger for the attack that ended his life? What if the murderer had nothing to do with rose breeding at all? Any one of the women at Bickleford Rose Festival might be the guilty party.

Did Felicity's investigation have to restart from scratch?

Felicity remained quiet and thoughtful as the interview was rounded off with a few questions from Alex about what Blanche planned to do next — she didn't yet know — and what would happen to the roses in the rickety-looking greenhouses.

Blanche had contacted the rose association for advice on what to do with the plants, but she'd heard nothing back. It was understandable. Colonel Bolt had seemed busy before but would now be under untold pressure since the accusations about Mr Merton's involvement in the swindle.

Blanche cleared her throat as Felicity and Alex stood up from the table. "You might do me a favour?"

Felicity was still rather numb from Blanche's revelations about Anthony Templeton being a seducer.

Alex responded. "What is it?"

"I would appreciate some eggs and some bread from the village." Blanche kept her chin held high. "I'm so tired of walking."

Jacques had fled with the van. With her employer deceased, Blanche had been abandoned. Was she to be pitied?

Alex nodded. "Of course."

It would add time to their journey and further delay to the turning in of his copy, yet it was the right thing to do. Felicity loved Alex for his approach in such situations, but she was quiet as they returned to the Alvis.

"You'd have preferred I turned her request down?" asked Alex. "I realise I'm not the one doing the driving."

"It's not that," said Felicity as they got into the motor and shut the doors.

"What is it then?" asked Alex.

Felicity's mind was whirring with everything she'd heard from Blanche, from Edna, from Leonora, from everyone to whom she'd spoken.

Was her investigation really back to the beginning?

What had she missed?

Felicity bit her lip.

Chapter Thirty-Six

THE NEXT DAY

"But... But what is it you will do over there?"

Lady Henrietta's words hung in the air of the little drawing room of Mrs Broughton's cottage. On the lap of the dowager's smoky-purple dress, Pip was squished into the generous layers of satin as Lady Henrietta stroked the Yorkie heavy handedly, distracted and rather concerned by the matters being discussed.

Felicity sat beside her grandmother, a cup and saucer with a fern motif almost brought to her lips for a sip.

It was finally happening.

"I should just like to see what comes my way," said Percy, somewhat apologetically. He was seated across the little tea table from Lady Henrietta in a brown two-button suit. He'd attempted to look smart for the luncheon, although his reddish-brown hair was always a little dishevelled.

Lady Henrietta frowned, as though she couldn't understand. "But where will you go?"

It was painful to see the dowager upset, but the situation came as a relief. And it had happened with no prompting besides Felicity throwing some serious glances in Percy's direction and a whispered *Will you tell her?* when her grandmother went to powder her nose.

Given the stalling of her investigation into Anthony Templeton's demise, Felicity felt oddly satisfied with the development.

Percy sighed. He looked pained. "The police said they're happy for me to travel as long as I keep them informed of my whereabouts. At least till this whole investigation business is finished."

Mrs Broughton glanced wide-eyed between Lady Henrietta and Percy. She'd done her best to make the luncheon a special affair. Having decorated the table with elaborate doilies, she'd chosen to wear a puff-sleeved floral frock with white lace trims, which made it difficult to say where the hostess ended and the table began.

Mrs Broughton's generous intention had been to distract Lady Henrietta from her misfortunes by holding a preparatory meeting for the war widows and orphans' fundraiser over lunch at her cottage on the edge of the village. The meal had gone swimmingly until dessert was served, although Felicity had to take some of the blame. Felicity had only confirmed to Mrs Broughton that she'd attend the lunch upon hearing Percy would also be there.

"It's a brave and admirable move, Percy," said Felicity, referring more to his announcement to Lady Henrietta than to his decision to leave England for the continent.

"Y-yes," offered Mrs Broughton gingerly. "Quite brave."

Percy smiled weakly at Felicity across the plates of uneaten strawberry fool. "Thank you."

"But what of your roses?" Lady Henrietta's tone implied she didn't agree one bit with Felicity's sentiment. "What of your mother's cottage?"

Percy nodded, his eyes in his lap. "I've let the British Rose Association know in case anyone would like to take over the breeding and propagating. The cottage would be for whoever would like to continue with the roses." He looked up. "Perhaps turn it into a proper nursery."

"That's it?" Lady Henrietta grimaced. "That's as far as you wish to take your mother's memory?"

Mrs Broughton looked frightened. "Yes, you must think of your mother," she offered, echoing the dowager.

Felicity kept quiet. Her grandmother had been awfully close to Pamela Colhayne, but did that outweigh Percy Colhayne's own desires?

Percy glanced up from his lap. "Yes, it's as far as I can go." He sounded calm. "I'd like to think I've done all I can to lay Mother's memory to rest."

Lady Henrietta looked with disbelief at her protégé. "But what about next year?" Her tone was forthright. "It could be a new start. Another chance at Best in Show." The dowager wouldn't give up easily.

Mrs Broughton leaned towards Felicity, her eyes still wide and fearful. She smelled of violet perfume. "Might I have a word with you in private before you and your grandmother leave?" she asked quietly.

"Of course," said Felicity. "If it doesn't take too long."

With Alex busy reporting on an armed robbery, and with her most recent thinking on the Anthony Templeton case not yet fully cooked, Felicity had been trying to re-concentrate on her articles for the Gentlewoman's Gazette. The already postponed deadline was only days away, and accompanying her grandmother to Mrs Broughton's luncheon had been an ad hoc interruption, albeit an important one.

"You're throwing away your talent, Percival," continued the dowager.

"Lady Felicity?" Mrs Broughton looked nervous, but hopeful. She eyed the doorway to the cottage's little entrance hall. "Might we?"

"Now?" hissed Felicity. She hoped to witness her grandmother at least accepting Percy's decision, even if the dowager could never agree with it.

Mrs Broughton nodded with some urgency.

"Very well." Felicity went to stand up, but there was a knock at the cottage door.

Mrs Broughton looked deflated. Her private discussion with Felicity would have to wait.

As the maid went to answer the knock, Mrs Broughton stood and went to the drawing room door.

Percy's gaze had wandered to the window under which the luncheon table was positioned, where Mrs Broughton's hollyhocks danced amidst colourful phlox. "I should like to think I might use my talent elsewhere. A return to painting, perhaps."

Felicity's grandmother had moved past her despair, at least. She seemed to be fuming. "Think about all those years of effort. Not just yours, my boy, but your mother's efforts as well."

There was no point blaming the romantic, easily distractible young man for the pain the dowager was feeling. Lady Henrietta had to take responsibility for putting too much of her hope and energy into Percy's situation. He had his own issues to deal with, after all. Everyone did.

"Perhaps you can help find a new tenant for Percy's cottage, Grandmama?" suggested Felicity, eager to ease the situation if she could. "Someone with a true passion for roses?"

Lady Henrietta gave Felicity a glare. This wasn't the direction in which her grandmother wished to take the discussion.

Mrs Broughton reappeared at the table. She had with her a small envelope.

"It's for you, Lady Felicity," said Mrs Broughton, handing the envelope over. "Those new people at the post office don't miss a trick, do they? How did they know you were here, I wonder?"

Felicity smiled at Mrs Broughton as she opened the envelope. "I believe there's a decent view of all the comings and goings in the village from the post office window." But when her eyes fell upon the text of the telegraphed message, she felt her cheeks grow pale.

To: Lady Felicity Quick
Bradley Court
Devon, England

From: Aboard SS Silvercrest
En route to New York

Date: June 21, 1922

APOLOGIES STOP CANT BE OF MUCH HELP FROM HERE STOP REMEMBERED SOMETHING STOP SOMEONE IN FLAT CAP ENTERED TENT AFTER PRESENTATION STARTED STOP DONT KNOW WHO STOP MIGHT BE NOTHING STOP GOOD LUCK STOP ETTY

Swallowing, Felicity glanced around her. Had anyone noticed the blood draining from her face?

Percy was still looking out of the window, and Lady Henrietta was staring daggers at her once-beloved protégé. Only Mrs Broughton was looking at Felicity.

"Might we have that private word, your ladyship?" she asked, perhaps too distracted by her own issues to notice the colour change in Felicity's cheeks. "I promise it won't take long."

"Of course," said Felicity, tucking the telegram into the pocket of her dropped-waist day dress and following Mrs Broughton into the cottage's narrow entrance hall. "What is it?" she asked, giving her head a little shake to perk herself up. She had to carry on as though nothing were wrong.

"I can't bear it anymore," hissed Mrs Broughton. "I simply have to tell you. My husband said I should just forget about the matter, yet every time I see your grandmother suffering, it's like a knife in my heart."

Felicity's head was almost spinning. "A knife?" Not another revelation about the case. Please, it was all too much.

"It's my fault, you see," continued Mrs Broughton, lowering her voice further. "Completely my fault that your grandmother has been excluded and ignored and that her life has become so difficult of late."

Felicity drew her eyebrows together. "I'm afraid I don't follow."

The dowager's voice carried clearly from the drawing room. She would not give up on trying to convince Percy to reverse his decision to abandon rose breeding.

Mrs Broughton glanced over her shoulder, her face lined with worry, the doily-like collar and cuffs of her dress quivering. "Mrs Winterpole was questioning Lady Henrietta's ability to be firm and to take the initiative, you see. She was questioning her ability to lead the decorating committee for the war widows and orphans fundraiser. I had the best intentions at heart. I always do. You know that, don't you, your ladyship?"

Huffs and sighs came from the drawing room as Percy stood fast.

"I know you do, Mrs Broughton," agreed Felicity.

Mrs Broughton blinked. "But don't you see?"

"See what, Mrs Broughton?" The contents of the telegram throbbed like a fresh bee sting in Felicity's pocket. It was almost impossible to focus on anything else.

Mrs Broughton looked like she might burst into tears. "I told Mrs Winterpole. I told her about your grandmother's altercation with Lord Anthony Templeton. If your grandmother has been cut out or refused from any activity or event, then it's all my fault." Mrs Broughton squeezed her eyes closed. "Oh, if I could do anything to make it better. Anything at all. But it does feel good to have told you, your ladyship. To confess."

"Mm-hmm," replied Felicity, her thoughts completely elsewhere, a plan already forming.

Mrs Broughton opened her eyes. "Your ladyship?"

"Yes?" Felicity gripped the telegram in her pocket.

"Are you not surprised by my admission?"

Felicity blinked at Mrs Broughton. "Do you wish me to be?"

"Well. I mean." Mrs Broughton didn't know quite what to say.

"Who of us witnessed my grandmother's outburst?" asked Felicity.

Mrs Broughton looked perplexed. "Why, it was yourself, myself, the victim, and his female assistant."

"And who of these witnesses has regular contact with Mrs Winterpole or any of the other relevant conduits through which such information might damage my grandmother's standing?"

"But I didn't mean any damage," hissed Mrs Broughton. "I intended quite the opposite. Wait." Mrs Broughton shook her head, her lace collar flapping. "You knew, your ladyship? You knew I was the source of the damage to your grandmother's reputation?"

Felicity narrowed her eyes at Mrs Broughton. She'd guessed quite early on, but what could she have done about it?

Balancing social interactions with the likes of Mrs Winterpole and Lady Henrietta wasn't easy for a woman like Mrs Broughton. Her drive in life was to be liked by everyone and to have everyone like one another. Even without her desperate testimony in the cottage hallway, it was always clear that Mrs Broughton wanted nothing but the best for Lady Henrietta.

Felicity had therefore focused on fixing the problem rather than lamenting its origins.

And there might still be a chance to fix it.

"Should you wish to make amends, Mrs Broughton," said Felicity, "I know of something you can do."

Chapter Thirty-Seven

Old Garden. China. Bourbon.

Many of the fields and valleys had been thick with mist on the dawn run over to Chagstock, but as the sun climbed in the pale sky, there was enough light to peruse the handwritten labels on the shelves of the British Rose Association's repository.

Moss. Portland. Centifolia.

Felicity had let herself in using the key supplied by Mrs Broughton and listened carefully, just to be sure. The painting of Lady Philomena Templeton, the association's founder, bore silent witness as Felicity traversed the entrance hall, grasped the thick wooden banister, and made her way upstairs.

The floorboards on the first floor creaked under carpeted runners, and the door to the repository groaned like an old galleon, but Felicity was confident of being alone in the building. Mrs Broughton had given her a detailed account of the regular comings and goings at the headquarters, and Felicity set off early enough to avoid bumping into anyone. Colonel Bolt likely wouldn't have objected to Felicity consulting the archives, but she didn't want anyone to peek over her shoulder and guess what she was doing.

Felicity had been wrong before. She had to be absolutely certain now.

Noisette. Hybrid Perpetual. Tea.

Felicity ran her fingers along the shelves as she read the labels. She had to work quickly but thoroughly. She needed something solid and utterly convincing to present to the police, because confronting people could be dangerous. Felicity owed it to Alex — if not to herself — to avoid taking such a risk again.

Felicity's finger stopped on the brass label holder.

Hybrid Tea.

Was this it?

She took down the first of the leather-bound ledgers and opened it on the broad mahogany table at the centre of the repository. The pages released a soft, musty scent.

"Goodness," whispered Felicity.

The columns were dense, the writing small, and the abbreviations unfamiliar. She flicked to the very front of the ledger, then to the back. There was no list to explain the abbreviations. This was a specialist's archive, listing rose breeds and their breeders from across the centuries. This wasn't a general resource for public use. She would have to manage.

Felicity scanned down the list of dates. She was in the early 1850s. The book finished in the 1880s.

She exchanged the ledger for the next one on the shelf, setting it down on the polished table. She flicked forward several pages. 1905. Closer.

She turned back. 1895.

Thud!

It was only a dull, distant sound, but it made Felicity pause.

She went to the window and gently pulled back the voile curtain.

Ripples refracted across one of the ornamental ponds at the front of the building, as though something had been dropped into it. A slender black cat was slinking across Chagstock's high street at a leisurely pace in the morning stillness. The Model T Ford was parked opposite the building's entrance. Further up the street, a delivery van stood outside the bakery with its back doors open.

The sound must have come from outside. To be certain, Felicity went to the repository's door, opened it a crack without making a noise, and listened.

Everything was still.

There was no need to be nervous, but Felicity had to move on with things. She might not even have the right rose type yet.

Returning to the reading table, she scanned the column containing the names of the breeders, but there was nothing of note. Surnames, initials, and titles were included in the ledger, but the name would have been different, then, wouldn't it?

She moved onto the columns describing the qualities of the roses that had been registered with the association, but what were the chances? There might not be any overlap in the attributes. It might be another type of rose entirely, or no rose at all, but Felicity had to try.

She began with the column entitled *Foliage*.

Simple. Compound. Serrated. Glossy. Downy. Silvery.

She turned the page, running her finger down the column.

She blinked.

Spiral.

Was it an abbreviation?

She went along the line, scanning the rose's other qualities. Under *Bud* was written *Pearl*.

Was it a hit? Was this a Templeton rose? The name of the breeder was not a Templeton.

The Honourable Miss P. Arundell.

Could P be for Pamela?

Even if it was precisely the rose Felicity was looking for, it wasn't enough to convince the police, was it?

More information on the Honourable Miss P. Arundell was needed. Was there a ledger containing information on the breeders?

As Felicity rose from her seat, an acrid smell touched her nostrils, causing her to wrinkle her nose. What on earth was it?

She looked out of the window. The street was still quiet. The

Model T was now the only motor. There was no one in sight. The smell was biting and unpleasant. It surely couldn't be the bakery. The customers wouldn't stand for it.

Felicity went to the repository door and cracked it open. She had to smack a hand over her mouth and nose to prevent herself from spluttering. The stench was so strong, it had to be coming from inside the building. Sharp and oily, it smelled like petrol.

But it made no sense. The smell hadn't been there when she came into the building.

Felicity opened the door further and listened.

Plop. Plop.

Liquid dripping.

And then the strike of a match.

Her blood ran cold.

Felicity dashed out onto the landing. "Stop!"

Chapter Thirty-Eight

"Lady Felicity?"

Standing at the bottom of the big wooden staircase, under the watchful eye of Lady Philomena's portrait, Percy Colhayne looked up at Felicity with confusion and bemusement.

Beside Percy's feet stood a petrol tin with its top missing. In his fingers was a lit match.

Between where Felicity stood at the top of the stairs and Percy at the bottom, the staircase was dripping with petrol. It had been splashed all about. Even the painting bore some of the liquid, which shone in the early morning light filtering through the windows beside the front door.

"Percy," said Felicity. "Please." Her breath caught. The whole building could go up like a torch at any moment.

Percy followed Felicity's gaze to the match in his hand. "Oh," he said, as though surprised to see it there. He blew out the flame.

Felicity put a hand to her heart, almost collapsing with relief. "Thank you."

How had Percy got in without being seen or heard? Felicity had been far too engrossed in the ledgers.

"What are you doing here?"

The question was Percy's.

Between her relief at the match being extinguished and admonishing herself for not noticing Percy's arrival, Felicity hadn't been quick enough to take control of the conversation. Yet words were the only thing that stood between a peaceful resolution and a firestorm.

"I was about to ask you the same thing." Somehow Felicity managed to sound mildly amused by the situation, even though her heart was banging in her throat and there was nothing whatsoever funny about the amount of accelerant thrown over the stairs.

Percy smiled sheepishly. He wore his rough gardening trousers and a loose linen shirt. With his half-messy hair, he appeared vaguely dashing in his own casual way. Yet his appearance was deceiving. Felicity, Lady Henrietta, everyone had been hoodwinked.

"Well, you can see what I'm doing," he said, casting his gaze over the staircase. "Caught in the act, aren't I? Rather embarrassing, really."

Felicity's instinct was to move towards him. Speaking across the distance of the grand staircase was impersonal. Such barriers needed to be broken down quickly if a resolution to the situation was to be found, which could surely only come about by gaining Percy's full trust. If it were possible at all.

But Felicity remained at the top of the stairs.

"Embarrassing?" she echoed with a little frown for emphasis.

If the worst came to the absolute worst, she would fly back to the repository, throw open the window, and jump out, hoping to hit one of the ponds. No one could walk away from such an incident unscathed, but Felicity might make it out alive.

"There's only me here to see you," continued Felicity. "After all we've witnessed together of my grandmother's unashamed attempts to get you into every flower related event going, I should hope there's nothing you could be embarrassed about in front of me." She smiled warmly.

Percy smiled back. The heel of his hand smacked against his

forehead. With his other hand, he squeezed his box of matches. "I feel so bad about all that."

Felicity's stomach felt awfully tight. She'd gone too far. She'd got too personal too quickly.

"Bad about all what?" she asked innocently while listening carefully for any sign of movement elsewhere in the building or outside.

Percy winced. "About everything your grandmother did for me. She was ruined when I told her I'd decided to step away from rose breeding, wasn't she? Absolutely ruined."

It was odd to hear him say this. Percy hadn't seemed upset at Mrs Broughton's luncheon the day before. He'd seemed rather distant. He'd always seemed removed from what was going on around him.

Felicity grasped the thick banister. It was slick with petrol.

"No, Percy," she said firmly. "You've not hurt her. Not in any permanent way. My grandmother's tougher than she looks." The statement was untrue, as Felicity herself had discovered, but Lady Henrietta was Felicity's grandmother to lie about, should the situation call for it. "She cares a great deal for you." Felicity softened her voice. "We all do."

Percy pulled at his shirt collar. "That won't be the case for long though, will it? I thought I might make a clean exit. There's no walking away from things now, is there?"

No walking away? Felicity's pulse raced faster. Percy was out of his mind. Thankfully, Felicity had at least a vague grasp of what had pushed him over the edge.

"You never intended to hurt anyone." Felicity's voice was soothing. "Did you, Percy?"

Percy's mouth fell open. "You know what I've done?"

To come out and say it would be too much. The matches were still in his hand. It had to be on his terms. Felicity needed to coax him into saying it first.

"I know you didn't intend to hurt my grandmother. You wanted to do your mother proud. That was all."

Percy frowned deeply. He attempted a smile, but it turned into a grimace. "What I did, I did for my mother, but I don't think she could ever be proud of me. Not now."

There was a pause. Felicity listened for any sound other than the dripping of the petrol on the stairs. For any sign they were no longer alone.

"Why would your mother not be proud of you?" asked Felicity innocently.

Percy bowed his head, the matches still clutched tightly at his side. "It was the first time I'd met him. My hopes were so high. My own fault, in a way, but my mother spoke so fondly of their time together. He'd told her to wait, and she did. She was the daughter of a viscount." He looked up at Felicity. "Did you know that about my mother?"

Felicity nodded. She'd seen the title in the ledger. Her grandmother spoke frequently and fondly of her dear friend Pamela Colhayne, whose maiden name Felicity was now quite certain had been Arundell, but the dowager had never mentioned Pamela's aristocratic background. Percy's mother had likely had no choice but to live a lie.

"She had offers of marriage that would have given her a comfortable life," continued Percy. "She should have been at Bickleford Rose Festival herself, you know. My mother was really that talented."

"I know." Felicity had seen the remarks in the ledger.

Rosa 'Whispering Fox' had been presented to the society in 1897. Percy would have been just a babe, and Anthony Templeton would have been long gone, but his memory was still very much alive in the mind of a woman in love. *A rose of truly exceptional quality* had been added under *Remarks*.

Percy looked up sadly. "He told her they would marry. He said he had to go to Africa and fight in the war there. He said she should wait for him. Only he never came back. She never heard a word from him. She assumed he'd died. He left her believing that." Percy averted his gaze. He wiped at his eyes with the heel of his hand.

"You must have been a good friend to your mother," said Felicity tenderly, "for her to have felt comfortable sharing such details with you." She had to keep him talking. What else could be done?

"My mother had no one to turn to. He'd ruined her whole life. Her parents were so disappointed and ashamed. She had to leave, invent a story for herself. Change her name. A woman on her own with a child. That's how she ended up here in Devon." Percy's voice shook. "And in the end, she died alone. Even I wasn't there for her."

"It wasn't your fault you were at the front," insisted Felicity. "And your mother wasn't alone. She knew you were thinking about her and loved her very much." It was important to move Percy away from self-reproach. It was too strong and unpredictable an emotion. "And my grandmother was with her. She had other friends around her, too. Your mother was loved by many."

"I couldn't believe my ears during that speech." Percy shook his head. He spoke as though he hadn't heard Felicity, his eyes fixed on the dripping stairs. "The special name he had for her. Red Vixen. She had flame-red hair. He had a thing for foxes. She renamed the cottage The Den in his memory."

"When you heard his special name for your mother," began Felicity, raising her voice so that it would be harder for Percy to ignore her words, "is that when you realised who he was?" Felicity had to connect with Percy. She had to keep him talking. Either get him to confess or put the matchbox down. Preferably both.

Percy looked up the stairs. "It took me a little while to understand. My initial reaction was confusion. Then amazement. Could my father really be Lord Anthony Templeton, the vanished son of the Templeton rose breeding dynasty?" He glanced up at the painting of the association's founder. "My mother never told me his name, but it made sense. The rose connection."

"Were you excited to meet him?" suggested Felicity.

Percy chuckled grimly. "I was so naïve. I imagined there must have been some mistake. That he hadn't realised that my mother had been waiting for him. Hadn't known he had a son. I even imagined we might have a connection." Percy drew in a shaky breath. "It was almost without thinking that I followed him as he passed behind the tents. I found him loitering beside piles of catering supplies. You know, I'd never imagined I would meet my father. I always believed him to be dead. I thought maybe he might even be touched to meet me." Percy's smile was bitter. "He made me feel like an absolute fool for even speaking to him."

Percy's actions had been so terribly wrong, but Felicity still felt a pang of sympathy for him. "What did your father say?"

"I mentioned my mother's name. Her maiden name. He had no recognition of it. Then I mentioned the special name he had for her. Red Vixen. He thought for a moment. Then he laughed. He said, 'If you think you're the only one... I've got no money for you.' "

Felicity gripped the banister. "Oh, Percy." She wanted to go to him, to comfort and calm him. To slip the matchbox out of his tensed fingers. But if she miscalculated, she could find herself running down a staircase engulfed in flames.

"And worse than that." Percy's brow furrowed with anger. "He said some rather rough things about my mother that I shall never repeat to anyone, for it was utter nonsense and balderdash." He was toying with the matchbox in both hands now, pushing it open and closed. "Balderdash."

Felicity's mouth felt dry. She'd never seen Percy angry before. Yet he was capable of more than just anger. He was capable of violence. Of taking the Best in Show prize winner's plate and aiming it at his own father's head.

"Your reaction was driven by pure emotion," said Felicity gently, doing her best not to sound desperate in her efforts to soothe. "It can happen to the best of us, Percy. It really can. You're not to blame." It was unlikely a jury would share this opinion, but honesty could not be Felicity's priority.

Percy shook his head. "You don't understand. It's not your fault, but you simply can't. Going to war changes you. I did away with so many men. I had no choice. It's you or them. You see the fear in their eyes, but I became numb to it." A tear rolled down his cheek. He palmed it away. "After my mother died, after I returned to England, I thought the roses would heal me, and they did. They really did. But he brought it all back. He set it all off again in my head. The way he reacted. The things he said about my mother. I felt the rage boiling up inside me. I couldn't stop myself."

Percy continued to push the matchbox open and closed.

"Stop yourself from what?" Felicity couldn't control the tremble in her voice. Was moving towards a confession going too far?

"I asked him, may I look at that plate you just won? He held the thing out to me as if it were worthless, as if he didn't care what happened to it. But it was heavy." The matchbox opened and closed. Faster and faster. "He was a monster. And I am his son."

"Percy, you're not a monster." Felicity had taken enough risk. She had to move the conversation onto safer ground. "Your mother loved you. My grandmother adores you. You said yourself, the war changed you. You weren't in control. Please, Percy." Felicity eyed the matchbox. "Why do this?"

Percy looked up at Felicity. His eyes were full of regret. Was she getting through to him?

"After I did it, I didn't know what to do. I hid his body. I went to the presentation. I felt numb. I felt nothing."

Felicity nodded her understanding, but her stomach twisted. When Lady Henrietta was suspected of involvement in Anthony Templeton's demise, Percy hadn't felt moved by her plight. He didn't care about the dowager. He didn't care about anyone but himself.

Yet Felicity had to continue to empathise with him. She had to get those matches out of his hand.

"It's normal to feel that way, Percy. But you're ready to make amends now, aren't you?"

Percy stopped playing with the matchbox. He pressed his lips together. "You know, I didn't imagine I would outsmart anyone. I expected to be caught. I was just waiting. I was simply amazed when all that con business came out. I couldn't believe my luck. I suppose I got overly confident. Started making plans for myself. Then when the con turned out to be just a temporary distraction... Well, I couldn't let go of my plans. My mother would want me to be happy, wouldn't she? The very least I could do was see to that."

So much of Percy's decision-making seemed based on his mother, from attempting to become a prize-winning rose breeder to defending her honour when Anthony Templeton insulted her memory. Pamela's impact on Percy had no doubt been amplified by his experiences in the war and her passing while he was away. It was a devastating cocktail of influences that severely hindered his ability to think straight.

The dripping of the petrol on the stairs had slowed, but there was still no other sound in the house or outside. Lady Philomena Templeton continued to stare down from her portrait, her gaze serene despite her descendants' attempts to destroy her legacy.

"How does setting alight the rose association headquarters fit into your plans to be happy?" asked Felicity.

Percy gave a little laugh. "I didn't want anything traced back to my mother or to me. But mainly my mother. She's been through enough. But that's why you're here, isn't it? You followed it all back to her, didn't you?"

Being dishonest on this point threatened to rile Percy. Felicity would side-step the issue instead.

"Your father gave your mother roses as gifts, didn't he?" she said, recalling what Leonora had said about her brother's thefts from the Rosarium shortly after he left home.

Percy nodded. "She'd been a keen gardener before that, but he made her quite mad about roses. You saw her records, too, didn't you?" he asked. "In the repository?"

"I just want to help you, Percy," said Felicity

"You sound like your grandmother. And I appreciate it. I really do. It's just..." He looked down at the petrol tin. "I don't deserve it. I don't deserve to get away. I thought I was doing right by my mother, but I see it now. She would be ashamed. She would be disgusted by me."

"Percy," said Felicity. She put a foot on the stairs.

"I'm a monster." His grip on the matches tightened. "Just like him. Just like my father." He picked up the petrol tin and turned the nozzle towards himself.

"Percy, no!" Felicity flew towards him, her feet splashing into the petrol on the stairs.

Percy jerked the contents of the tin onto himself, dousing his hair, shirt, and trousers with the acrid liquid.

"Go!" he bellowed. "Leave!"

Felicity's heart pushed into her throat as she stood on the stairs before him. Was she supposed to dash past him to the front door?

There was a sound outside. The scraping of stone.

"Percy, please." She edged towards him, holding out a hand. "Give me the matches. Don't do this."

Tears mixed with the petrol on Percy's cheeks. He held out the matchbox. With shaking hands, he pressed it open. "I said go!" he roared.

"No!" Felicity lunged towards him. "Don't!"

Bang!

The front door of the building slammed open.

Chapter Thirty-Nine

The blooms in the courtyard of the British Rose Association headquarters perfumed the air as the sun climbed in the sky. The day would likely be a hot one, but while the sunshine warmed the stone bench upon which she was seated, Felicity continued to shiver. Her tailored linen blazer, pleated skirt in a matching dove-grey, and cream georgette blouse were still rather wet. Her ribboned straw cloche, which sat on the bench beside her, was soaked beyond repair.

The drama on the staircase was now over, replaced by the to-ing and fro-ing of countless policemen. The sweetly scented courtyard was an oasis of peace, but on the opposite side of the stone table to Felicity, Chief Inspector Luscombe looked anything but relaxed.

He pinched a hand over his forehead and looked down at his notebook. "Explain to me again your purpose for being here at dawn, your ladyship. I'm still failing to understand it."

"My apologies, Chief Inspector." Felicity had already explained everything. Being still rather shaken by her encounter with Percy, she'd perhaps spoken in a way that had been hard to follow. "I shall start again, from the beginning. The deceit to win the Best in Show prize was uncovered the day we saw one another at the Dingles' nursery. Was it not?"

The policeman nodded stiffly.

"I suspected that might have been the end," continued Felicity, "as I'm sure you did, too. It sounded as though Clive Dingle had assumed responsibility for Anthony Templeton's demise. When that turned out not to be the case, I had to go back to the beginning."

The corners of the chief inspector's mouth pulled downwards with displeasure. Felicity wasn't supposed to have been investigating, but there was little point in chastising her now.

Though the sun warmed the back of her blazer, Felicity's teeth chattered as she spoke. "It was possible the motive behind the killing had nothing to do with roses. At least, not directly. Your own investigations classed the method as an act of passion, likely without premeditation."

The chief inspector eyed Felicity suspiciously. "Go on."

"I heard from Blanche Ernault that Anthony Templeton had something of a history with women, and not at all in a pleasant way."

The policeman raised an eyebrow. It was an indelicate subject.

Felicity continued, regardless. "Blanche had assumed Anthony's end to be related to his behaviour with women, but that would have opened up the suspect pool exponentially. And I remained convinced that the speech Anthony gave was the trigger. The timing and, well, the choice of weapon supported this. At least in my mind."

The policeman continued to regard Felicity sceptically. "And why didn't you come to us with this information?"

"I would have loved to, Chief Inspector, but I wanted to present you with evidence instead of a vague set of ideas." Felicity offered a smile that was simultaneously apologetic and slightly sarcastic. "I don't wish to waste your time or that of your men."

There was something in the narrowing of the chief inspector's gaze that implied he wouldn't have dismissed her ideas. Might he even regret having sent Felicity away when she requested his help with her grandmother?

"What brought you to the rose association's repository?" The policeman's tone was flat.

"A telegram from the singer, Mr Etty. He was kind enough to

answer an enquiry we sent to the steamer upon which he was travelling. We asked what he witnessed at the flower show around the time of the misdeed."

There came another raised eyebrow from the chief inspector.

Felicity had actually sent the singer a barrage of questions, almost all of which Mr Etty had ignored. But that didn't matter. What was important was that he'd responded, and the information he'd shared had been pivotal. At least in Felicity's thinking on the case.

"Mr Etty responded to say he saw someone arriving slightly late for Mr Shakerley's presentation. Someone in a flat cap. He didn't know who."

Chief Inspector Luscombe frowned deeply. "Your ladyship," he said sternly. "The testimony of a witness is evidence that you should have shared with the police."

Felicity blinked innocently. She could indeed have handed Mr Etty's telegram over to the chief inspector, but she'd needed to act quickly. "I didn't wish to cause offence by implying you and your men hadn't already gathered all the relevant testimony, Chief Inspector. Especially not when you'd given the witness in question special dispensation to leave the country."

The policeman shifted uncomfortably on the stone bench. "How did you know it was Percival Colhayne that Etty had seen?"

"I didn't," said Felicity. "I merely suspected it. So I came here to check. I wanted to be extremely sure. The ledger's still open on the table upstairs, although I still don't think it would have been enough to share with you and your men. It contains hints rather than actual evidence."

Chief Inspector Luscombe looked grave. "It was a rather grim and yet fortunate coincidence that Colhayne himself showed up. Not that I would wish harm on you or anyone else, your ladyship."

Felicity's stomach gave a little squeeze as she remembered the petrol soaked stairs and the matchbox in Percy's hand. "I had indeed not expected to see anyone at such an early hour."

"Yet you took precautions." The policeman cast his gaze towards the shadows at the edge of the courtyard.

"Don't look at me." Alex stood with his notebook and pencil in his hand at the edge of the little garden, his grey three-piece suit somehow not remotely wet.

Considering Alex's contribution to the outcome of events, Chief Inspector Luscombe couldn't object to him writing down quotes from Felicity's side of events, and Felicity of course had no opposition to being quoted for Alex's article, even if the publicity was never her favourite part of such situations. In any case, a stop-press had already been made in the Western Daily News' morning edition. The full details would be shared with readers that afternoon. It had been scoop after scoop for Alex since Bickleford.

"It wasn't my idea to stand guard," he added with a smile in Felicity's direction. "It was Lady Felicity's."

She smiled back at him, her shivering subsiding a little.

Alex had been on watch in his Model T opposite the rose association's headquarters. The set-up had its weakness, however. Percy had used a back street and a window at the rear of the building to gain access, so Alex hadn't seen him.

The chief inspector returned his steely attention to Felicity. "I cannot condone how you gained access to the building—"

Frowning, Felicity cut him off. "I simply borrowed a set of keys."

"—and clearly any conversation we ever have about your investigating falls on deaf ears."

Felicity folded her arms over her chest but said nothing. It was perhaps better not to make any promises in this arena.

The policeman sighed. "But I can say that it's thanks to you we don't have even more destruction and chaos on our hands."

Felicity lifted her chin a little. Despite the lacklustre delivery, she would take the compliment in the spirit it was intended. "Thank you for saying so, Chief Inspector."

"And it's also thanks to you, Mr Cooper." Chief Inspector Luscombe nodded in Alex's direction.

From his motor parked opposite the building, Alex had watched the window of the rose association's repository. He'd had a view of the crown of Felicity's straw cloche while she was sitting at the table perusing the ledgers. She'd moved away from the table a couple of times. On the last occasion, when she didn't reappear quickly enough, Alex went to check.

After quietly approaching the building's front door, Alex heard voices. It was Felicity and Percy. He couldn't risk looking through either of the windows at the side of the door to see what the threat was, for fear of being seen. Then he caught a whiff of the petrol.

"I tried apologising to Colonel Bolt for the damage," said Alex somewhat wryly to the chief inspector, "but he seemed rather preoccupied."

In a feat of strength, Alex had emptied one of the large ornamental plant pots at the building's front entrance and filled it with water by scooping from the pond. He'd then kicked open the front doors and heaved the pond water at Percy, drenching his clothes and, crucially, his matches.

Despite everything that had happened, the colonel, who arrived shortly after the police, had seemed particularly upset by the missing plant pot and half-empty pond, which disrupted the symmetry at the front of the building.

"I've also apologised to Lady Felicity." Alex winced at her.

Felicity had been almost within reach of the matches in Percy's hand and therefore caught in the deluge.

"Rather a little damp than smouldering," she said, having no complaints about being hit by the water thrown by Alex.

While still dripping, Felicity had dashed to the secretary's office to use the telephone to summon the police. After relieving him of his matches, Alex had remained with Percy, although there'd been no need to restrain him. Percy sat on the staircase, put his head in his hands, and wept until the police arrived.

"But what I found doesn't matter now, does it, Chief Inspector?" said Felicity. "You have a confession."

I did it. I'm the one. You can take me away, Percy had said as he'd offered his wrists for cuffing when Chagstock's local sergeant arrived, looking stunned and bleary-eyed from the early call out of bed.

The chief inspector frowned. "I should still like you to show my officers what you came across in the repository and how you suspect it links Colhayne's mother to Anthony Templeton. There's a case to be made, but what kind of case exactly, I can't yet say."

"Murder?" pressed Alex, his pencil poised. "Or manslaughter?"

"I can't yet say," repeated the policeman firmly.

"But it can be reported in the afternoon edition that Anthony Templeton's killer is now in custody, can't it?" pressed Felicity. Lady Henrietta was foremost in her mind.

The policeman knitted his fingers and leaned forward on the stone table. "Well."

"Can't it?" repeated Felicity.

It was the end. Wasn't it?

Chapter Forty

SEVERAL WEEKS LATER

Swallows chirruped and danced low in the sky. Guests mingled and chatted under bunting that fluttered in the warm afternoon air. Linen-draped trestle tables groaned under the weight of mountains of cakes and sandwiches.

Bradley Court's elegant rose garden had more life in it than it had done in years, possibly decades, and Lady Henrietta could take all the credit. But her recovery from everything that had happened since Bickleford Rose Festival hadn't been as immediate as Felicity had hoped.

Following Percy's arrest, there was no more room for suspicions around who ended Lord Anthony Templeton's life, but it was understandably still an enormous blow to the dowager. Upon returning from the rose association's headquarters, Felicity had been forced to tell her grandmother almost all the details. Lady Henrietta insisted on nothing less.

"Doing away with one's own father on the first encounter is simply horrific," she told Felicity, her cheeks quite white from the shock of it all. "And it's dreadful to think how poor Pamela suffered so terribly without even knowing it. When she passed on, she was still quite obsessed with Percy's father. If only she'd known the truth about him."

"It's all quite awful, isn't it?" Felicity patted her grandmother's hand and did her best to be of comfort, but Lady Henrietta had continued to look pale and wear a haunted expression for several days.

Yet now, under the brilliant blue of the summer sky, Lady Henrietta's cheeks were bright pink, her natural charm and wit were on full display, and the guests were gathered around her like moths to a flame.

But just because Lady Henrietta had organised her own fundraising event all by herself, it didn't mean the dowager had no use for her granddaughter.

A maid in a black-and-white uniform arrived with a curtsey before Felicity. "Excuse me, your ladyship. Lady Henrietta requests your presence."

Felicity looked out across the crowded rose garden. The dowager was craning her neck, the feathers on her hat bobbing, her hand at the throat of her light burgundy dress with lace trimmings. Having caught Felicity's gaze, she gestured for her granddaughter to join her.

After politely dismissing the maid, Felicity turned to Alex with an apologetic sigh. In a smartly tailored grey three-piece suit, he didn't look at all out of place among the well-heeled crowd in the rose garden.

"Well, that was over before it began," said Alex, smiling with amusement. They'd only just found a moment together on the sidelines of the event and had exchanged barely a sentence or two.

"I remain hopeful that we'll get to speak for more than just a few moments," said Felicity. "It's really been far too long."

Felicity's profile as something of a celebrity had grown even further because of her involvement in the solving of the Anthony Templeton affair. Practically everyone at the garden party wished to shake her by the hand, and Alex had work to do. Lady Henrietta had insisted that he report on her event for the Western Daily News.

The pair weren't just in demand that afternoon, however.

Over the past few weeks, Felicity hadn't been able to shake free of her duties for the Gentlewoman's Gazette. Her brother Jasper had negotiated the coverage of the flower show affair with the magazine's editor and without obtaining Felicity's approval until practically the last minute. Luckily for Jasper, he was still away on business and conducting everything via telephone, although Felicity planned to say some rather stern words directly to him when he returned to Bradley Court.

Alex, meanwhile, had been busy not only with reporting on the aftermath of Anthony Templeton's demise but also on several other important stories, including the appearance in court of a famous charlatan clairvoyant.

It left little time for tea and buns at their favourite Exeter tea house. Indeed, they'd hardly seen one another at all.

Alex smiled warmly at Felicity. "Go to your grandmother. We can talk later. I promise."

"I'll hold you to it." Felicity gave Alex's hand a subtle squeeze before punting off through the crowds in the rose garden, the skirt of her pale blue silk tea dress wafting behind her.

The scent of expensive perfume mixed with the heady smell of Lady Henrietta's collection of roses. The colours worn by the event's attendees all seemed to complement the pastel pinks and satin whites of the blooms. It was a beautiful scene.

As Felicity drew closer to her grandmother, her skin prickled with wariness.

In a prim little toque in pale daffodil-yellow that balanced the greens of her dress, Mrs Winterpole stood next to Lady Henrietta, her expression somewhat less enthusiastic than that of many other guests at the party. Colonel Bolt was also present. He had on a smart pinstripe suit, but he leaned heavily on his ivory-topped walking stick and looked rather ill-at ease.

"Here she comes now," reassured Lady Henrietta as Felicity approached the little gathering.

In a bright red bow tie and with his spectacles evenly positioned on the bridge of his nose, Mr Shakerley was also part of the group. At Lady Henrietta's side, Mrs Broughton wore an impractically wide Merry Widow hat with trailing ribbons and a puff-sleeved frock.

"Yes," agreed Mrs Broughton. "Here's Lady Felicity."

Felicity had never discussed Mrs Broughton's confession with her grandmother. Had Mrs Broughton told Lady Henrietta that she'd spread the news about the altercation with Anthony Templeton? Perhaps it had been enough that she'd admitted what she'd done to Felicity. By lending her keys, Mrs Broughton had, after all, played a small role in saving the British Rose Association from destruction.

Pip was also at Lady Henrietta's side, tucked under her elbow. The Yorkie was ready to follow Felicity's grandmother into battle on any day, as long as there were some of his favourite foods tucked into her purse. The little dog watched her interlocutors with bright, attentive eyes and much sniffing of the air, no doubt scenting the richness of the food on the trestle tables.

"Felicity, dear," said Lady Henrietta as Felicity navigated a group of guests selecting drinks from a tray to join the hostess' huddle at the centre of the rose garden. "I was just explaining to Colonel Bolt, Mrs Winterpole, and Mr Shakerley what exactly I was trying to achieve with relocating the fundraiser for the war widows and orphans to our home here at Bradley Court."

After her initial shock at the revelations related to Percy, his mother, and Anthony Templeton had settled, Lady Henrietta had entered a phase of deep contemplation. It lasted only a couple of days, but Felicity had never witnessed anything like it in her grandmother. She was quiet but not sad. Active in the garden and around the house, but not venturing far afield.

Whenever Jasper telephoned, Lady Henrietta only wished to hear about his recent business meetings. When speaking to Felicity, she was happy to listen to updates about the progress of Felicity's magazine articles. She had very little to say for herself, offering barely an opinion on any matter. On the telephone one evening, Jasper had said to Felicity, "Do you think we ought to call the doctor?"

But when the period of contemplation ended, it was clear a new phase had begun.

"Felicity, I shall head into town this afternoon for a meeting with the War Widows and Orphans Relief Fund," Lady Henrietta had announced suddenly over lunch one day. "I shall inform them we'll hold the annual fundraiser here at Bradley Court. In the rose garden."

Felicity had drawn in her chin. It was her grandmother's prerogative to do what she wished at Bradley Court, especially in Jasper's absence, but such bold decisions were rarely made without discussion.

"Are you sure?" asked Felicity.

"Quite," had come the dowager's answer, without hesitation.

With Percy now completely out of the picture, Lady Henrietta was focusing on her own wishes. Her own needs. She was her own new project, and it didn't stop with the garden party. Felicity was pleased to have been proved wrong when it came to her grandmother's resilience.

"It's lovely that you could all be here," said Felicity to the little group after a round of polite greetings. "Grandmama has worked so hard to make this event special."

Lady Henrietta looked extremely proud at Felicity's words, as did Pip.

Mrs Winterpole gazed about the garden with a mixture of discomfort and wonderment. She looked rather humbled by the event. Not just by the decorations and the food, which were luxurious and perfectly executed, but by the guests.

There were all the usual suspects from the region's floral societies, both staff and volunteers. Rose breeders and other nursery owners were also in attendance, those detained at His Majesty's pleasure excepted. The inhabitants of Lower Diddleton were also invited as a gesture of neighbourly good will.

But Mrs Winterpole blinked in awe at the actors, writers, government ministers, and some rather important-looking people that even Felicity didn't recognise.

The music-hall singer Mr Elliot Etty had come all the way from London for the event, though it was a fleeting visit, as he was taking the ferry from Penzance for a well-deserved holiday in the Scilly Isles. He explained he was exhausted following a successful tour of the

United States and a few exclusive concerts in London, including one for the king's household.

Mr Etty had brought with him a gaggle of other well-known faces, and the discreet selection of journalists and society reporters that had been hand-picked to attend the event — Alex included — lapped up their presence, magnesium bulbs flashing.

"You have indeed excelled yourself, Lady Henrietta," said Mrs Winterpole. Her voice was small, but there was no hint of bitterness to her words. The compliment was genuine. It was impossible not to be impressed by the dowager's achievements.

Would Mrs Winterpole one day apologise to Lady Henrietta for taking matters too far when she heard about the dowager's falling out with Anthony Templeton? It would be unlikely to make any difference. Lady Henrietta had moved on without Mrs Winterpole's apology, and there was nothing that could prevent the two widows going to war with one another the next time bulbs had to be chosen for the village green.

"Yes, I quite agree with Mrs Winterpole," said Colonel Bolt, turning to Lady Henrietta. "The ingenuity and resourcefulness of women such as yourself, your ladyship, is an untapped resource. I'm very pleased to have taken steps to make better use of it."

In the wake of Felicity's confrontation with Percy at the rose association headquarters, the pressure of the situation was simply too much for Colonel Bolt, and he became sick for a spell. His illness, however, hadn't stopped the clean-up and then normal running of the association.

The colonel's secretary had called Mrs Broughton, who had alerted Mrs Winterpole, and the women had rallied a platoon of enthusiastic volunteers, who quickly cleaned up the mess and got the normal business of the association flowing again. Even the organisation's finances — which Colonel Bolt had found a little overwhelming to manage, though he wouldn't admit it — had been straightened out by women accustomed to running the treasuries of the various societies and foundations for which they volunteered.

Lady Henrietta, too, had played a small part in the resurrection of the British Rose Association, mainly via donations. She had her own projects to concentrate on now.

"By the time I returned to my post," said the colonel, "things were running more smoothly than ever."

"We're very lucky to have a leader like you, Colonel, to rally the troops," said Mrs Winterpole generously, for she had been the main orchestrator of the association's activities in the absence of its president. "And we're also extremely grateful to Lady Felicity, of course. If it weren't for her, there'd be no association."

"Oh, I'm not sure about that, Mrs Winterpole." Felicity was becoming better at accepting compliments and gratitude for her efforts, but she was always alert to credit being attributed where none was due. "The association is surely far more than a building full of records. It's about the people."

"Very true, dear," said Lady Henrietta.

"Very true," echoed Mrs Broughton, nodding along, the ribbons on her wide-brimmed hat flapping about.

Also nodding, Mrs Winterpole seemed to approve of the sentiment. Then she frowned. "You know, I still cannot forgive myself."

Lady Henrietta chuckled. "Please, Mrs Winterpole. It's water under the bridge." The dowager was determined to be magnanimous in her triumph.

Mrs Winterpole shook her head primly. She had something other than Lady Henrietta's past suffering in mind. "Not noticing that Mr Colhayne wasn't there for the start of Mr Shakerley's presentation. That he came in late and took a seat only after it had begun. How could I have missed such an important detail? I must have been so distracted by that timepiece. My husband swore by the watch with his manoeuvres in the navy, you know, but I suppose it had become rather stiff with age."

Lady Henrietta gave a little roll of her eyes. "Please, Mrs Winterpole. You were not the only one to be rather drawn in by Percival's charms." The dowager had thoroughly moved on from any sense of mistake or regret in her efforts regarding Percy. "There wasn't anyone among us who could even imagine what he was truly capable of. And can we not remain focused on the positive? For today, at least?"

Mrs Winterpole straightened, adjusting her toque. "Oh. Quite. We must, of course, not ignore your achievements, your ladyship," she said, returning her attention to Felicity. "And the brave actions of your colleague, Mr Cooper. And all those splendid articles in the Gentlewoman's Gazette and in the Western Daily News."

Felicity smiled. "That's kind of you to say." It indeed felt better to focus on the positive. "We should congratulate Mr Shakerley, too," said Felicity, turning to the bow-tied rose expert. "I understand your new book has found quite an audience."

Mr Shakerley's eyes twinkled. He fiddled with his spectacles, making them slightly crooked. "You're quite correct, your ladyship." The events from Bickleford Rose Festival had shone a spotlight on rose breeding, and the launch of Mr Shakerley's book had ridden the wave of interest. "It's gratifying to know that so many people care about the origins of and traditions related to British roses. And that we shall have so many new breeders and those skilled in the arts of nursery practice joining our community." Mr Shakerley raised his eyebrows at Lady Henrietta.

The dowager returned his gaze knowingly and rather proudly. Lady Henrietta and Mr Shakerley had met several times over the previous weeks. Indeed, in her new phase of focusing on her own projects, Felicity's grandmother had built bridges with some rather interesting characters.

Crash!

"What the—" Colonel Bolt turned sharply.

A footman had dropped an empty tray onto the stone path at the edge of the garden, and the chaos was spreading. Guests stepped back. Gasps went up. A corridor was being created through the garden, rose bushes trembling like the parting of waves.

And then there they were.

Woof! Woof! Woof!

Two Jack Russells, one with black patches and one with tan spots, encircled Lady Henrietta, barking and jumping, their braided leather leads trailing on the ground.

"Oh!" cried the dowager as Pip growled and struggled in her arms.

Woof! Woof! Woof!

Felicity shot a glance across the garden. Havelock was storming through the guests in the dogs' wake, his face like thunder.

She looked around for Alex but couldn't see him.

"Goodness!" Mrs Broughton watched with alarm as Pip continued to struggle in Lady Henrietta's grasp.

The dowager indeed seemed to have difficulty containing the Yorkie. "Master Pip, would you please— Oh!"

With a mighty push of his paws, Pip sprang out of the dowager's arms and took flight towards the Jack Russells, who danced on their hind legs, jaws snapping, ready to meet him.

Chapter Forty-One

"Flossie! Daisy!"

His beefy proportions testing the integrity of a brown pinstripe suit, Havelock arrived on the scene just as Pip's paws reached the grass and the little Yorkie began squaring up to the two Jack Russells. But the burly gardener was too late to grab their leads.

"Heavens!" cried Mrs Broughton as the dogs piled onto one another, growling and yelping with excitement. Guests scuttled backwards as the canines tussled on the lawn.

"Gentle now!" boomed Havelock.

Lady Henrietta chuckled.

The three dogs were engaging in rambunctious play, teeth snapping the air, growls aplenty, and tails wagging hard.

It was a familiar scene, the two energetic Jack Russells having spent much time at Bradley Court over the past weeks, and Pip having made his fair share of trips to Templeton Manor. They had been a little wary of one another at the beginning, but were now the perfect playmates, the Jack Russells and the Yorkshire Terrier being well matched in size and energy.

Slipping gracefully through the crowds, Lady Leonora Templeton arrived beside Havelock, looking effortlessly beautiful in a simple dropped-waist frock in sage-green crepe and with her dark hair roped elegantly into a chignon at her nape.

Leonora put a gentle hand on Havelock's arm. Her touch triggered him to drop his fists from his hips and stand in a less aggressive manner. With Havelock relaxed, Leonora smiled in amusement at the dogs.

"That's quite enough," said Lady Henrietta, plucking something from a pocket hidden in the satin folds of her burgundy dress. She held her hand high in the air. "Dogs!" The dowager's voice was authoritative.

Pip, Flossie, and Daisy ceased their play. All canine eyes were on Lady Henrietta's hand.

"Sit!"

The little dogs' rear ends hit the lawn immediately.

"Paw!"

Each dog raised a forefoot.

Felicity smiled. Her grandmother was just showing off now, but why not? She had come far with her dog training. Felicity was much happier about leaving Pip in her grandmother's company now that the Yorkie was at least having to work for his treats instead of being spoiled.

"Good dogs." Lady Henrietta leaned forward to award each of the three terriers with a charcoal biscuit.

Havelock shook his head in disbelief. Might he take inspiration from Lady Henrietta for keeping Flossie and Daisy under control?

"Now," continued the dowager, "you may continue your play, but not in the rose garden. Is that understood?"

The dogs, still sitting, cocked ears and tipped their heads, their eyes firmly fixed on Lady Henrietta. They had a desire to listen and to please her, but they hadn't a clue what she was asking. The dowager's canine communication skills still required fine tuning.

Leonora nodded to Havelock.

The gardener picked up the Jack Russells' leads. "Come on, girls," he said in his usual gruff tone.

"You may let them off in the orchard," said Lady Henrietta.

Havelock grunted his acknowledgement of the instruction as Pip went bounding off after the tethered Jack Russells, and the threesome tumbled along the path to the orchard together.

Leonora watched them leave, smiling tenderly at both her dogs and her gardener.

"Lady Leonora," said Lady Henrietta, "how wonderful that you could join us on this special day." She turned to Colonel Bolt. "We have Lady Leonora to thank for the wealth of roses on display in the garden today, including several varieties created by my dear late friend, the Honourable Mrs Pamela Colhayne."

Leonora had been with Lady Henrietta to Percy's cottage on a number of occasions. Using the ledgers from the rose association, they identified several floral varieties that Pamela had lovingly created and that were still true to the forms Pamela had intended. Putting her rose-hunting skills to good use, Leonora had even located a couple of specimens that had almost suffocated among the brambles at the edge of the garden.

"Oh, yes," said the colonel, leaning on his stick to get a better view of the rows of blooms rescued from Pamela's garden. "Some very fine plants."

"There are a few of my own among the display." Leonora gave a subtle nod towards the fascinated visitors weaving in and out of the lines of rose bushes in pots that had been transported from Templeton Manor and carefully arranged among the dowager's own plants.

"Rosa 'Flossie's Frolic' was most deserving of Best in Show," said Mrs Winterpole admiringly.

"Most deserving," echoed Mrs Broughton.

Leonora smiled politely but said nothing.

Mrs Winterpole and the platoon of volunteers running the rose association in Colonel Bolt's absence had taken swift action to reassign that year's Best in Show prize. There was only one finalist in the running who wasn't either deceased or in rather a lot of trouble with the police, so the prize went to Leonora by default.

Colonel Bolt used his stick to gesture to a potted rose with rich green leaves and full, rounded flowers in ethereal alabaster white. "But Rosa 'Toddy's Serenity' is the true triumph here today, your ladyship," said the colonel reverently. "I've never seen anything like it."

"Thank you," said Leonora, with a hint of melancholy.

Toddy had been a childhood nickname for Anthony Templeton. The rose was Leonora's way of remembering her brother, whose demise she mourned in a very private way, but mourn it she did. Everyone was once but an innocent child.

"'Toddy's Serenity' is indeed quite spectacular," agreed Mr Shakerley, his eyes narrowed behind his wonky spectacles. "And thoroughly unique. Quite a departure from the typical Templeton roses. And rather a welcome departure, I must say."

Continuing to smile, Leonora flashed a glance at Lady Henrietta. Despite the pain of everything that had happened, the drama and loss had brought the two formidable women together.

After the rescue mission to Pamela's cottage, a new friendship had been born. Discussions of ancestry and about how the Templetons and Quicks collaborated on the birth of the British Rose Association rapidly developed into new ideas. The fates of Edna Dingle and Blanche Ernault even served as inspiration to the broad-minded Lady Henrietta and Leonora.

Edna, without her husband's help and guidance and despite many years working in the trade, hadn't enough skills to run the Dingles' nursery alone. She knew enough about plants but not about the running of things. The business side had been men's work.

Not that it would have been easy to resurrect the Dingle name in the plant-selling world. The newspapers had been zealous in their reporting when Clive appeared on trial for the attack on Mr Merton and his attempt on Felicity.

Lady Henrietta and Leonora felt Edna ought not to be left to become destitute, however. A place for her was found as a garden assistant at a large estate close to the prison where Clive would serve his sentence.

Blanche was a little trickier to assist, as she didn't know the first thing about plants. Leonora was grateful for the dedication Blanche had shown her brother, and she offered to find Blanche a suitable position at another estate, perhaps as a lady's maid or as a tutor of French.

Blanche refused the offer, although it wasn't entirely clear why. Perhaps she was simply too proud to accept the help.

The Frenchwoman instead announced she would travel to London to seek employment. Leonora had paid for her train ticket, but it had been weeks since anyone had heard from her. It was hoped that Blanche wouldn't land in further difficulty, although London was perhaps a more suitable location for her than the Dorset countryside.

"'Toddy's Serenity' smells absolutely divine," cooed Mrs Broughton.

"It really does," agreed Felicity. She'd learned a lot about roses over the past weeks but, going forward, would be happy to offer only the opinions of a layman on the topic. "Congratulations."

"Thank you." Leonora straightened. "But it's not just about the plants, is it?" Leonora threw her question to Lady Henrietta.

"Of course not." The dowager's eyes widened. "And look, here's our woman of the moment."

Chapter Forty-Two

As a kitchen maid, Janey Whedon wasn't normally to be found above stairs at Bradley Court. But in her best dress and a sweet little straw hat, she looked prim, presentable, and full of nerves as she approached Lady Henrietta in the summer sunshine, the polite chatter of the garden party and the scent of roses swelling around her.

Mrs Winterpole looked at Mrs Broughton in confusion. Colonel Bolt widened his eyes at Mr Shakerley.

Felicity could see from the twinkle in her grandmother's eyes that the dowager was thoroughly enjoying herself.

"Janey is the first of our recruits." Lady Henrietta put a proud hand on the girl's shoulder. "Aren't you, Janey dear?"

Janey flicked an anxious yet excited gaze at the group. "Y-yes, your ladyship."

"Recruit?" Colonel Bolt leaned hard on his walking cane. "I'm not sure I follow."

"Would you like to tell them, Lady Leonora?" offered the dowager.

Leonora raised her elegant chin slightly. "We're opening a horticultural school for women and girls. The Lady Philomena Institute of Garden Arts, named in honour of my ancestor. The first cohort begins next month. It's a collaboration between the Quick and Templeton families."

Lady Henrietta nodded with satisfaction. "We hope to provide opportunities for training and perhaps even start a few careers."

"For there's nothing wrong in this day and age with a woman who wants her own career, is there?" Leonora raised an eyebrow at Felicity.

Felicity smiled. She couldn't disagree.

Colonel Bolt looked rather stunned. "Th-that's very impressive." Even if it still didn't feel quite normal to him, the colonel had learned not to underestimate women's capabilities. "Very impressive, indeed."

Lady Henrietta beamed. "Oh, Colonel. I'm so glad you think so."

Mrs Winterpole narrowed her eyes at Mrs Broughton. "You knew about this?" she asked.

Mrs Broughton swallowed and nodded, the ribbons on her hat dancing in the breeze. "I shall assist with the teaching of flower arranging," she said, a tremble in her voice. Mrs Broughton must have made a concerted effort to withhold news of the school from Mrs Winterpole.

Lady Henrietta looked pleased with Mrs Winterpole's surprise. She'd given Mrs Winterpole her own taste of being excluded. It would have been much easier if the two widows could simply agree to share ideas and collaborate, because their interests overlapped so thoroughly. But then where would be the fun in that?

"Flower arranging is an element of the training you're very much looking forward to, isn't it, Janey?" enquired Lady Henrietta encouragingly.

Janey nodded with enthusiasm. "Oh, I'm looking forward to all of it, your ladyship. My grandmother used to have a beautiful little garden. I'd love to have just a scrap of her talent."

Leonora smiled warmly at Janey. "Should you develop a particular talent for roses, I shall be looking for apprentices to work in my Rosarium."

Janey blinked with surprise, then bobbed a curtsey. "Thank you for the opportunity, your ladyship. I shall do my best in every class."

Felicity smiled. The horticultural school was good for everyone. Lady Henrietta had a new project and many enthusiastic protégés with whom to work. The likes of Janey Whedon would be offered new chances. The world of gardening would be enriched by new, female talent, meaning traditions like the Templeton roses could continue with fresh perspectives.

"Mr Shakerley has also agreed to contribute." Lady Henrietta lifted her brow in the rose expert's direction.

"Oh, really?" This was news even to Felicity.

Mr Shakerley averted his gaze with a touch of false modesty. "I'm creating a course that will teach even the most novice of flower breeders how to recognise the most important traits in successful plants." He cast a glance at Janey. "I've never taught girls before, but I'm sure it can't be too difficult."

Leonora frowned at the plant expert. "Don't worry, Mr Shakerley. I will be checking your lesson plans." Leonora would certainly ensure that Mr Shakerley's classes were free of condescension towards the young women.

"We shall organise our own event to celebrate the launch of the school," said Lady Henrietta. "We don't wish to steal the spotlight from the fundraising for the War Widows and Orphans Relief Fund today. But we thought you should know." The dowager gave the kitchen maid another proud pat on the shoulder. "We're very much looking forward to seeing what young women such as Janey might achieve."

Janey smiled with a mix of pride and nervousness. Felicity beamed reassuringly at the girl. There had been a time when Lady Henrietta felt unsure about careers for women. Had Felicity's own trajectory influenced her grandmother's thinking on the matter? It was entirely possible.

Colonel Bolt cleared his throat. "If the British Rose Association can help in any way—" He glanced at Mrs Winterpole. "—we should be glad to hear it."

"Yes," said Mrs Winterpole a little stiffly. Her exclusion from the school project perhaps still stung. "Absolutely."

"Now, it's very interesting you should say that, Colonel," began Lady Henrietta, stepping closer to the colonel, deftly sealing off his attention for a private discussion.

"And what's next for you, Lady Felicity, if I may ask?" Leonora's question was posed quietly, with a curious yet challenging twitch at the corner of her lips.

Felicity continued to find Leonora's manner somewhat difficult to read. Thankfully, her aloofness didn't bear out in her personality and allegiances. The difficult time she'd had growing up with parents who'd been harsh with her and her brother meant she'd developed a hard outer shell. Underneath, however, was a caring, sensitive soul.

"I have my last contracted articles for the magazine to finish. After that..." Felicity broke off, allowing her gaze to wander briefly across the garden. She knew what she wanted. How might she express it?

"More detective work?" suggested Leonora. "At least, I would hope so. I don't suppose I'll ever be able to thank you enough for your investigation into what happened to my brother. And for saving my nephew's life."

Despite all he'd done, Leonora acknowledged Percy as family. She'd tried to meet with him, but he'd so far rejected Leonora's requests to visit him in prison. Indeed, he'd turned down visits from everyone, Lady Henrietta included.

Percy had yet to be tried for his wrongdoings, but he was in the care of a psychiatrist, so it was possible the worst of all penalties wouldn't be used against him. Might Leonora and her newly discovered nephew have some kind of relationship in the future?

Felicity couldn't imagine what she might say to someone who had done away with Jasper, whether or not they were related to her. Everyone, however, no matter their misdemeanours, ought to be treated with dignity.

"You don't need to thank me," said Felicity. "It's enough to know that the resolution has brought peace of some kind."

"I understand you consider yourself a journalist foremost," continued Leonora. "You make that clear in your magazine byline."

It was touching how Leonora followed Felicity's periodical pieces.

She wasn't a typical reader of the Gentlewoman's Gazette, but that had been part of why the magazine had wanted Felicity to write for them, to attract a new audience. A more modern sort of woman.

"It would be a true shame for the world to be deprived of your obvious capability for detection." Leonora smiled wryly. "But I suppose it must be difficult to decide what to do when one has talents in so many arenas. Luckily for me, I was brought up to do one thing only."

Felicity's gaze had once again drifted over to the other side of the rose garden. "Yes," she said a little absent-mindedly. "That indeed could be the case."

"Everything all right?" The sudden, gruff enquiry came from Havelock. He'd arrived at Leonora's side with a flush in his cheeks, the two plaited leather leads coiled in his big bear-paw hand, and the dogs presumably still dashing about in the orchard.

"Yes, Mick," said Leonora. "Thank you." She gave the burly gardener a brief but tender smile.

He grunted in acknowledgement but remained at her side. He clearly disliked letting Leonora out of his sight for too long, and she seemed perfectly accustomed to his ways.

It would not have been proper to enquire into the precise nature of their relationship. Perhaps they'd never discussed it themselves. What was obvious was that Leonora and Havelock understood each other and cared for one another a great deal.

Felicity's attention snapped away to the other side of the garden.

"Would you please excuse me?" apologised Felicity to Leonora and Havelock. "There's someone I need to speak to rather urgently."

Chapter Forty-Three

Alex had reappeared in the garden and gestured to Felicity from the other side of the parterre rose beds. She nodded her acknowledgment but didn't go to him directly.

Ducking under pergolas teeming with aromatic flowers and dodging footmen carrying trays of drinks, she wove in and out of the glamorous guests enjoying the beautiful blooms, the warmth of the sun, and coupes of champagne.

Slipping down a narrow path alongside a tall yew hedge, Felicity glanced over her shoulder. Alex was following, as she knew he would. He held his homburg to his chest, a hand smoothing the side parting in his dark blond hair, a smile on his handsome lips.

Arriving at a wooden bench under an arbour covered in heavily scented jasmine, Felicity took a seat and waited for Alex. The wood of the bench was smooth and warmed by the sun. The chatter from the fundraising event rose softly in the background. It was one of Felicity's favourite spots for sitting and reading whenever she found the time, which wasn't often these days.

Alex balanced his hat on his knee as he took a seat beside Felicity. "I got called indoors. Jasper telephoned. He sends his love."

Felicity frowned. Alex was teasing. It wasn't at all the kind of thing her brother would say, though she knew Jasper loved her very much.

"Checking up on you, was he?" Felicity asked.

"Wanted to make sure I had all the angles on Percy's case covered, in addition to your grandmother's garden party."

"You're doing an admirable job keeping everyone happy."

Alex half-smiled. Concern flickered across his scarred brow. "Percy's defence is aiming for a manslaughter plea. They'll be presenting him as weak of mind."

Felicity nodded slowly. She and Alex had already discussed such a defence as a strong possibility. Percy hadn't suffered the unluckiest of all outcomes while in the trenches, but his time spent on the front had seriously affected him.

"At least you can put it in the paper now."

Alex nodded. "Jacques has returned to France. He'll face a military trial. Charged with *insoumission*. Failing to present himself for conscription."

"Might he be..." Felicity swallowed. An image of the firing squad flashed through her mind.

"Very doubtful. That's not really the approach these days. The public can't stomach it, for one thing. Hard to say exactly what will happen, given the circumstances in which he was captured."

Felicity gently wafted her hand to encourage a slightly dozy bumble bee away from the silk flowers on her straw hat and towards the jasmine. "The circumstances of Jacques being investigated as part of the Best in Show swindle, you mean?"

Alex looked down at his homburg. "If it weren't for that, Jacques wouldn't have been extradited. The warrant for his arrest couldn't be ignored, but people would rather the police spent their time on other things these days. It's possible he'll get off rather lightly."

"Although unlikely we'll ever see him again."

"I think his contribution to British rose breeding has, indeed, ended. Say, I didn't tell you about Percy's time in France, did I? Quite uncanny, really. Mirrored his father's trajectory somewhat."

Felicity wrinkled her brow. "In what way?"

"Both of them spent time in *chateaux* serving widowed princesses or countesses from the *ancien régime*. Percy worked as a gardener. It's not entirely clear what Anthony was up to exactly."

Given Anthony Templeton's proclivities, Felicity wasn't sure she wished to know too many of the details. "How's Mr Merton?"

"I put a call into the hospital just this morning," said Alex. "My contact there suggests the fellow might be malingering. Not something I'll be putting in the paper, of course, but it's understandable. Sounds like he'll face civil litigation for his involvement in the con at the flower show."

Felicity cocked her head. "Who'll bring the case? The rose association?"

Alex nodded. "Colonel Bolt doesn't sound incredibly enthusiastic about it, but there's apparently a team at the association dedicated to prosecuting Merton. All working on a voluntary basis."

A smile passed over Felicity's lips. Women of any age should never be underestimated.

"And considering roses weren't the only type of flower Merton was judging," continued Alex, "it's possible there'll be several solicitors waiting to speak to him. No wonder the chap doesn't want to wake up."

The police still hadn't been able to interview him, but they'd deduced that Mr Merton's motive for influencing the prize-giving had been money. In Mr Merton's name, they'd uncovered a holiday booked to Egypt with the bill still waiting to be paid, an order for a Bentley 3 Litre with a dealer in Plymouth, and a tab open at a rather exclusive clothing shop in Torquay.

The police's theory was that Mr Merton, who had been spotted by flower show staff lurking behind the marquees, had been waiting in the wrong location. He likely wished to talk to Anthony Templeton about the money owed to him. Money Anthony likely had no intention of paying.

Instead, it had been Percy Colhayne who followed Anthony to the rendezvous location where Mr Merton was supposed to be waiting, and Percy had his moment alone with his father.

"Do you know when you might come back to the paper?" Alex's tone was casual, although it wasn't his first time asking Felicity this.

She sighed. They used to see much more of one another before she started writing for the Gentlewoman's Gazette. Investigating the flower show affair had flung them back together, but now they were once again so busy in their separate ways. Was it destined always to be like this? Was there not another way they might spend time together?

"Everyone keeps asking me what I might do next—"

"I'm so sorry." Alex looked crestfallen. "It was a selfish question."

Felicity put a hand on top of his. "I know you don't want to pressure me."

Alex looked relieved. "Never."

"But I'll admit I'm confused."

"Understandable." Alex wrapped his strong, gentle fingers around Felicity's hand. "You're a fantastic journalist and an amazing investigator. Which path do you wish to take?"

Felicity fired him a sharp glance. "I wasn't fishing for compliments."

Alex admired a meadow brown butterfly that had landed on the crown of his hat. "What's confusing you? Or may I guess?"

Felicity narrowed her eyes, amused. "I should love to hear your guess." Over time, she'd grown more comfortable with Alex's knack for reading her ideas almost before she'd fathomed them herself.

"The paper was your first love and you're loath to give it up. Yet you're a natural born detective and would like to help more people in the way you're so good at." Alex watched as the butterfly opened and closed its orange and brown wings. "In summary, you're torn."

"Go on."

"And then there's the magazine. The Gentlewoman's Gazette. You don't enjoy it, but you don't wish to disappoint Jasper or remove yourself from journalism altogether."

"How do you do it?"

Alex watched as the butterfly took flight. He turned to Felicity. "Do what?"

"Know me so well."

Alex smiled. "Do I?"

Felicity frowned. "Or am I that easy to read?"

Alex gave her hand a squeeze, his palm big and warm. "Let me reassure you it takes rather a lot of puzzling to work out how you think."

Felicity's heart pumped harder. She knew what she wanted. She saw it clearly before her.

"I wish to meet your family," she said.

Alex's eyes widened with surprise. "You do?"

Felicity swallowed. She was taken aback by what she'd said, even though she'd thought about it a lot. Even before she'd accidentally grabbed his hand during that wedding they'd attended together. Her mind kept returning to the situation.

Alex knew Felicity's family. He was good friends with her brother, Jasper, and had got to know Lady Henrietta and even Pip exceedingly well. It felt only right that Felicity present herself to Alex's kin. It was highly unusual for the woman in a courting couple to initiate the activity, however, and Felicity certainly never imagined she would blurt it out so bluntly to stun even herself.

But despite her surprise at what she'd said, Felicity was not ashamed.

She nodded firmly. "I do wish to meet your family."

Alex continued to look at her wide-eyed for a moment. His face softened. He smiled. "A trip to London, then, is it?"

Felicity gripped his hand harder. "I should like that very much."

Alex wrapped his other palm on top of hers. "You don't know how happy that makes me."

Felicity's heart hadn't beat so hard since they were in the medieval rose garden at Bickleford. When she and Alex stood facing one another. They'd been so close. She'd thought about it many times. They'd gazed at each other in much the same way as now, on the bench beneath the jasmine. Leaning towards one another—

Yap! Yap!

Felicity jolted up straight, her hand slipping out of Alex's and flattening on her chest.

It was Pip. Of course, it was Pip. Again, they'd been interrupted. Goodness, the Yorkie had given Felicity's heart a jolt.

"Hello there, Master Pip," said Alex good-naturedly.

Pip stood before them, tail wagging. He was pleased with himself.

Yap!

"I thought you were playing with friends in the orchard?" said Felicity a little tetchily. It wasn't the ending to her secret meeting with Alex for which she'd hoped.

"Lady Felicity?" Someone else was coming along the path beside the yew hedge.

Felicity stood up and swept her hands over the silk of her dress. Alex put on his hat. Pip turned towards the newcomer, tail wagging.

A woman with a jet-black bob wearing a slim-cut skirt and jacket in muted coral taffeta and spectacles with smoked lenses approached the bench.

"May I help you?" asked Felicity politely. Her heart was still recovering from her close encounter with Alex and the surprise from Pip, but at her grandmother's event she was both an ambassador for the Quicks and — thanks to the Gentlewoman's Gazette — for career women in general.

Yap!

Pip was still wagging his tail with enthusiasm. Felicity bent down to grab him, but he nimbly dodged her grasp, wriggled through the hedge, and ran off barking, presumably back to the orchard and his friends. Had he guided the woman with the black bob to Felicity and Alex's hideout? Certainly not on purpose.

The new arrival waited patiently as Felicity failed in her attempt to grab the Yorkie. She held out a hand. "May Lee. How do you do?"

Felicity shook the woman's hand. Alex was also introduced.

"You're a reporter, aren't you?" May looked with concern at Alex. "Can I request we keep this conversation confidential?"

Alex held up his hands. "I can leave, if you prefer."

"Mr Cooper will stay," said Felicity. At that point in time, she had no desire to be separated from Alex for any reason. "Whatever we discuss will not appear in the papers. What is it you wish to speak to me about?"

May returned her attention to Felicity. "I've been sent to engage your services."

"Sent by whom?" asked Felicity.

"At this stage, I'm afraid I cannot say."

"What do you mean by 'my services'?" Felicity was more than a little intrigued.

"As a private detective."

Felicity shot a glance at Alex. He looked excited but raised his eyebrows questioningly.

How did Felicity feel?

Felicity responded with a wide-eyed blink. She was interested. Goodness, she was interested. But was she ready? Was this the right next step?

"What would be the nature of the investigation?" asked Felicity.

"The precise details of the endeavour will be explained to you should you accept the invitation for a meeting. My employer requests your presence in Mayfair. Based on what you hear at the meeting, you may accept or decline the offer."

Again, Felicity exchanged glances with Alex. The timing of the proposal was uncanny. They'd just been talking about a trip to London.

"When does your employer wish to see me?" asked Felicity.

"We've booked a compartment for you on tomorrow's Riviera Express." May tipped her head, her sharp black bob swinging at her cheeks. "Do you accept the invitation?"

Felicity mentally rifled through her plans for the coming period. Lady Henrietta was extremely busy with her new projects, and Jasper was still away on business. Felicity had only her magazine articles to work on, although she'd become adept at obtaining deadline extensions.

She turned to Alex. Was it too soon? Were things moving too fast?

Alex's dark blue eyes sparkled. He gave Felicity a little nod.

Felicity turned to May. "I shall be on the London train tomorrow."

Claim your free Lady Felicity Quick ebook!

Sign up for my email newsletter and you'll get **Murder at Afternoon Tea** absolutely free.

This exclusive story isn't available anywhere else.

As a newsletter subscriber, you'll also receive writing updates, special offers, and peeks behind the scenes...

Use this link to sign up and claim your copy today:
https://BookHip.com/XMGPNZC

Read the next in the series...

Murder by the Thames

A Lady Felicity Quick 1920s Cozy Mystery
Book 8

A stroll along the River Thames reveals breathtaking views of the Tower of London, Big Ben ... and a body in the water!

England, 1922. London is a dazzling change from Lady Felicity Quick's life in rural Devon, and her first case as a professional private detective is proving a rousing success.

Investigating a string of daring thefts at an exclusive Bond Street jeweller has introduced Felicity to bustling theatres, lively music clubs, and the glamour of London's high society. It's also brought her closer to Mr Alexander Cooper, the London-born journalist on whom Felicity is rather keen.

But when a jaunt to the river takes a sinister turn, Felicity is drawn into an even deeper mystery involving the most fascinating and fashionable denizens of England's capital. Beneath the glitter, there's a world of secrets and danger — including a troubling connection to the family Felicity dreams of joining through marriage.

Can Felicity solve the case and make sense of her future with Alex? Or will London's darker side leave her dreams — and her very existence — adrift in murky waters?

If you love witty and determined heroines like Lady Hardcastle and Maisie Dobbs and the twist-filled historical mysteries of Helena Dixon and Agatha Christie, then don't miss Murder by the Thames!

Murder by the Thames will be available soon!

A Note From The Author

Thank you for reading this Lady Felicity adventure! I truly hope you enjoyed reading the book as much as I loved writing it.

If you have a moment, I'd be incredibly grateful if you could leave a review. On Amazon, Goodreads, or wherever you prefer.

Your thoughts not only mean the world to me but also help other readers discover new books to love.

Thank you so much for your support!

Warmest regards,

Rosie

The Lady Felicity Quick Mystery Series

Murder at Afternoon Tea

(Novella | Exclusive for Newsletter Subscribers)

Murder on the Village Green

(Book 1 | Available Now)

Murder at a Country House

(Book 2 | Available Now)

Murder at the Tea Rooms

(Book 3 | Available Now)

Murder at the Ball

(Book 4 | Available Now)

Murder on the Coast

(Book 5 | Available Now)

Murder at a Boarding School

(Book 6 | Available Now)

Murder at a Flower Show

(Book 7 | Available Now)

Murder by the Thames

(Book 8 | Coming Soon)

About the Author

Rosie Hunt is a British author of cozy mysteries both puzzling and historical. Her books include the Lady Felicity Quick mystery series set in the green and pleasant countryside of southwest England in the 1920s.

A history addict and former journalist, Rosie grew up immersed in the worlds of Poirot and Miss Marple. This early exposure to baffling murder mysteries rather coloured her outlook on life, and it was only a matter of time before she began writing her own.

Rosie loves clotted cream, knitting, and Golden Age crime fiction, and she'll never miss an opportunity to visit a National Trust property. She lives with her husband and their four-pawed overlord on a river in Northern Europe.

Join Rosie's mailing list:
bookhip.com/XMGPNZC

Follow Rosie on Facebook:
facebook.com/RosieHuntAuthor

Printed in Great Britain
by Amazon